The Black Swan, *Rose in the Mist*, and *Irish Gypsy*

Praise for Ana Seymour . . .

"Ms. Seymour has outdone herself again . . . *The Black Swan* is like sipping fine wine—it's intoxicating."
— *Rendezvous*

"Ana Seymour takes her legion of loyal readers into a fascinating new realm of medieval lore."
— *Times Record News* (TX)

"Ms. Seymour has captured the historical era and given us a romance filled with wonderful characters and several unique subplots . . . a highly enjoyable read."
— *Romantic Times*

"Exciting . . . The story line is loaded with authenticity. . . . The characters are intelligent and warm. . . . Fans of this subgenre already know that they see more of the era when Ana Seymour is the author, and this tale enhances her deserved reputation."
— *BookBrowser*

"[Seymour is] again filling pages with her mastery of plotting and the sweet joys found in family, friends, and the simple pleasure life affords. . . . It is always a joy to read a novel of this caliber."
— *Under the Covers*

"Readers will be enthralled as they follow spunky Jennie's struggles to keep her family together with a never-give-up determination. Superb."
— *Bell, Book & Candle*

Maid of Killarney

Ana Seymour

JOVE BOOKS, NEW YORK

This is a work of fiction. Names, characters, places, and incidents either are the product of the author's imagination or are used fictitiously, and any resemblance to actual persons, living or dead, business establishments, events, or locales is entirely coincidental.

MAID OF KILLARNEY

A Jove Book / published by arrangement with
the author

PRINTING HISTORY
Jove edition / December 2002

Copyright © 2002 by Mary Bracho
Cover art by Bruce Emmett

Visit our website at
www.penguinputnam.com

ISBN: 0-515-13415-5

A JOVE BOOK®
Jove Books are published by The Berkley Publishing Group, a division of Penguin Putnam Inc., 375 Hudson Street, New York, New York 10014.
JOVE and the "J" design are trademarks belonging to Penguin Putnam Inc.

PRINTED IN THE UNITED STATES OF AMERICA

10 9 8 7 6 5 4 3 2 1

One

John Black hunched in his saddle and tried to ignore the rain seeping down the back of his neck. His stallion, Greybolt, looked as if he felt just as soggy and cold as his master.

He gave the animal a pat, and water splashed from the horse's thick coat. "Forgive me, old boy," he said. "I'd remembered Killarney as a beautiful, sunny land."

Warm sun and brilliant skies painting the backdrop for a panorama of emerald green hills and ice-blue lakes. That was the picture he'd retained from his childhood. He supposed it had rained, back in those days, now two score years ago, but what he remembered was the sun.

He sighed. Perhaps the Riordans had been right. It was time for him to rest a spell. All three Riordan brothers had urged the plan after the last round of talks between the rebels and the English queen had failed. John Black had struggled for peace for so many years that he'd forgotten what the word meant. He no longer knew what it felt like to feel at peace.

"Get away from the fighting for a while, John," Cormac Riordan had urged. "Far away. Go home to Killarney. You could stay with Niall and Cat and the boys. You know that Cat would love to show you her sons."

That had been the deciding factor. Not the rest, but the thought of seeing the daughter of his lost love. How Rhea would have been proud if she could have lived to see her two lively grandsons.

He looked around and tried to see if he could recognize any familiar landmarks through the rain and fog. The road had become narrower and muddier as he neared the Valley of Mor, where Catriona O'Malley Riordan and her husband, Niall, served as lord and lady over the O'Malley lands. If memory served, he'd soon reach Banburn, the little village at the western end of the valley.

There should be an alehouse in the village, and he was tempted to stop for a hot drink and a few moments by the fire before continuing. "How would you like some time in a dry barn?" he asked Greybolt. "Or should we press on and hope we arrive at O'Malley House before the road washes away from under your feet?"

Greybolt continued plodding straight forward without lifting his head. The horse had been through nearly as many years of fighting as he had, and John looked forward to giving him a well-deserved rest. He continued talking, in spite of the animal's lack of interest. "Niall Riordan's stables are the pride of the south. Perhaps he'll have some sleek fillies for you to enjoy."

For just a moment John tried to remember the last time that he, himself, had enjoyed a sleek "filly." Too long. Hell's bells, Black, he chided himself with a touch of amusement. You're too old to be getting itchy in the saddle at the sudden thought of a warm and willing wench.

He almost missed the turn to the village.

"Throw her in! Hurry, before anyone comes."

John drew up his horse at the sound of boyish shouts.

"Do we dare? She'll sink like a bloody rock."

"If she's a witch, she'll float."

John squinted to see through the mist. The voices had come from the edge of a small pond where three boys were gathered, two of them carrying what appeared to be a squirming bundle. With a frown, he headed toward them.

"Whoa there, lads!" he shouted. "What's going on here?"

All three of the boys' heads turned in his direction.

"I told you, Des," one said. "Now we're in for it."

"Shut your mouth," the other boy replied. "It's a stranger, and he's alone. He knows nothing of us. Get rid of her, then run."

The two carrying the bundle heaved it into the water. Then all three boys sped around the back edge of the pond and disappeared into the trees. John pulled Greybolt to a halt and jumped down. Whatever the boys had thrown into the pond had, indeed, sunk like a rock. He feared it wasn't a bag of unwanted puppies.

The rain suddenly started coming in driving sheets as he raced to the edge of the pond. Without wasting what could be crucial time trying to see into the dark water, he plunged in. The cold was a shock even to his already sodden body, but he forgot the discomfort in a wave of relief as his fingers closed on a sheet underneath the water. The cloth was wrapped around a solid mass that was definitely not puppies.

Pulling the form behind him, he kicked toward shore. When his feet could touch bottom, he pulled the bundle into his arms and walked up the bank. He'd distinctly heard the boys shout something about a witch, but even if he had believed in such things, the bundle he held could be no witch. It was a child.

He stumbled once on the wet bank, then placed the bundle on the reeds and knelt beside it. Quickly, his hands shaking from cold and alarm, he untied the cords and pulled the sheet away to reveal a girl, her lips white and her face already turning the grayish blue of death.

"Christ Jesus," he muttered. He lifted the apparently lifeless form in one arm, turned her over, facedown, and pressed hard into her midsection. Instantly water gushed from her mouth and she began coughing.

When no more water came from her mouth, John righted her and laid her back on the bank. "Easy now," he said. "You'll be better in a moment. You've had a bit of a drink."

The color was already returning to her face. Her eyes fluttered opened and stared up at him, wide with fear.

"I won't hurt you," he assured her. "I've just pulled you out of the pond. You're safe now."

The sudden burst of rain was once again easing into a drizzle, though John scarcely noticed. He was now soaked through, and so was the poor little mite he had plucked from the pond. Her eyes were midnight blue, as dark as the murky water behind them. She appeared to be breathing normally. He put his fingers along the side of her neck. She cringed at his touch, but said nothing as he felt her life's blood moving in a reassuringly normal rhythm.

"Can you speak?" he asked her, removing his fingers and sitting back. "What's your name?"

She gave a small shake of her head.

"Don't be afraid," he told her. "Whoever those boys were who were trying to hurt you, they've gone—run away like the cowards they obviously are."

He thought he detected a slight smile on her lips,

which had turned from white to a still-bluish pink. "What were they doing with you?" he asked.

Once again, the only reply was a slight shake of her head, along with a noticeable shiver.

"We have to get you dry and warm," John said. "Where do you live?"

She bit her lip and remained silent.

John struggled to keep the exasperation from his voice. "Listen, lass. I'm trying to help you. We need to get you out of those wet clothes and into a warm bed. I'll take you to your family, but I need to know where they are."

She lay on the ground, watching him, her shivering now turning into violent trembles. With a sigh he leaned over and picked her up, still half wrapped in the sheet. "If you can't tell me anything, I'll take you into the village and see who knows something about—"

"Nay!" Her voice was surprisingly strong.

He looked down at her. Her eyes were darting around in panic. "I'm only trying to help you, child," he said gently. "I'll take you wherever you say, but we must get you inside before the chill turns to fever."

"I live in Whistler's Woods."

He shifted her to a better position in his arms and pulled off the cords that still clung to her, then used the wet sheet to wrap her more securely. "Whistler's Woods? I'm not from here, lass. You'll have to show me the way."

She nodded and settled in his arms without objection. Struggling with his soggy bundle and his own wet clothes, he somehow managed to pull himself and the girl up on Greybolt's back. "Which direction?" he asked when they were firmly in the saddle.

She stretched a small hand out from underneath the sheet and pointed toward the other side of the pond. John nudged Greybolt and the horse started to move.

"Now will you tell me your name?" he asked. She was in front of him on the saddle, and he could no longer see her face.

"Daphne," she said after a long moment.

It was an odd name for a bedraggled village girl, and John would have liked to question her more—about the name and about what had led to the near-fatal incident at the pond. But he could feel her shaking against him and decided that the questions could wait until he got her safely to her home.

She spoke nothing further on the ride, simply pointing whenever he asked the way. They had left the road and were traveling on an uneven path that forced Greybolt to pick his way slowly through the mud. Finally her hand came out to point one last time, and she said, "It's just there. I can walk the rest of the way."

The rain had stopped, but the late afternoon hour was adding to the gloom. John could just make out a small thatched cottage through the trees. "I'll see you inside," he said, holding her firm as she twisted in an apparent attempt to slide off the horse.

"I pray you, sir," she pleaded. "Let me go."

John lifted her back into position. "Nay, I'd see you tucked warm in bed and be sure you're none the worse for wear after this day's adventure. As your rescuer, I've something of a stake in your welfare."

She seemed to suddenly realize for the first time what he had done for her. She turned around to face him and said, "You have my gratitude, sir. You saved my life."

"Aye, child, I did, and now I'll not have you risk it again through lack of proper care. Do you live with your mother and father?"

"My mother." There was reluctance in her tone.

"Well, then. I'll speak with your mother. You should be put to bed with a plaster and fed hot ale."

She looked miserable and afraid, her face pinched and her hair falling around her shoulders in wet tangles. "Prithee, let me go by myself. I'll give my mother your instructions. I promise. But please don't come in to see her."

John frowned. Was the girl afraid of her own mother? The thought made him angry. Anyway, what kind of a mother would let her child get into the situation Daphne had found herself in that afternoon?

"Are you afraid she'll beat you, child?" he asked her. " 'Twill not happen if I have anything to say about it."

Daphne's eyes filled with tears, and she shook her head, but she stopped struggling to get out of his grasp.

Surprisingly, the broken path became smooth as they neared the cottage, and there were neat rows of primroses on each side leading up to a wooden door, which opened as John pulled Greybolt to a stop and swung from his back.

In the doorway was a tall, slender woman. Her clasped hands went to her throat as she cried in a strangled voice, "What's happened?" Then before he could answer, she was running toward them. "Is she hurt?"

The anguish in her tone immediately banished his suspicion that Daphne's mother was uncaring or cruel. "She's going to be fine, mistress," he told her.

Daphne added her reassurance. "I'm fine, Mummy," she said, as the woman reached them and held out her arms for the child. "I can walk."

John let his charge slip from his arms to stand, but when she tried to take a step, she stumbled on the bunched-up sheet. "Best let me carry you inside, child," he said.

Daphne looked at her mother, who gave an imperceptible shake of her head. "I thank ye, sir, for all your help, but I'll be fine now with my mother."

The tall woman had put a protective arm around her daughter. "I'd know what transpired here," she said. Now that the initial scare was past, her voice was rich and composed.

"I've just rescued your daughter from a pond at the edge of these woods," John said.

"From Cotter's Pond?" the woman asked in surprise. "I thought you were back in your aviary all this time, Daphne. Remember you promised me you'd not wander off like that again?"

The girl nodded, obviously ashamed.

"What happened at the pond?" her mother asked. "Did you fall in?"

The girl had begun shaking again. "Mummy, I'm cold," she said.

John gave a nod. "The explanations can wait. This child must get between warm blankets and drink something hot."

He made a move to pick her up again, but Daphne stepped to one side, stumbling again.

"I'll take her," her mother said, picking the child up easily. "Could you just pull away the sheet?" she asked John.

He did so, then watched as the mother and daughter started up the path to their cottage. There had been no invitation for him to follow. In fact, he got the distinct impression that neither Daphne nor her mother wanted anything to do with him, but the remaining vestiges of his former profession made him reluctant to leave a patient without being sure that she was receiving proper treatment. After a moment's hesitation he followed the pair up the path.

He came to a halt at the threshold, his mouth opening with surprise. This was no poor villager's home. Though the front room was small, the table and chairs were elegantly carved. A finely stitched tapestry hung along one wall. Across the room was a case that held over a dozen bound books. John gave a low whistle. The books alone were worth more than a simple peasant could hope to earn in a dozen years.

The woman and girl had disappeared through a doorway at the back of the room. He crossed over to it and peered inside. Mother and daughter sat side by side on a big bed. The mother had her arms clasped around Daphne and was rocking her. Silent tears coursed down the woman's face.

Cautiously he stepped into the room. "Truly, mistress, there should be no lasting effect of the mishap."

The woman looked up at him. Her blue eyes were lighter than her daughter's, but the bitterness shining out of them made them appear almost as dark. " 'Twas no *mishap*," she corrected, half spitting the word. Evidently her daughter had told her the truth about the incident.

"Nay," he agreed solemnly. " 'Twas vile mischief by a trio of miscreants, and they should be called to account for the deed. I shudder to think what would have happened if I hadn't come along."

The woman looked embarrassed as she suddenly realized her lapse of manners. "Forgive me, sir. You have my gratitude. My daughter may owe you her life."

He shrugged off her thanks. "Yet if we stand here discussing the matter, we are once again risking it. She needs to be put to bed."

The woman looked wary. "I shall do so, sir, as soon as you leave us."

John shook his head. "I'd see her properly treated before I go. May I know your name, mistress?"

She stood. "My name is Lily. And once again, I thank you for your help, but now I'm asking you to leave us."

She had the bearing of a noblewoman, and her

speech was unlike the dialect he remembered being used by the humble folk of Banburn. Who were these people? he wondered, looking from the mother to the daughter. There was little enough resemblance between them. Daphne's hair was dark, whereas her mother's was the color of rich honey.

"I'm a doctor," he was astonished to hear himself say. It was an admission he'd not made for over twenty years. "I'd like to see that she's well."

The woman appeared to be hesitating, but finally she said, "I'll take care of her."

Behind her on the bed, Daphne was beginning to shake again. "Zounds, woman, I don't see that you're doing much of a job of it at the moment."

He should just go and leave the troublesome wenches to themselves, he told himself with a snort of irritation. Though years of campaigning and sleeping on the run had inured him to hardship, the cold from his soaking was beginning to creep into his innards, and he did not have the humor to stand here arguing with a stubborn woman.

She appeared to be studying him. "You're a doctor?" she asked. "Truly?"

He had been once. "Aye," he said.

She hesitated. Finally she said. "Step out of the room while I get her into bed. Then you can see to her."

Her tone gave the impression that she was doing him a great favor, rather than the other way around. "Do you mind if I warm up at your fire?" he asked with a sardonic half-smile. "I'm rather wet."

"Oh!" She looked him up and down as if it was the first time that she'd noticed him. He imagined he made a sorry picture in his bedraggled state. "Of course, warm yourself," she said. "Put more wood on, if you like. It's in the woodbin just outside the door."

He nodded and walked out of the room. What an

odd day. The woman had said she was called Lily.
She'd given no family name. He went to the fireplace
and turned so that his back could feel the warmth of the
flames. Then once again he began to study the contents
of the room, including the bookshelves. Daphne and
Lily. A Greek goddess and a flower, living in an isolated cottage deep within the woods. Who *were* these
people?

The fire crackled behind him as he waited. He could
smell the steam as his sodden woolen leggings ab-
sorbed the heat of the flames. He wished that he were
the one climbing into a warm bed, he thought, stifling
a yawn of exhaustion. If the mysterious Lily had a
barn, he'd be tempted to bed down there. It would, in
fact, serve a double purpose, since he could then see
how his patient was faring in the morning before he
continued his journey.

"I've changed my mind," came Lily's determined
voice from the doorway.

He turned around in surprise. "I beg your pardon?"

"I've seen to Daphne. She's faring well. She's almost asleep. We have no further need of your services."

She could as well have been dismissing a lackey
who had displeased her. John raised an eyebrow. "My
services?"

"Daphne's never seen a doctor, and I warrant she's
done fine without."

"And how many times has she half-drowned in a
cold pond?"

The woman's gaze wavered, but she said, "I'm
sorry, but we prefer to be alone. I'll thank you to leave
us be."

John looked beyond her to the door of the bedchamber. If he had thought the girl at risk, he would
have bullied his way in to see her no matter what her

mother said. But his impression had been that the girl had taken no lasting harm, and in view of the mother's adamant refusal, he saw little choice but to leave.

"Very well, mistress," he said. "If you find the effects of this night lingering, please send for me. I shall be staying at O'Malley House. Do you know it?"

"Aye." She nodded, but after a moment added, "Though I'll not be sending for you."

John shook his head. He was suddenly too tired to argue further. Without another word, he began walking toward the door.

"Doctor," she said. When he paused, she continued, "I *am* grateful for what you've done today."

He gave a curt nod.

"And I'd ask one more favor of you."

That surprised him. "What would that be, mistress?"

"I'd ask that you put aside all memory of what you have seen and done this day."

"That is the favor you'd have of me?" he asked, confused. The water had left him feeling muddled enough, and now he had to contend with a woman who made no sense.

"Aye," she said firmly. "I'm asking that you forget that you ever laid eyes on my daughter . . . or on me."

He gave his head a little shake of disbelief. "Mistress, I will leave you and your daughter alone, since you ask me, but I can assure you that it will be a long time before I forget the events of this day."

She made no reply, simply stood watching him, her expression holding neither warmth nor pleading. He waited another moment, then shook his head again and walked out of the cottage.

TWO

"So you met the witch of Whistler's Woods?"

John lifted his head at his host's question. It was past midnight, but he and his friends Catriona and Niall Riordan were still sitting in the dining hall of their home, O'Malley House. John had arrived just after dark, weary to the bone, but dry clothes and a hearty dinner had given him renewed vitality. He'd listened eagerly to his hosts' tales of rebuilding the O'Malley lands that had been illegally taken away from Catriona when she was fourteen. The beaming couple had proudly presented him to their two young sons, Lorcan and Padraic. It had been a congenial evening, providing exactly the warmth and sense of family that Cormac Riordan had predicted when he'd urged John to travel to Killarney.

"The witch of Whistler's Woods? That little girl's no more a witch than I am queen of England," John replied with a snort.

"Not the girl, the mother," Niall clarified. "There have been murmurs about her for years. This is the first I've heard of accusations against the daughter."

"It's bloody nonsense. Neither one of them is a witch."

Niall nodded agreement. "I'm not sure I even believe in such things."

"Nor I," his wife agreed firmly.

"Why do people say these things of them?" John asked.

Niall shook his head. "Likely no reason at all, as is the case with much malicious gossip."

Catriona added, "It goes against the sensibilities of some of the good people of Banburn to think that a woman can live by herself and raise a child in the bargain."

"She has no husband?" John asked.

"Nay, nor has she ever had, as far as anyone knows. She uses no surname. She seems to have no family and no friends." Catriona's brown eyes were soft with feeling. John knew that she herself had gone through her own years of feeling alone in the world after her father died and she was whisked off to exile in England.

"How can she live?" John asked. He found himself strangely curious, even though the secretive Lily had made it clear that she wanted nothing to do with him.

Niall shrugged. " 'Tis a bit of a mystery. Though she comes to market and sells baskets sometimes."

"Baskets?"

"Aye." Catriona's eyes danced. "They're beautiful. Truly works of art, I'd call them." She rose from her chair and walked over to a chest at one end of the hall. Opening it, she took out a reed basket, dyed black and beautifully twisted into the shape of a swan. "I asked her to make this one for us, since the black swan is the symbol of the Riordans."

John shot a smile at Niall. "But no longer a sad one." Some had said that the black swan had been a silent symbol of mourning for the generations of Riordan brides who had died within a year of their weddings.

Niall grinned back. "Nay, since all three Riordans have produced brawny offspring and kept their wives healthy in the bargain, I'd say the curse of the Riordan brides is past."

"Good. Though I believe in curses even less than I do in witches. But tell me, is there nothing else that has caused the rumors? Surely it's not only because the woman lives by herself. There must be widows in town in like circumstance."

Niall shook his head. "Lily is simply not like other women. There's something about her that's different."

John remembered his impression that the woman had not been of humble origin. "Does no one know her background?"

"Nay," Catriona answered. "She just appeared one day, years ago, with the child. And then, of course, there's the deformity. People are so cruel—"

"The deformity?" John interrupted in surprise.

Niall and Catriona exchanged a glance. Finally Niall said, "The girl. She has the Devil's Foot. Surely you noticed it."

"I mislike that term," Catriona chided her husband gently. "The girl's foot is twisted. Did you not see her walk?"

John shook his head. Thinking back, he'd only seen Daphne take a couple of steps, and those had been more like stumbles. He'd attributed it to the encumbering sheet around her legs.

"Sometimes that condition can be corrected," he said. "Do you know if she's been seen by a physician?" As soon as he asked the question, he remembered the girl's mother saying that she'd never seen a doctor. And Lily had made it obvious that she did not intend to change that.

"I doubt it," Catriona answered. "As I say, they keep to themselves. It's a pity. The girl comes with her mother to market, and she's a pretty little thing."

"Aye, and the mother's a beauty, as well," Niall added. Catriona shot him a reproachful glance. His expression turned sheepish, and he added quickly, "Of course, she pales in comparison to the beautiful mistress of O'Malley House."

John was amused at his friend's hurried effort to placate his wife. He watched as the two exchanged loving smiles. Suddenly there was an intensity to their expressions that excluded John and the entire rest of the world. John sat back in his chair, quietly content. Though the relationship between Niall and Catriona had begun with a double betrayal that had almost cost both of them their heads, the two had eventually found that rare harmony of souls that makes the trip through life so much richer.

It was something John himself had never had. It had been his destiny to travel life alone. But he could, at least, rejoice in the young couple's happiness.

He cleared his throat. "I suspect 'tis past time for me to seek my bed," he announced loudly.

Catriona's cheeks turned pink.

Niall stood with a grin. "No doubt. You've had a hard day, old man," he said.

John smiled. When he and Niall had traveled together to the spectacular London court of Queen Elizabeth, it had been a joke between them that John, in spite of being nearly double Niall's age, had matched him in vigor and had always seemed to be able to draw twice the number of court beauties. He stood and gave a little bow first toward his hostess, then his host. "It has been a hard day, if truth be known, and I *am* not as young as I used to be—"

"Which is why I intend to give you several lengths

lead when I race you in the morning," Niall teased. "Greybolt against my best mount. It will be just like the old days."

"The day I need you to give me a lead riding Greybolt will be the day I'm dead and buried, you young pup," John retorted.

Catriona laughed at the men's taunts, but said, "You'll not forget that you've promised Lorcan and Paddy to take them riding in the morning, and I'd not have them learning bad examples from the wild ways of their father and their uncle John."

"Uncle John?"

Catriona smiled at him. "I've told the boys that they may call you uncle, if that's acceptable to you."

John felt a curious swelling of his throat. "I'd be honored, child, as well you know." The swelling grew as Catriona smiled, then walked around the table to take her husband's outstretched hand. Niall pulled her against his side, put an arm around her, and dropped a kiss on her cinnamon-colored hair.

"Will you need anything further?" Catriona asked John.

He smiled. "Not a thing. I can see myself to my chamber. Now take that husband of yours to bed before he forgets that company is present."

Catriona gave a girlish giggle that would lead no one to believe that she was chatelaine of an estate and mother of two youngsters. "Good night then, John," she said. "We're happy to have you here."

Niall pulled her toward the doorway, bidding John good night with an offhand wave and a mumbled, "We'll see you in the morning."

John watched them leave with a smile. Young love. In his own case, it had turned tragic and changed the entire course of his life. But when it had happy results, there was nothing better.

• • •

"But, Mummy, did you not think the gentleman was kind?" Daphne asked.

Lily pursed her lips and continued brushing the tangles out of the girl's hair. Daphne had slept soundly all night. The fear that had gripped Lily from the moment she'd seen her daughter in the arms of a stranger, her face white and pinched, was beginning to fade. "He appeared to be kind enough, child, but 'tis best not to trust appearances."

"I was so afraid when he pulled me from the pond, but he spoke gently, and his arms felt strong and warm." Daphne's expression was suddenly older than her years. "I felt safe," she concluded after a moment.

Lily gave a shudder. She remembered arms that had felt strong and safe. Arms she had thought would protect her from the cruelty of the world. She had put her faith in an illusion, and she was not about to let her only child make the same mistake.

"The man is gone, Daphne. There's no need to think about him further."

Daphne pulled her head away from her mother's hand and took the brush. "I can do it myself, Mummy," she said with some irritation. "I'm no longer a baby."

Lily let the brush go and sat back on the bed with a sigh. "Of course not. It's just that it was overly tangled this morning after your fall in the lake."

"I didn't fall," Daphne corrected.

"I know." She watched in silence as Daphne continued to work on her hair. Deep inside her chest, Lily could feel the familiar welling up of love that often came over her as she contemplated the miracle of her daughter. She never ceased to be amazed at how this beautiful, special being could have come out of betrayal and dishonor. But lately there had been an element of disquiet along with the wonder. When Daphne

was small, it had been easy for her to create a world for
just the two of them. But, as her daughter had just insisted, she was no longer a baby, and yesterday's incident had proved that their magical world was no longer
safe.

"Are you angry with me, Mummy? I didn't mean to
snap at you about the brush," Daphne said, looking up
with worried eyes.

Lily put her arm around the girl and gave her a
quick hug. "Nay, I'm not angry with you, Sweetcakes.
I'm angry with the boys who did this thing to you."

Daphne bowed her head. "They didn't like my
foot."

Lily winced. "They are rude louts, Daphne. You
must not care what they say or think. Ignorant people
are often cruel to people they don't understand."

"I don't think the gentleman who saved me saw that
my foot was wrong."

"I'm sure it would have made no difference to him
if he had." At her daughter's skeptical expression, she
gave a sad laugh. "What nonsense is this, Daphne? Are
you thinking that he would have thrown you back in
the water if he had seen it?"

"Nay." The girl did not look entirely convinced.

Lily rocked her back and forth. "Ah, my darling,
darling child. You are warm and bright and perfect.
You must not begin to believe that you are anything
less."

The sunny smile returned to Daphne's face. "You
say those things because you are my mother," she
teased.

"I most certainly do," Lily agreed, giving her an affectionate tap on the nose. "But they also happen to be
true."

Daphne jumped up and put the brush on the washstand. "Shall I fetch some berries, Mummy?" she asked.

Lily smiled. The berry patch was on a steep hill that was difficult for Daphne to manage, but she never hesitated to volunteer for the task of picking. "Just bring enough for breakfast. I intend to go later to choose the ones I want. Then this afternoon we'll make a nice potage."

Daphne nodded and started across the room with her halting steps. Lily watched until she disappeared out the front door, then allowed the tears that had been threatening since the previous evening to finally fall.

How could anyone have been so cruel to her beautiful child? She had long ago learned that life wasn't always fair. She'd learned to deal with injustice, and there had been times when she had thought the lessons hard. But until now, she had no idea how agonizing it would be to face an injustice to her child. It appeared that keeping her daughter isolated in their little haven in Whistler's Woods was no longer enough to shelter her from the outside world. And the worst of it was, she had no idea what she was going to do about it.

"Will you take me next, Uncle John?"

John smiled down at the oldest Riordan boy, who was a miniature of his father. "Aye, Lorcan, after Paddy's ride, 'tis your turn."

"Could I ride him by myself, Papa?" Lorcan asked Niall, who stood by the rail of the corral watching John's antics with his sons.

"Nay. Greybolt's too powerful a mount for you to try just yet. But you may ride on him with your uncle John after he's finished touring Paddy."

Lorcan looked disappointed, but did not argue.

Padraic, with the typical attention span of a three-year-old, was already tiring of the game. He bounced in the saddle in front of John and lisped, "Wanna go pony ride."

Each boy had his own personal pony, though Padraic was only allowed to ride in the ring next to his father or mother.

John pulled up next to Niall and handed down his younger son. Then Niall gave five-year-old Lorcan a boost up on Greybolt's tall back.

"Can we ride outside the ring, at least?" Lorcan asked.

John looked at Niall, who gave a nod of permission. Greybolt had patiently ridden in circles inside the fence for long enough. Now, as John gave him his head, the horse bolted for the freedom of the gate.

"Woo-eee!" Lorcan cried, hanging on to John's thighs.

"Is it too much speed for you, lad?" John asked. "Are you frightened?"

Lorcan threw back his head and laughed, unconsciously imitating his father. Apparently Lorcan had also inherited his father's love for fast and reckless horses.

"Hold on tight, then," John said. "We'll have a run."

By the time the two returned to the stables, Lorcan's cheeks were red and his eyes were dancing with excitement. "We went like the wind, Papa!" he shouted to Niall, who was walking around the ring alongside Padraic on his pony.

Niall grinned as John dismounted and lifted Lorcan to the ground. "So you're teaching my son wild ways on a horse," he said to John. "Ruining all my sage and sober advice."

"I'd give a pretty purse to see you sage and sober on a horse, Niall Riordan," John retorted.

Seeing that Lorcan was once again running around on his own two feet, Padraic decided he, too, had had enough riding. He slid to the ground and was off after his brother, chasing him around the ring like a dog after a cat.

"They're bonny lads," John told Niall. "You must be proud."

"Aye. To think there was a time when I'd thought to be content raising nothing but horses for all my days."

"That was before you met a certain red-haired rebel spy."

Niall grinned. "Aye. I believe I was lost from the first moment I glimpsed her there in the grand corridor at Whitehall Palace. Remember? I told you that her beauty rivaled the roses in the queen's garden."

"Aye. And I remember warning you straight off that she was a flower of the prickly variety. Though even I didn't realize that the wound would prove fatal."

"Aye. As if I didn't already have two older brothers telling me what to do, I've had to put up with your nagging over the years. And the damnedest part of it has always been that all three of you are right, more often than not."

The two men laughed and lapsed into silence for several long minutes, remembering their past adventures as they watched the antics of the new generation of Riordans. The boys had begun a wrestling match on the ground, which was still muddy from the previous day's rains. In spite of his smaller size, Padraic seemed to be holding his own with his big brother.

"I'd best get them back to the house," Niall said after several minutes. "Their mother will have my hide for turning them into such ragamuffins."

John smiled. "I can imagine you and Eamon engaged in the exact same activity not too many years back."

"You have the right of that, not because it's been few years since our childhood, but because both my brothers still feel the need to show me their strength now and then, even though we are old married men."

"And you can still beat them both hands down."

Niall grinned. "Aye." He jumped over the fence rail and walked toward his sons. "'Tis a draw, lads," he declared. "And I believe you both deserve a berry tart for your efforts. Though we'll have to see what your mother has to say about those clothes."

John watched fondly as his friend gingerly grabbed the back of his sons' tunics and pulled them out of the mud. Cormac had been right, he thought again. It was soothing to be here. Comforting to remember that the world was not all war and dying.

"I'll need to find these scamps a bath," Niall told him. "Shall we put off our race until later this afternoon?"

John nodded. The boys were squirming and giggling in their father's grasp. "Do you need assistance?"

Niall shook his head and started toward the house. "I'll see you at the noon meal."

"Aye. I'll see to Greybolt, then I'll be up."

Still smiling, John walked his horse back to the O'Malley stable. Like the rest of the buildings on the estate, it was of recent construction. All the original buildings had been burned by the soldiers of Henry, Lord Wolverton, who had secretly seized the O'Malley lands against the orders of the queen. John had met a number of treacherous men in his life of political intrigue, but Wolverton had been one of the most evil. It was fitting that he had died before he had ever been able to enjoy his ill-gotten estate.

Now the O'Malley lands were back with their rightful owner. They would make a fine legacy for the two active youngsters Niall had just carried away. The boys were a lively twosome, and if they grew up to be like their father and Riordan uncles, they would be fine young men, nothing like the ruffians he'd seen yesterday by the pond.

The sudden memory erased the warm feeling he'd had all morning. He thought of Daphne's white face as he'd first seen it when he had opened the sheet. She could well have died. It was irritating to think that neither Daphne nor Lily were likely to pursue the matter and see that the boys were called to account for the deed.

And what of the "deformity" his hosts had mentioned? When Lily had carried her daughter into their cottage, he'd thought it was due to concern over the incident. Now he wondered if it had been so that he wouldn't see the girl walk. How badly was she affected by the condition? he wondered. He'd been away from medicine for many years, but he continued to study the subject, eagerly learning the latest treatments whenever he could find new information.

He finished stabling Greybolt and wandered back out into the yard where the two boys had recently been happily scrambling around. Could Daphne run? Had she ever been able to join in games with the village children?

The questions continued to nag him as he walked slowly back to the manor house. By the time he reached the massive front entrance, he'd made up his mind. His race with Niall would have to wait another day. He had a call to pay this afternoon. Whether or not the mysterious Lily welcomed his visit, he was a doctor, and he intended to see how his patient was faring.

Three

The path into the little cottage did not look quite so abandoned when it was lit by sunlight streaming in through the trees. Greybolt had no trouble finding the way, and the distance seemed much shorter than it had the previous day in the cold rain.

By the time they reached the clearing where the house stood, John was rethinking the wisdom of coming. If the woman wanted nothing to do with the outside world, then who was he to force himself upon her? But the sight of the child kneeling alongside a row of flowers resolved his doubts. He stopped for a moment at the edge of the trees, watching her. She hardly resembled the little girl he had rescued. Her cheeks were full and pink, her blue eyes sparkling as she talked to a sparrow perched on a primrose branch. The drab little bird appeared not the least bit wary of its human companion.

"If you wait here, I shall bring you more bread crumbs," the girl was saying. "Or you can go back to the aviary where you belong. But you must not eat Mother's flower seeds or we won't have this pretty garden for you to visit."

John smiled. "Good day, Mistress Daphne."

The girl and sparrow both turned at the sound of his voice. The bird flew away, but the girl froze in place.

John swung off his horse. "My apologies. I fear I've scared off your little friend." Daphne's alarmed expression made her once again resemble the half-drowned girl from the previous day. "I didn't mean to startle you. I came to see how you are recovering," he explained.

He could see her struggling for composure as he walked toward her. "I thank you, sir, but, as you can see, I'm perfectly well again. There is no need—"

"Is your mother inside?" he asked.

She hesitated, then shook her head. "She's gone to gather berries."

"Ah." John thought for a moment. Perhaps it was fortunate that Lily was not here. He could begin to get Daphne on his side before her mother had a chance to chase him away again. "Then I shall wait for her. I have something to ask her. Do you think you could play hostess until she returns?"

Again there was a long hesitation, then Daphne nodded. As she got to her feet, John could see that she held one leg at an angle while she put her weight on the other. "Did you sleep well after your dunking?" he asked, smiling.

She nodded. "Until midmorning. Mother called me a slugabed."

John laughed. "I'd say you deserved an extra nap after that experience." He wanted to ask her about her leg, since he felt she would talk about it more freely without her mother present, but he'd have to get her to trust him before he broached the subject. "What were you doing just now? Tending the flowers?"

"Aye. The birds peck at the seeds sometimes, so I have to bury them. They mean no harm," she said quickly, as if worried that he might hold something against her little winged friends.

"I suspect they're just hungry, like all other creatures."

She appeared relieved. "Aye, 'tis why I've made a special place behind the house to feed them. Do you want to see it?"

"I'd be honored," John said.

"We call it my aviary," Daphne said, leading him around the side of the cottage.

"Aviary? That's a fancy word."

"It comes from the Latin." She crinkled her nose. "I don't like Latin much, but Mummy says I must study it anyway."

Latin? The girl may live in the woods, but apparently she was a scholar. The path narrowed and she went ahead, allowing him to get a good look at her feet. On one she wore a simple leather boot. The other was wrapped in rags. As she limped along, he could see that a piece of leather was stitched to the bottom of the cloth. The twisting of the foot was outward, which was encouraging. It was the easiest kind of irregularity to treat. He had a moment of the special elation he always used to feel when he sensed that he would be able to help one of his patients. He could help this child. He was sure of it.

"The birds don't mind if I'm here, but they won't stay when there's a visitor," she said with some apology as their arrival produced a mass fluttering of wings.

John looked around in wonder. The trees behind the house formed a semicircle, and almost every one had some kind of little birdhouse or feeder trough. Many of them were skillfully woven baskets. "Are these all for birds?" he asked with a low whistle.

"Mostly birds, but also bunnies, squirrels, field

mice, ferrets. There's a hedgehog who comes around sometimes. I call him Homer, after the storyteller. Though I doubt that Homer the Hedgehog knows any Greek," she added with a giggle.

Did she know Greek, as well as Latin? John wondered.

"My name is Greek," she added, absently brushing out the floor of one of her birdhouses.

"It's from a goddess, is it not?"

"Aye, Daphne. She lived in the country and rejected all the suitors who came to pursue her until they turned her into a tree so she wouldn't have the bother. I'd not like to be a tree, though. I'd rather be a bird. Or even a hedgehog." She looked over at him with a grin.

He wanted to help this girl, he thought with an urgency he'd not felt for years. "Your aviary is wonderful, Daphne."

"You can see it out the back window of the house. Then the birds will come back. Would you like to go in and have something to drink?"

"I'd like that very much." He followed her into the cottage, wondering how he should broach the subject of her foot. He didn't want to rush things, but he had a feeling that it would be easier to talk with her before her mother returned. "Daphne," he began carefully, "as I told your mother yesterday, I'm a doctor."

She turned around to him and pulled her skirt around to hide her leg, in a gesture that he suspected had become habitual. She nodded, but seemed to ignore his comment. "Would you care to sit down?" she asked, motioning to a bench by the big fireplace.

"Aye," he said, taking a seat.

"Is ale agreeable?" Though he could tell she was nervous, her manners were as fine as the lady of a manorhouse.

"Aye." He watched her move around the room,

fetching a mug from a shelf and a pitcher from a wooden cupboard. She seemed comfortable with her gait, though her twisted foot dragged as she walked, slowing her.

"Have you and your mother ever thought to talk to a physician about your foot?" he asked finally, after she had steamed the ale with a poker from the fire and handed him the mug.

"My foot?" she asked, her eyes darting away from him.

"Aye. I see that your right foot twists outward a bit. I wondered if you'd ever had any treatment for it."

She looked back at him, her lower lip quivering slightly. "My mother says we're all the Lord's creatures, no matter the shape or size."

He felt a wrench in his chest. Obviously, the subject was painful for the child, but he couldn't help her if he couldn't get her to talk freely. "Your mother is entirely right. But sometimes the Lord doesn't mind if we improve a bit on what he's produced."

"My mother says there's naught to be done."

"She may be right there, as well. But she may not. I've seen many people with a foot just like yours who have managed to make it much straighter in order to walk better."

Her eyes widened. "You've seen people with a foot like mine?"

"Aye, child. 'Tis a common enough thing."

"There's no one like me in all of Banburn."

"I warrant there's no one as pretty as you in all of Banburn, either," he said with a smile.

For the first time she gave a shy smile in reply.

"Would you sit beside me on the bench here and let me look at your foot?" he asked.

The smile died quickly. "I warrant my mother wouldn't like it."

He warranted the same, which was why he was trying to hurry her. If he could get a good idea of her condition before her mother came back, he would know better whether he had a chance to help her.

"I only want to look at your foot, Daphne. I promise that's all I will do."

The girl looked as if she were about to acquiesce when a voice from the open doorway startled them both. "Touch her and I will kill you."

John looked up, and his first impulse was to laugh. Lily stood framed in the door. In one hand she held a basket full of small red berries. With the other she grasped a heavy sword, its weight causing her arm to twist toward the ground.

John was careful to keep his expression serious. He rose from the bench and said evenly, "Good day, Mistress Lily. Your daughter and I have been waiting for you."

She lifted the tip of the sword toward him. "I'll ask you to leave," she said.

He walked slowly toward her. Where had she obtained such a weapon? he wondered. The blade glinted razor sharp in the sunlight, and the workmanship on the hilt was extraordinary. He'd seen dukes and earls with poorer armaments. "What do you intend to do with that thing?" he asked, motioning toward the sword.

"Whatever I have to."

He smiled at her. "There's no need for you to do anything other than to give it to me before you cut yourself."

She made a feeble attempt to waggle the sword at him. "I've told you to leave," she said.

He continued walking toward her. "That's a two-handed sword, mistress. You might want to put down your berries before you engage me in combat."

She looked uncertain for a moment, then leaned backward out the door and bent to one side to place the basket of fruit on the ground outside. John took the opportunity to spring forward. He anticipated little difficulty in snatching the blade from her hand, but he found her grip unexpectedly tight. The berries went flying as she dropped the basket and grabbed the weapon tightly. The sword jerked backward, cutting him across the palm of his right hand. Bright red blood spurted from the gash.

John and Lily looked at each other, equally astonished. Then Lily cried, "Oh," and let the sword clatter to the ground.

"Mummy!" Daphne cried. "You've stabbed him!"

Recovering from his surprise, John bent to retrieve the weapon. The cut was not serious. He'd had worse. But it was producing impressive quantities of blood. "Let's put this out of harm's way," he said, walking over and placing the sword on the mantelpiece. Then he turned back to Lily, who still stood in the doorway, her face white.

"Heaven save me, I didn't expect . . . I didn't mean . . . I've never—" she stumbled.

"Never fear, madam. No one would take you for a practiced swordsman. Now may I trouble you for a rag?" he asked, lifting his dripping fingers. "I appear to be bleeding all over your floor."

This jolted her to action. With Daphne looking on in fascinated horror, she pushed him to a seat on the bench and brought rags and a pot of water from the fire. "Is it bad, do you think?" she asked as she gently washed his hand.

"I believe I shall survive," he replied, hiding a smile. It was almost worth the sting of the cut to see the transformation from the haughty woman who had twice ordered him from her house.

She continued cleaning his hand, rinsing the bloody rag in the basin of water, but every time she wiped away the blood, more would seep from the wound. Her expression was remorseful as she looked up at him. "Shall I stitch it closed?" she asked.

This time he let his smile show as he picked up one of the cloths she'd brought. "If you would just help me tear this into a strip, I'll bind it tightly enough to stop the bleeding. I've been stitched a time or two," he added, "and I don't relish the experience."

When the bandage was ready, John deftly wound it around his hand, finishing the job with a neat knot that he tied with one hand and his teeth.

"So you really are a doctor," Lily said slowly when he had finished and sat back against the bench.

"Aye, that I am. Though I've not been active in the profession in recent years."

"What do you do now?" Daphne asked. "You're not from Banburn, are you?"

"Nay, lass, though I was born hereabouts. These days I'm from nowhere and everywhere. As to my occupation, why, I've had many over these past years." He shot a rueful glance at the blade on the mantel. "For one thing, I've been known as one of the best swordsmen in Ireland—until today."

Daphne giggled, and the sound seemed to brighten the room. "Imagine that, Mummy," she said. "You've bested a real swordsman."

"I did no such thing," Lily said hastily. "It was an accident."

"Where did you get such a weapon?" John asked again. He stood and walked over to examine the blade. "It's magnificent. And how did you come to have it with you today? Surely you don't use it to pick berries?"

"The sword is an . . . an heirloom. I took it with me

today because—" She glanced at Daphne, then back at John. "I'm not sure why I took it. 'Twas a whim."

John's face grew serious. "Perhaps you feared a visit from the boys who harmed your daughter yesterday. I'd not blame you. They should be dealt with. Is there no magistrate in the village you can go to?"

Both mother and daughter remained silent.

"Do you know who they were?" he asked finally. "I'll go into the village myself and find the scoundrels."

"'Tis best forgotten," Lily said after a long moment.

John looked from mother to daughter in disbelief. "They could have killed her—they nearly did. How can a thing like that be forgotten? What if they make another attempt?"

Lily drew herself up, and once again she turned into the arrogant woman of the previous day. "We intend to be more careful in the future," she said coolly. "Daphne has developed a bad habit of wandering off by herself, but she's promised me that she won't do it again."

John felt his temper rising. "Good God, woman, don't be foolish. There are laws to protect people—"

"Laws are for regular people," she said. "Not for the likes of Daphne and me."

John shook his head, and turned to Daphne. "Child, I mean no disrespect to your mother, but you should know that laws are for everyone. And if anyone *ever* tries to hurt you again, you run and scream for help. You'll find that people will help you. Most people in this world are not like those boys."

"Some folks in the market smile at me," Daphne told him shyly.

"Of course they do, and they would help you, too, if you were in trouble. Remember that." He glanced over at Lily, whose expression had grown stormy.

"Aye, some folks smile," she said bitterly. "And some folks point and murmur behind their hands about the witches of Whistler's Woods. If you haven't already heard the tale, you soon will. So don't be telling my child that 'tis a benevolent world. I know better."

Daphne's smile had disappeared. John let out a long breath. Years ago when he'd been practicing his profession, one of the first lessons he'd learned was that the heart was much more difficult to cure than the body. Something had poisoned the heart of the woman who was watching him with such hostile eyes, and her daughter was now suffering the consequences.

"Will you at least let me look at her foot?" he asked.

Lily shook her head. "I apologize for having cut you. The truth is I wish violence on no man. But I meant what I said when I came in with the sword. You're not to touch my daughter—ever."

John glanced at the girl, who was watching their exchange with an expression of misery. Daphne was on the verge of blossoming into a lovely young woman, in spite of her bad foot. Did her mother think to keep her isolated forever?

Tears filled Daphne's big eyes. He gave her a wink of reassurance and forced himself to speak pleasantly to her mother. "I will honor your wishes, mistress, but should you change your mind, please remember my offer. I believe your daughter would walk more easily with a brace. And such a device may even be able to correct some of the problem."

"As far as I'm concerned, Dr. Black," Lily said icily, "my daughter has no problem. Now I would ask you once again to be about your way and leave us in peace."

He bit back a retort. The woman's refusal to discuss Daphne's condition was not helping her daughter, but if she continued to be adamant, there was little he could do. "Good day, then, madam," he said after a long moment.

She nodded without speaking.

He walked over to Daphne and crouched down to speak directly to her. "You're a special lass, Daphne. I'm proud to have met you." She gave him her timid smile. He straightened up, resisting the impulse to put a hand on her head. "Don't forget you promised bread to your friend outside."

"I won't."

He smiled, then turned and walked out of the cottage, closing the door behind him.

Lily didn't say anything after their visitor had left. She took the basin of water and a clean rag and knelt to scrub angrily at the bloodstains on the floor. After a moment of rubbing, she dipped the rag in the basin. The water was already so bloody that the cloth came out scarlet. With a sigh of disgust, she threw it back into the water and stood up. Lifting the basin from the floor, she said, "I need to fetch more water."

"Shall I do it?" Daphne asked.

Lily shook her head.

"I warrant Dr. Black shouldn't come around here any more," the girl said gravely. "He makes you angry."

Lily paused on her way to the door. In her heart she knew that her behavior did not come from anger, but from fear. She turned back to her daughter and set the basin on the floor. "Sweetcakes, you're happy here with the life we have together, aren't you?"

Daphne did not hesitate. "Of course, Mummy. You know I am."

Lily smiled. She'd been abandoned by family and mistreated by the world, but there were moments when she looked into her child's eyes and considered herself to be the luckiest person on earth. "I'm happy, too. And

I don't intend to let anything change the life we have together here. That's why I sent Dr. Black away. He wants to change things."

Daphne went over to put her arms around her mother's waist. "I don't think he'll come again, Mummy. After all, you did nearly cut his hand off."

Lily gave a little shiver. "'Twas hardly that. I believe Dr. Black thought it was just a little cut."

Daphne turned her face contentedly into her mother's side as Lily returned her daughter's embrace. "He was rather brave about it, wasn't he, Mummy?"

"Aye." Brave and skillful, she thought as she remembered how the doctor had deftly bandaged his own wound. Once again she asked herself the question that had been torturing her since the man's first visit. Was she wrong to reject his offer of help? Was it fair to Daphne to refuse to consider a treatment that might make things easier for her?

"In any event, I warrant he'll not be wanting to risk a repetition," Daphne said wistfully, disengaging herself from her mother's arms. "Still, it was exciting to have a visitor, wasn't it?"

Lily stepped away and once again picked up the basin. "I suppose so."

She started toward the door, then stopped as Daphne said, "Mummy?"

"Aye?"

"Do you think Dr. Black was telling the truth about my foot? I mean, about being able to make it better?"

Lily felt her heart crack inside her chest. "I—I'm not sure, Sweetcakes."

Daphne limped over to the corner of the room and picked up a basket of old bread. "I reckon now we'll never know," she said matter-of-factly. Then she moved past her mother toward the door. "I'll go out with you. I'm going to feed my birds."

Four

Catriona turned around on the seat of the wooden cart with a gentle sigh. Her two sons were tumbling around on the bed of the little wagon, locked in one of their endless wrestling matches. "Lorcan! Paddy!" she admonished. "If you don't sit nicely like big boys, I warrant Uncle John will not want to take us to market ever again."

John hid a smile. The youngsters' antics had not bothered him in the least, but for Catriona's sake he was willing to serve as the excuse for a lesson in manners. "I myself was just thinking 'tis a shame that Paddy and Lorcan aren't old enough to drive this rickety old thing," he said with a casual glance behind him. "I could use the help."

Lorcan pushed his brother away and pulled himself to a kneeling position behind the seat. "Why, I'm old enough, Uncle John. Papa lets me drive it."

"Does he now? I'd have said 'tis too hard a task for such a little tyke. The wheels are none too steady and require a firm hand."

Lorcan scrambled over the backrest of the seat and pushed himself between his mother and John. "I can hold 'em as steady as anyone," he promised. "I done it hundreds of times."

"Ah, I hadn't realized we had an experienced teamster in the family," John said gravely, handing the cart reins to the boy at his side. The lumbering vehicle required little guidance.

As expected, the move triggered a small, indignant voice from behind him. "I can drive, too, Uncle John. Papa lets me."

Lorcan looked back with a contemptuous glance at his little brother. "You can only drive sitting on Papa's lap, Paddy. You're too little."

Catriona shook her head and rolled her eyes at John. She'd been an only child, and was a female to boot. He supposed that it was difficult for her to accept what seemed to him normal male rivalry. He turned around in his seat to address the smaller boy. "I reckon your papa is a good teacher, since I see that Lorcan is doing such a fine job at the reins," he said. "When you're the age of your brother, I've no doubt you'll be doing as well as he. In the meantime, on the way home today you may sit on my lap and show me how you drive with your papa. Is that a bargain?"

The boy nodded, his good humor restored.

John ruffled a hand through the child's tousled hair, then turned back facing the road.

Catriona leaned against the backrest with a smile. "You're good with them, John. You'd think you had a dozen of your own at home."

"I don't even have a home, my dear, much less a dozen children."

Catriona thought for a moment. "Well, you have O'Malley House. It's your home whenever you want it."

"I know, lass, and glad I am of it. You must know that I hold you dear as any daughter I may have had. If your mother had chosen me instead of your father, you'd be my daughter in truth." He put his arm casually around Lorcan and gave a slight extra tug to the rein the boy held in his right hand, causing the old plow horse to veer slightly toward the center of the road.

"I can do it, Uncle," Lorcan insisted.

"I know you can, lad. You're doing just fine."

Catriona was frowning. "'Tis not too late, John. You're still young enough to have a family of your own."

John laughed. "'Tis not the years, but the life they've been put to. I reckon 'twould be a brave lass who would take on a grizzled old soldier like me."

"You're neither old nor grizzled," Catriona argued with a huff of indignation. "Why, in London, you had more ladies surrounding you than the court tailor showing the latest fashion. You had the lady Arabella quite fascinated. She confided it to me."

"Your friend Arabella was a sweet thing, but I suspect her deepest thoughts went little beyond the latest court gossip. And she was young enough to be my daughter."

"Her age doesn't seem to bother most of the older courtiers. Arabella was one of the most sought after of Elizabeth's ladies."

"Because many old men are simply looking for young flesh to make them remember their livelier days. The simpler the maid, the better, so as not to cause the old goat undue taxation in keeping track of his young wife."

Catriona laughed, but shook her head. "Ah, John, such cynicism is unlike you. I'm not accepting your version of yourself as the weary warrior, tired of life. I've seen your romantic side, don't forget. I still have the book with the tender words you once wrote to my mother."

John could feel his cheeks grow warm in an uncharacteristic flush. "That was long ago, child. Before you were born, in fact."

"And what of it? Would you make me out to be that ancient?" she teased.

He chuckled and clapped a hand on Lorcan's shoulder. They were arriving at the edge of Banburn, where a number of stands had been set out for the weekly market. "You are at least old enough to be the mother of a fine teamster," he said lightly. "And I should be old enough to know better than to engage in this kind of discussion with a lady."

The topic was dropped as John helped Lorcan steer the cart under a tree and pull it to a stop. Then the boy crawled over John's knees to drop over the side of the wagon to the ground. "I'll tie her up, Uncle!" he shouted. "Papa taught me the knots."

John grinned at the eager boy, then climbed down himself and held his arms out to help Catriona and Padraic. The market beyond them was already bustling with activity. The sounds of voices and horse-drawn carts were punctuated by regular singsong shouts as the vendors touted their wares. Tantalizing smells arose from the row of cook fires—sizzling meat and the yeasty scent of fresh bread pasties.

Suddenly the years seemed to slip away, and John was a boy again, arriving to market with his own family—his parents and brother, now all gone. The sounds and smells seemed to curl their way inside him, leaving him with a deep, warm sense of satisfaction.

Catriona stepped beside him and tucked her arm under his elbow. "I'm not giving up, John," she said archly. "I've decided we need to find you a lady, and when I set my mind on something, I usually get it. Just ask Niall."

John gave her fingers a pat. The day was too perfect

for argument. "I wish you success in the venture, my dear. But don't blame me if my growling stomach finds me more interested in yon baker's sweet tarts than any of the feminine beauties Banburn may have to offer."

"But, Mummy, we haven't been to market in weeks. You said we might go next time."

Lily sighed. She and her daughter had been up since dawn. They'd taken their morning bread and cheese on an expedition to pick wild apples from the far corner of the wood. It had been a pleasant morning, and Lily had hoped that it would make Daphne forget the promised visit to the market. Now as they sat at their table, peeling the harvested fruit, Lily tried to steel herself against the disappointment in her daughter's voice. It was made more difficult by the fact that Daphne's tone was simply sad, not pouting. Her daughter rarely became petulant, even when Lily had to turn down her requests to expand the horizons of the small world her mother had created for her.

"I know, Sweetcakes," she told her, "but that was before the incident with the boys."

"And before Dr. Black came to our house."

"Aye. 'Twould be safer if we didn't show ourselves for a time. We have everything we need here."

Daphne scrunched her forehead, deep in thought. Finally her face brightened, and she said triumphantly, "We don't have any more honey. Not a drop. How are we to make apple tarts without honey?"

With a sinking feeling, Lily put down the apple she'd just peeled and rose to her feet. "Are you sure?" she asked.

"Aye, I looked for some in the crock last night to sweeten my ale."

Lily walked over to the wooden pantry and pulled open the door, though she knew that it was unlikely that Daphne was mistaken. They only had one crock for honey, and it was, indeed, empty.

"You yourself said we should make the tarts today, Mummy, since the apples wouldn't keep."

"We could put them in vinegar—" Lily stopped as she watched the sparkle dim in Daphne's eyes. "Do you really want to go, in spite of those boys?"

The light in Daphne's eyes rekindled, carefully. "Aye, I do, ever so much. I don't care about them when I'm with you. And in any event, we probably won't see them. They're not from the village, you know."

Lily knew. From her daughter's description, she had guessed the identity of one of the boys who had tried to harm Daphne, though she hadn't yet decided what she was going to do about it. "Perhaps you're right—we're not likely to see them at the market."

"Nor Dr. Black, either," Daphne added with a wisp of regret.

"I reckon Dr. Black would have little business in the Banburn market," Lily agreed. The thought was reassuring. She closed the pantry door. "Very well, we'll go." As Daphne jumped to her feet, she added, "Just to get the honey. Then we'll have to hurry back if we're to finish our pies before bedtime."

"Can we just look at the ribbons, Mummy?"

Lily smiled. There had been a time in her life when she, too, had loved pretty things. "Aye, Sweetcakes, we'll look at the ribbons. I might even buy you a new one to keep that hair from tangling so."

"I'm going to change to my green frock," Daphne said, beaming. "Mayhap we'll find a ribbon to match." Then she started toward the bedchamber using the lopsided gallop that was the closest her bad leg would allow to a run.

•　•　•

John had thoroughly enjoyed his day. To Catriona's amusement, he'd been even more enthusiastic than her sons at sampling the tasty wares of the food sellers.

"I'll just have one more tart, then I'm done," he said finally as they came to the end of the row.

"So shall I," Lorcan said, holding a hand over his stomach in imitation of his Uncle John.

"I should think you'd had enough," Catriona demurred. "You'll have a bellyache and keep Nanny up all night long."

"How about we divide one?" John suggested with a wink. He pulled a coin from his purse and handed it to the seller, who nodded his thanks and passed over a sticky pastry.

By the time the transaction was completed, Lorcan's gaze had strayed to the middle of the road, where Padraic was trailing along with some of the village boys who were playing a game of hoops. "I'll eat my half later!" he shouted, running into the fray.

John chuckled and popped the entire cake into his mouth. "I warrant I'll be the one with the bellyache," he observed.

Catriona laughed. "At least your belly is of a size to handle all that food."

John looked down at his flat middle with mock worry. "Are you calling me paunchy, lass?"

"Nay, though I daresay a few more weeks with us—" She broke off as John's expression suddenly changed.

"Those three boys across the road, watching the game," he said tersely. "Do you know them?"

Catriona squinted. The trio was standing in silence, eyes on the children in the middle of the road. Their dress was generally finer than the village youngsters. "I believe 'tis the O'Farrell lad and his friends, the Crawley brothers. Why?"

John absentmindedly licked the stickiness from his

fingers. "I'm not sure. They put me in mind of the boys who threw the little girl into the pond the night I came. 'Twas too foggy to see their faces, but the size is right, and something about the way they're standing there together."

Catriona gave a low whistle. "I hope you're wrong. The O'Farrell boy is the son of Nevin O'Farrell, the Earl of Lymond. He's lord of Lymond Castle."

John tried to take himself back to the scene that afternoon at the pond. He'd heard the boys shouting, but their voices had revealed little about their origins. In Killarney the speech of the gentry was about the same as the more humble village folk. But one of them had used something that could have been a name. "What's the tall one's name?"

Catriona thought for a moment. "That's the O'Farrell boy. I think they call him Desmond. In truth, we've not had much to do with the family. Niall says we shouldn't forgive them for looking the other way when Wolverton took over my lands."

Desmond. That didn't sound quite right. John wished he could remember more clearly. "How about the others—the Crawleys?"

"Named after their father, both of them. People call them Harry One and Harry Two."

John gave a brief smile, but continued watching as the tall boy in the middle signaled to his companions and the three turned to walk up the road toward the center of town. "I can't understand why the girl and her mother won't identify the culprits," he said finally.

Catriona shrugged. "Perhaps the girl didn't know who they were. They may not have been from around here."

John shook his head. He'd had the feeling that Lily knew who had attacked her child, and since she would not accept his help in dealing with the matter, he could only assume that she had her own plans for preventing a repetition of the incident. He flexed his still-sore hand. Surely she didn't think she could protect her daughter with a sword she'd barely been able to lift?

"Why, there they are. Why don't we ask them?" Catriona asked, surprising him out of his reverie. He turned to look as she pointed to the end of the food stands. There, with her daughter's hand clasped firmly in hers, was the exasperating Mistress Lily herself. She was dressed in a dark purple gown with a full kirtle and long bodice that accentuated her graceful form. She held a big gray crock that nestled on the curve of her right hip. John felt a sudden increase in the temperature of the warm afternoon.

"So they *do* come into the village," he said.

"Aye. Remember I showed you the swan basket she made for me? I see them here regularly on market day, though they never seem to have much to say to any-one."

John glanced out at the melee in the middle of the road. "Shall I retrieve your two pups so that we can go pay our respects?"

Catriona shook her head and began to stroll toward Lily and her daughter. "We'll leave the boys at their game. As long as I stay within sight, they'll find me when they're tired of playing."

He was sure that the two females they sought spotted him immediately, but they made no move to meet them as John and Catriona approached. Once again he noticed that Daphne pulled nervously at the side of her dress as if to be sure that her twisted leg was hidden from view. The gown was a pretty green that made her bright blue eyes sparkle the color of a Killarney mountain lake. A matching green ribbon tied back her long hair.

"Good day, fair ladies," he said, smiling first at the

girl, then her mother. He pointed to the crock and added in an aside to Daphne, "Have you come for more flower seeds to feed to the birds?"

"Good day, Dr. Black," the girl said, returning his smile. She looked pleased to see him. Then she turned toward Catriona and bobbed an awkward curtsy.

"I believe you are acquainted with my friend, Lady Riordan?" John asked Lily, who had yet to speak.

She gave a kind of regal nod, but did not repeat her daughter's curtsy. "Good day, my lady," she said. Then she acknowledged John's presence with a murmured, "Dr. Black."

There was a moment of awkward silence. Finally Catriona said to Lily, "I was telling Dr. Black that you and your daughter make quite miraculous baskets. I still have the black swan you fashioned."

Some of the stiffness went out of Lily's expression. " 'Twill last a lifetime with proper care," she said. "I'm glad you like it, my lady."

John looked around at the marketplace, then back to Lily. "Have you just arrived? You may have come too late. I fear between myself and Catriona's two boys, we've nearly depleted the entire row of its wares."

"We're here for some honey," Daphne clarified. "To finish the apple tarts."

"Mmmm. If I hadn't already received one insult today about my thickening girth, I'd be tempted to follow you home to sample them." He patted his middle as he spoke, and saw that Lily's gaze rested for a moment on his flat abdomen, then slid away.

"Perhaps you could—" Daphne's voice faltered as she glanced nervously at her mother, but then she continued, "Perhaps you could come for some on the morrow. They won't be finished until late in any event." Drawing herself up with some boldness, she added to Catriona, "You'd be welcome as well, my lady."

John glanced at Lily, whose expression had once again become rigid. He reached to lay his hand briefly on Daphne's shining black hair. "I thank you, lass. Though, of course, 'twould be for your mother to say if we were welcome or no."

Lily watched her daughter's bright face with a feeling of helplessness. She'd tried to devote herself to giving her child so much love that she would never feel the lack of the friends and family that surrounded most normal people. But the few glimpses she'd had of how readily Daphne responded to John Black's warmth deepened her awareness that she could never hope to be her child's entire world. It was a realization that had been coming to her gradually, and all at once it seemed quite clear. She must do something to provide Daphne with more opportunity to meet people. But she had no intention of beginning with the man whose hand rested on her daughter's head. Somehow she sensed that allowing John Black into their sheltered existence would wrest things out of her control, and Lily did not intend to let that happen.

"Dr. Black has many more important things to do than eat apple tarts, Daphne," she said coolly.

"On the contrary. The consumption of apple tarts happens to be high on my list of important activities," he said smoothly, giving Daphne another wink.

Blast the man.

Fortunately, the lovely young woman at the doctor's side changed the subject. "John has told me what happened the other day at Cotter's Pond," she said to Lily. "What a terrible scare. Is your daughter fully recovered?"

Lily turned to Lady Riordan with some relief. Though she'd rather not discuss the incident at the pond, it was preferable talking to anyone other than Dr.

Black, whose gray eyes watched her as though he could read every one of her secrets.

"She's recovered, aye, thank you."

"Dr. Black saved my life," Daphne added.

Catriona smiled at the girl. "He's a handy fellow to have around, is he not? He saved my life once, as well."

Daphne's eyes grew round. "Did he rescue you from a pond?"

"Nay, but he helped me recover when I lost my first baby."

Lily glanced at the doctor, who was shaking his head. "You were strong and healthy, lass," he said. " 'Twas nature that cured you. I did virtually nothing."

His modesty was unexpected. In her other life before Daphne's birth, Lily had lived in a world where the advice of physicians was sought for the smallest illness. She'd never held a good opinion of the profession. She remembered them as being an arrogant lot, with remedies that often harmed as much as healed. John Black appeared to be different. But as she knew all too well, appearances could be deceiving.

Lady Riordan was addressing her again. "So we wondered if Daphne recognized the boys who did this to her?"

The young woman's concern was so apparent that it was impossible to take offense at the directness of her question. Still, Lily wasn't ready to answer it.

"Nay, I fear she did not know them," she answered calmly.

"I did not know their *names*, Mummy," Daphne corrected. "But I knew them. I've seen them a number of times around the woods. They—they've watched me before."

Lily shifted the crock in her arm. "I beg pardon,

Lady Riordan, but we must be taking our leave. I'm afraid this honey is quite heavy."

"Forgive me," John said. Before she knew what he was doing, he had pulled the jar out of her grasp. "It certainly is too heavy for you to be carrying all the way back to the woods. We shall take you back in our cart."

Daphne clapped her hands together with glee, but Lily's feeling of dread deepened. " 'Tis not necessary," she said. "I'm used to carrying things. Anyway, the road through the woods is too narrow for a wagon."

"Not this one. It's only a small cart. It will travel your road just fine."

Lily tried her refusal again. "We really enjoy the walk—"

"Rubbish. No one enjoys walking with a heavy crock like this. I insist. We'll deliver you home. Do you have further business here today?"

With a sinking heart, Lily shook her head. "Nay, we were ready to leave."

John smiled. "Good. I'll fetch the boys and we'll be off."

Five

John was surprised to see that only a few moments after he had seen the entire group settled in the little cart, Catriona and Lily were talking as comfortably as if they had been old friends. There was no evidence of any difference in their stations, though Catriona had been raised in the high society of London. Of course, he had no idea where or how Lily had been raised. From the first time he'd met her and seen her cottage, he'd suspected that she was not a simple peasant. Now he was certain of it. Peasants didn't teach their children Latin and Greek.

It was a warm day with a bright blue sky. Holding the reins loosely, he leaned back in contentment and let the two women carry the conversation.

He'd helped Daphne climb into the back section with the boys. Both Padraic and Lorcan had glanced curiously at her twisted foot, but neither one had asked about it. Daphne herself had so far remained quiet during the trip, even though John had had the feeling that she was excited to be riding with the Riordan family.

"Forgive me, Lily," Catriona was saying, "but don't you get lonely living out in the woods all by yourself?

Wouldn't you care to join in more of the neighborhood activities?"

Lily smiled at her new friend, but shook her head. "Daphne and I are happy where we are. We have each other, and that's all we need."

John gave a rueful smile. Lily might be responding more readily to Catriona than she had to him, but the end result was the same. The woman wanted to be left alone.

Catriona frowned as she lowered her voice and observed, "Perhaps you are happy enough, but is it the best thing for your daughter? I would think her at an age where she would like to be among other young people."

"Like the ones who tried to drown her the other day?"

The stiffness had gone back into Lily's posture. Catriona reached to put a conciliatory hand on her arm. "Nay, not like those. But there are many good people she could get to know."

"We like things as they are," Lily said with a cold tone that ended the friendly conversation they had been having.

They rode along in silence for several minutes. Finally John glanced back at the children and asked, "Are you all comfortable? Are these lads behaving like gentleman, Daphne?"

Daphne smiled at the two boys, who returned the gesture with shy smiles of their own. "We are fine, Dr. Black. 'Tis kind of you to offer the ride."

"We couldn't let two ladies walk home on a warm day like this, could we, lads?" he asked.

The boys shook their heads. "Is it hard for you to walk on that foot?" Lorcan asked Daphne, pointing to her leg.

Daphne flushed, but seemed to realize that the question was one of simple curiosity. Neither one of the boys appeared at all repulsed by her oddity. To John's surprise, she pulled her dress up slightly to show them her foot as she answered, "It causes me to limp, which makes me tired after too long a walk," she explained. "Mostly I worry about how it looks when I wobble along. Sometimes I feel like a broken old rocking horse."

Lorcan and Padraic giggled, but Lorcan said, "Nay, you can hardly tell. I only saw it when Uncle John lifted you into the wagon."

Daphne nodded. "Climbing is hard."

She offered the explanation of her lameness with a complete lack of self-pity, John noted. The horse gave a sudden jolt as they turned into the narrow path through the forest. John pulled back on the reins to steady the animal, wincing as the leather strap pulled against his bandaged hand.

Lily looked at the bandage with a flush of guilt. "Is your—is your hand better?" she asked.

"Aye," he answered, willing himself not to react to the sudden pain. The leather had pulled straight across the wound. It hurt like hell.

"My mother stabbed your uncle with a sword," Daphne told her companions with a slight air of pride. "She was protecting me."

Catriona turned sharply to look at John, and he gave an inward groan. He'd told his hosts that he'd injured his hand on a piece of fence wire. " 'Twas an accident," he said weakly.

"I didn't mean it," Lily offered at the same time.

Catriona looked from one to the other, as if waiting for a further explanation, but when neither spoke, she said quietly, "I'm sure," and lapsed into silence.

Embarrassed at being caught in a blatant lie, and

with his hand throbbing, John was glad when the cart pulled within sight of the little cottage.

"Why, this is a lovely place!" Catriona exclaimed. "What beautiful flowers."

"I thank you, milady," Lily said hurriedly. She jumped down from the wagon without waiting for John's help. Then she went around the back to assist Daphne. Finally, lifting out the big crock, she added to John, "Thank you both. You've been very kind."

Without another word, she seized her daughter's hand and started up the path to the house. Daphne turned back to wave at the boys, her expression wistful.

When the mother and daughter had neared the house, Lorcan said, "I think Daphne would have liked us to stay and see her house, Mummy."

Catriona looked thoughtful. "Perhaps another time. I believe Daphne's mother is a bit fearful of visitors."

"Why?" the boy asked, as if the concept was totally foreign to him.

Catriona smiled sadly at her two boys. "Maybe she worries that other children will make Daphne feel bad about her foot."

"We didn't make her feel bad, did we, Mummy?"

"Nay. I think Daphne knew that you thought no less of her because she has one foot a little different from yours."

Lorcan nodded, then seemed to forget the subject as Padraic pulled him back down on the wagon bed to play.

John had been maneuvering to turn the cart around in the small space of the narrow path. Finally headed the right direction, he looked over at Catriona with a sigh. "I lied about my hand," he confirmed.

She nodded. "I must say I wondered why."

He shrugged. "I'm not sure. It just seemed that Mis-

tress Lily's reputation had suffered enough without
adding mayhem to the list. And, truly, 'twas an accident. I was pulling the sword out of her hand and cut
myself."

"But she was threatening you with it?"

"Aye. She was worried that I'd come to hurt her
daughter."

Catriona shook her head. "Ah, John, your expres-
sion softens when you look at her—at both of them.
I've only seen that look in your eyes a few times.
They're reached you, somehow."

"Aye," he admitted simply.

Catriona was silent for a few moments. Finally she
said soberly, "I hate to say it, but I'm afraid you'd be
wiser to put the thought of them out of your head. Lily
obviously wants neither help nor company. And next
time you try to offer either, the wound might be to
more than your hand."

John nodded. It was the same advice he'd been giving himself since he'd first set eyes on Lily and her
daughter. Perhaps this time he was ready to listen.

Lymond Castle was the oldest structure in eastern
Killarney. Some said it had been built on the ruins of a
druid temple and that spirits of the ancients still walked
the grounds on holy days. Its lord had carried the title of
Earl of Lymond for as long as anyone could remember
and had traditionally stayed aloof from the other landed
gentry in the area. The present earl had kept himself
even more distant, which only contributed to the rumors
that he had secretly aided in the seizure and burning of
the O'Malley lands years before.

Lymond himself was bothered by neither the isolation nor the rumors. He preferred the company of his
prize hunting falcons to anything human. He'd duti-
fully taken a wife and sired a son on her, then shunted

her off to a far corner of the castle to live out her life like the poor mouse she had always been.

His son, Desmond, represented the only complex factor in his orderly existence. Sometimes when he looked at the lad who was now growing tall and assuming a decided resemblance to his father, Lymond felt an unaccustomed warmth. Most of the time the lad represented little more than a nuisance. Recently he'd sometimes become an outright bother.

"I told you to stay away from Banburn, and to most particularly stay away from those two wretches living in Whistler's Woods," he told the boy as Desmond stood in front of him in the castle antechamber. Lymond's knuckles were white around the large Lymond seal he held clasped in his right hand, but he did not raise his voice. Nevin O'Farrell never raised his voice.

"We left as soon as we saw them in the market," Desmond said. He was tall and too slender, in the way of boys who had suddenly grown too fast for their own body, but his face was long with strong, aquiline features, like his father. Son of privilege, he'd already discovered that between his fine looks and his father's purse, the favors of any whore or milkmaid in the county were his for the taking.

"Would you have me chain you below in the donjon for a few months until you get some sense into your maggoty brain?" his father asked. "If you and your idiot friends had killed that girl, you'd be headed for the gibbet. Earl's son or no. Have you understood that?"

"Harry One said she was a witch and would float. Anyway, we'd all had too much ale and—"

Lymond pounded the seal on his desk. Desmond gave a little jump and craned his neck in discomfort. "I don't want to hear more about that . . . unfortunate incident. I just want you to stay away from Banburn and

Cotter's Pond and Whistler's Woods and the entire area. I never want you to see that girl again, or, more to the point, for her to see you."

Desmond dropped his chin and nodded.

Lymond watched his son's bowed head for a moment, then stared over at the fire blazing on the hearth, lost in thought. "If you only knew the mischief you could cause—" He stopped.

Desmond's head came up. His expression changed from chastened to crafty. "I never even had to tell you about the event, Father, but ever since I did, you've been in a bad humor. The cripple doesn't know me, and likely never will. Why do you care about her?"

Lymond's gaze switched from the fire back to his son. "I care nothing about her. But I have only one heir, and I don't fancy seeing him swinging on Gallows Hill."

"Who is she?" Desmond persisted. "Who is the witch of Whistler's Woods?"

Lymond's expression went blank. "She's nobody. Now leave me and remember what I've said. When we reach London, I want you on your best behavior."

Desmond continued to look thoughtful as he made his way out of his father's office and up the castle stairs.

"Catriona asked me to talk with you, John," Niall said bluntly. "She's worried that you've become taken with this witch person."

The two men had met early that morning to hold their long promised race, but the rain had returned, so they ended up talking, perched on two bundles of hay under the wide eave of the stable as the rain pelted down around them.

"I thought you didn't believe in witches," John said with some amusement.

"I don't. But this Lily person is odd, you have to admit. Cat says you lied for her." When John remained silent, Niall added, "I thought John Black never lied."

"'Twas a harmless enough tale."

"To protect this woman. Whose name you don't even know."

John couldn't decide whether to be irritated or amused. "I've seen more than forty-five summers, Niall, almost as much as you and Cat put together. I believe I can take care of myself."

Niall grinned at his friend. "I told Cat as much. But she made me promise to talk with you just the same."

"She made you promise?"

Niall's grin deepened. "Let's say, she made it worth my while to do her the favor."

"Ah, my friend," John said with a sigh, "you don't know what a lucky man you are."

Niall looked out through the rain at the stable yard and the gentle green hills beyond. "Aye," he said softly. "I do."

John reached over to punch his shoulder. "Then enjoy what you have and stop spending time worrying about an old campaigner who's probably overstayed his welcome under your roof."

Niall looked at John in surprise. "You're joking, I trust."

"Nay. I was thinking 'tis time for me to leave this Eden and get back to the real world of war and politics."

"You've not yet been here a fortnight. We'd expected to have you for months."

"I serve no purpose here, Niall. I thought I could use a time of idleness, but I find myself itchy. I'm beginning to feel like a useless old helmet, thrown to the edge of the battlefield."

Niall looked at his friend with concern. "Cat is

counting on having you as part of our household for the winter, at least. Anything less would do her a great hurt."

Now it was John's turn to look out at the rain. It would be cold up north. And lonely.

"I shall have to leave you one of these days," he said finally. "I'm not quite ready to be tucked away and fed coddled milk and bread. I've a bit of life in me still, you know."

Niall grinned. "I don't believe 'twas with coddled milk that you drank me under the table last night." His expression grew serious again. "I know you'll have to leave, John, but not yet. Cat wouldn't hear of it. She'll think the witch of Whistler's Wood drove you away." A sudden gust blew the rain under the eave, wetting them. Niall stood. "Forget this talk of leaving. Let's go inside for some warm dinner."

John stood more slowly. "'Tis kind of you and Cat to want me," he said. "I warrant I can stay through the holidays."

Lily could feel the cold creeping through her as she made the final turn into the still-familiar pathway to the castle. The trail was heavily shaded, but the thick trees were not the cause of her shivering. It was a deeper cold, one that she hadn't been able to escape, even after all these years. If she'd had her choice, she'd never set foot anywhere near Lymond Castle, ever again.

It had taken her nearly a week to decide to come, but once the decision was made, she'd taken quick action. She'd left a surprised Daphne with a pot of stew simmering on the stove for her dinner, and had told her daughter that she might not return the entire day. It would be the first time she'd left her for such a length of time. When Daphne had asked for details of her plans, she hadn't lied, but she hadn't told the whole truth.

"I'm going to Lymond Castle to visit Aunt Maired," she'd said.

"But Aunt Maired has always visited us here." Daphne had looked puzzled. "May I go with you?"

"Nay, child, 'tis a long, long walk. I'll have to keep a brisk pace if I'm to be back before dark."

She'd left the girl disappointed and more than a little nervous, but she trusted Daphne to keep her word and stay near the house while she was gone. As long as she didn't venture beyond the little haven Lily had created for them deep in the woods, she would be safe.

Just for today, she prayed silently. Keep her there, and keep her safe. She was beginning to understand that it would be impossible to keep Daphne confined in their small world forever. It was that knowledge that had put her on the path to Lymond Castle. She had to ensure that the incident at Cotter's Pond would never happen again. She'd told Daphne the truth about her destination. But it wasn't her sister-in-law Maired she'd come to see. Maired would be of little help in her current mission.

She didn't underestimate her sister-in-law. Maired had her own strength and had made the best of her life with a man whom Lily considered to be a monster. Over the years Maired had been Lily's only connection to her past. The sweet woman had visited the cottage in Whistler's Wood several times a year, often bringing touches of Lily's past—a piece of furniture or a treasured book. She'd also pressed money on her exiled sister-in-law. And Lily had taken it, for Daphne's sake.

But today Lily had not come to see Maired. She'd come to Lymond Castle to see the earl—her brother, Nevin O'Farrell.

Lily had almost reached the stable yard behind the

castle. Through the trees she could see the imposing
North Tower where she'd often played as a child. The
tower had been her fantasy world, a place where a
young girl could truly believe that one day a shining
knight would arrive to bring her a world of love and
magic.

She stopped, still within the shelter of the trees,
looking up at the tower. Memories flooded through
her. The shining knight had arrived, a handsome
Englishman, but he'd brought neither love nor
magic. She smiled at the thought, pleased that the
memories had turned to irony—a great improvement
on the raw pain that had accompanied them for so
many years.

It was past midday. She didn't have much time if
she was going to see her brother and return before dark.
He'll be even less happy to see you than you are to see
him, she told herself firmly, trying to gather courage.
And more surprised.

She'd rehearsed her speech endlessly the entire
night, lying awake in bed next to Daphne. She'd be
calm and determined, she'd decided. She'd show no
curiosity about the castle that had been her home for
twenty years. She didn't care what he had done to it,
what changes he had made. She'd state her case, then
leave.

"If you want the Lymond family secrets to stay secret," she'd tell him, "you will see that your son never,
ever comes near my daughter again."

It would be enough, she was certain. Nevin's weak-
ness had always been fear of the truth.

She'd come by the back way where the old castle
walls had long since crumbled. She was tempted to
scramble over the ruins and slip into the castle by the
small rear door and find her way to Nevin herself. She
imagined he'd be in the antechamber, behind the big

desk where her father had spent so much of his time. His two children had been forbidden to enter the cold room.

But in the end she decided that sneaking in would be a sign of frailty, so she marched around to the front and imperiously told the guard at the gate to admit her. She didn't know the liveried man, and he appeared to have no idea who she might be, but, evidently deciding that she appeared to represent no threat, he raised the ancient wooden door, allowing her to enter.

More memories came as she crossed the castle yard—some happy, some bittersweet. There was the old buttery where she had played with her cats among the barrels of ale. She'd adopted a number of the furry creatures over the years, taking them to live in her own bedchamber, thus rescuing them from a life of hunting their own prey in the cold castle barnyard.

She glanced expectantly at the little shed as she passed, almost as if she expected little Inky to come pouncing out at her from behind one of the barrels.

She'd remembered the castle yard as a busy, bustling place. Today the only occupant was a servant sweeping on the far side. Once again, she didn't recognize the man. He looked up as she walked across to the castle, but said nothing.

The main castle building itself seemed smaller than she remembered. As she approached the front portico, the tall iron doors creaked open. Someone from inside had been watching her approach. It was another servant she didn't recognize, dressed in the same livery as the man at the castle gate.

"May I help you, madam?" the man asked.

"I'm here to see Nevin O'Farrell," she said, careful to keep her voice strong and loud.

The servant looked her up and down, a faint smile

of confusion on his face. "My lord is not in residence," he told her after a long pause.

Lily suddenly felt light-headed. She'd not anticipated that Nevin would not be here. "Will he be here later this afternoon?" she managed to ask.

The servant shook his head. "As I said, madam, he's not currently in residence. Lord Lymond has gone to London."

Lily bit her lip. "Then I'll see the lady Maired."

"My lady is with my lord," the man said, showing the first touch of irritation.

"Have they gone for an extended visit?" she asked.

"London is a very long distance," the man observed.

A safe distance, she thought. "What about the boy?"

"I beg your pardon?" The man was beginning to close the door.

"Their son? Did he go to London with them?"

"Aye, madam. Master Desmond accompanied his parents."

At least, then, the problem was solved for the moment. The tension that had been building up toward the anticipated reunion with her brother began to drain from her, leaving her tired. She'd walked all morning, and now would walk all afternoon, without rest. But at least she knew that Desmond O'Farrell was all the way across the channel from her daughter.

The servant continued to stare at her. She gave him a nod, then turned to walk away.

After a moment he called after her. "May I tell Lord Lymond who was calling, madam?"

Lily thought for a moment. She turned back to the man. "Aye. You may tell Lord Lymond that his sister paid him a call."

The man looked dumbfounded. "Er—did you say his *sister*, madam?"

"Aye, his sister."

Then she turned and strode away across the yard. Let that start the rumors spinning in the castle gossip mill, she thought with some satisfaction. It would serve Nevin right. And if he didn't like it, he could just come and tell her so.

Six

Uncle John was giving the Riordan boys a fencing lesson. It had become a favorite activity with them in the month John had been staying at O'Malley House. Of course, the "swords" were little more than roughly whittled sticks, but the combatants appeared to be fiercely engrossed in the battle as Niall strode down to the stable yard in search of them. He grinned. His two youngsters had the seasoned veteran pinned against a fence.

"Have you come to rescue me?" John shouted as he approached.

"You appear in need of it."

"Aye. You didn't tell me that you'd bred two fierce warriors." His words were punctuated by the *click-clack* of the wooden swords. As he approached, Niall could see that John's position was not dire. With his long arms and expert skill, he was easily parrying the blows of both his little opponents, but had let himself be backed into the fence corner to add to the suspense of the contest.

"Do warriors get a break for dinner?" Niall asked. His sons were so intent on their fight that neither one had so much as turned to look at him. Even Padraic, at his young age, was lost in intense concentration. Perhaps John was right, Niall thought, his grin dying. Like countless Riordans before them, his sons were born to fight. He could only hope that the fragile peace with England would hold so that they would never have to.

"Cat's waiting for us," Niall said as the relentless *click-clack* continued. "We've visitors for the noon meal."

John looked over at him sharply and let his sword arm fall to his side. The two boys took advantage of the sudden breach to give their uncle a whack on each side of his ribs.

"Visitors?" he said with a slight frown, reaching for his opponent's hands to stop the onslaught. "Again?"

Niall's grin reappeared. "She'll not give up, John. Cat is determined to find the woman who will make you want to stay and settle down here in Killarney. I've told her you're too old and too bloody stubborn to ever fall for one of these sweet neighborhood colleens, but you know Cat when she gets an idea in her head."

John deftly plucked the swords from Lorcan and Padraic. "Sorry boys, the fight is over for today." At their looks of disappointment, he rubbed his sides and added, "You've bested me, I vow. An old man like me can only take so many blows in a day."

"Will you fight us, Papa?" Lorcan asked.

"Nay, son. We can't keep your mother waiting."

"Even if she is a misguided meddler in other people's lives," John muttered to Niall after the boys had started running up toward the house.

"But a sweet meddler, you'll admit," Niall argued. "She only does it out of love for you." The explanation did not smooth the frown from John's face. "And in any event, I believe you'll like the Bartons."

John groaned. "And the Barton *daughter.* How old is she?"

Niall glanced away. "I believe she's . . . er . . . she's over sixteen, I'm sure."

"Sixteen?" John looked over at his friend. "Niall, what's that wife of yours thinking? Last week 'twas Mistress Dunwoody who was to inherit a vast estate in the south and, oh, by the way, as the only child of a doting old fool was a wee bit spoiled, as evidenced by the fact that she slapped your maid for bringing the meat too cold."

"Aye," Niall agreed. "That was a mistake, but—"

"And the week before 'twas the Widow O'Farlane, who would give anything for a new husband to warm her bed, especially since she'd somehow lost every hair on her head, which she felt the need to demonstrate by removing her wig every ten minutes."

Niall chuckled. "'Tis a small neighborhood. There are not too many maids still eligible. But truly, John, you'll enjoy the Bartons. Sir Thomas has been traveling in the East and has news of the peace negotiations."

John looked gloomy as he trudged beside Niall toward the house. "I'll be happy to hear Sir Thomas's news," he said. "I'll be less happy to have him dangle his lovely daughter before me like a piece of bait in front of a fat trout."

Niall laughed and clapped his friend on the shoulder. "Ah, John, you've managed to evade the hook thus far. I doubt that Sir Thomas will prove to be a skilled enough fisherman to catch you. But just play along. Consider it a favor to me, for it keeps Cat in a good mood."

"Which profits you everything and me nothing," John returned dryly.

Niall's eyebrow went up. "Sure now, if it's envy I

hear in that tone, perhaps you'd best give Mistress Barton a look after all."

John shook his head. "I've committed a number of sins in my long life, Niall, but to date cradle robbing is not one of them."

They continued the trip up to the house in silence.

"How many estates have been taken?" John asked.

Sir Thomas Barton looked grave. "Six that we know of so far. Taken without ceremony and handed over to English lords. Apparently Elizabeth has decided that giving away land in Ireland is an easy way to repay her favors. Never mind that the land belongs to someone else."

"And has for generations," Niall added.

They were seated at the long Riordan dining table—Catriona and Niall at the two heads. Cat had motioned John to a seat next to Cecily Barton, who to his eye appeared to be little older than his friend of the woods, Daphne. She was thin as a reed with a long, straight torso that had not developed even the barest of feminine curves. John had shot Catriona a disapproving look, as he obliged by courteously helping the girl to her chair and sitting next to her. But his main attention through the meal had been on Cecily's father, Sir Thomas. The man had brought disturbing news about the increasing tensions in the area.

"Are there plans to do anything to stop this?" John asked. "When I came here, I was aware that a rebel movement was reassembling in the north under O'Neill's nephew. Has contact been made with them?"

Sir Thomas was a good-humored, ruddy-faced man who looked as if he'd rather be spending time with his hounds and a houseful of grandchildren than dealing with political concerns. He sighed and leaned back in his chair. "Fine meal, my lady," he said to Catriona.

Then he turned back to John. "I'm afraid the problem is that we've not been able to organize ourselves here like they have in the north. As a result, the English have been able to pick us off, one by one, without repercussions. I wish to hell we had an O'Neill among us to provide some leadership."

Black shook his head. "Once the countryside is dotted with English land owners, 'twill be harder than ever to stand against them. I would think your neighbors would understand that and want to do something quickly."

"The most powerful barons don't seem to trust each other," Sir Thomas replied. "Then, too, they may have reason. We know for a fact that some of the landed gentry in the south have worked for the English in the past. In return for keeping their own lands, some have been willing to betray their fellow countrymen."

Niall leaned forward. "Some like who?" he asked sharply. "We need to know who our enemies are. I don't intend to see the O'Malley lands back in English hands."

Sir Thomas took a swallow of ale. "'Tis rumored that the Earl of Lymond and his entire family are now in London shaping their own bargain with the English."

"The Earl of Lymond? Nevin O'Farrell?" Catriona asked in surprise.

"Aye."

She turned to explain to Niall and John. "My father knew the current earl's father. The family always stayed mostly to themselves, but I believe my father respected the old earl. When he died, I remember Father was worried that his son was not yet ready to take over such a vast estate."

"Are we talking about the family of the boy we saw in the marketplace that day?" John asked her.

"Aye, we saw the current earl's son—Desmond. You thought he might have been one of the boys responsible for—" She broke off her sentence, apparently not wanting to go into the details of the incident with Daphne in front of the dinner guests.

John had no desire to open the subject, either, but it was interesting to learn that the son was not the only member of the O'Farrell family whose deeds were questionable. He didn't like to think that such people were neighbors to the Riordans . . . or to Lily and Daphne. "So these O'Farrells are meeting with the English?" he asked Sir Thomas with a frown.

The portly knight nodded, then glanced at his daughter, who had said almost nothing the entire meal. "My Cecily has been to London and Paris, as well. She's a well-educated young lady. Her mother, God rest her, saw to it. Dr. Black, you must hear her sing."

The girl blushed furiously, and John shifted in his seat. Sir Thomas was not much older than John, himself. Why would any man want a son-in-law his own age? Cecily was a pretty little thing, and would no doubt have little trouble finding a fine young man to provide Sir Thomas with the descendants he obviously craved.

Catriona smiled at the girl. "We'd love to hear you sing, my dear," she said, rising. "Wouldn't we, husband?" She looked for support to Niall, who looked almost as miserable as John.

"Of course," he mumbled. " 'Twould be a pleasure."

"Then shall we retire to the drawing room?" Catriona asked, seemingly unaware that she and Sir Thomas were the only ones in the group who appeared pleased with the plan.

John stood and pulled back Cecily's chair, then offered a hand to help her rise. Her own hand was ice cold and shook as she placed it in his. The bright red flush of her cheeks had traveled down her neck, mottling her pale skin.

"Mistress Cecily," he said with sudden decision. "Please forgive me, but I will have to postpone the pleasure of hearing you perform. I've several tasks requiring my attention this afternoon."

The girl shot him a look of thanks.

Catriona looked surprised, but said graciously to Cecily, "Perhaps we can persuade you to return on another occasion, my dear."

Cecily looked as if she'd been given a reprieve from the gallows. "I'd be pleased, milady."

Catriona came around the table and put her arm around the girl, pulling her away from John's side. "Shall I show you my garden before you leave?" she asked, glancing back at John with a look of reproof.

His hostess's disapproval did not bother John in the least. He offered his excuses once more to Niall and Sir Thomas, then strode quickly out of the house, making a straight line for the stables. He'd lied, again. He had no tasks to perform that afternoon. But anything was better than sitting in Catriona's drawing room while Sir Thomas tried to show off his poor little daughter like a brood cow up for auction. He felt warm and itchy and slightly ill, and was quite certain that none of it was due to Catriona's goose dinner.

It wasn't until he'd set Greybolt galloping across the meadow behind O'Malley House and up out of the valley that he began to feel better. The wind blew sharply against his cheeks. He breathed it in as if to cleanse away the stuffy air and heavy odors of the past two hours.

Greybolt did not seem to need a direction, and for a time John paid little attention to where he was going, as long as it was away from Sir Thomas and his prize. He told himself that he was surprised when he recognized the familiar path into the woods, but somehow he'd known that he was heading here. The conversation at dinner about seeing the O'Farrell boy had put her in his mind. Put *them* in his mind, he corrected himself. Lily and Daphne.

Something had changed. Lily couldn't quite put her finger on it, but it seemed that Daphne was not quite the same since the incident at Cotter's Pond. Of course, the experience had been terrifying, and perhaps that was the cause of her new attitude. Or it might have had something to do with the involvement of the doctor. Daphne had asked about him several times since they'd last seen him, the day he and Lady Riordan had given them a ride home in their cart.

Whatever the reason, Lily was growing increasingly uncomfortable. She found herself paying more attention to her daughter's walk, noting the girl's difficulty in a way she hadn't for years. She studied Daphne's face when she wasn't looking, and realized that it was becoming the face of a woman, not a girl. For the first time she noticed that Daphne's thin figure was beginning to fill out. Her breasts were growing under her straight, little girl dresses. The sight made Lily's mouth grow dry with a kind of panic.

The most disturbing change had been Daphne's insistence on spending more time alone. Up to now, mother and daughter had been practically inseparable. Except for occasional excursions to pick berries or to catch a few fish in the nearby stream, Daphne had shown little desire to venture off by herself. Now it seemed that she was seeking solitude almost every day, much to Lily's distress.

The trip to Lymond Castle had given Lily some comfort with the knowledge that Desmond O'Farrell was out of the country, but there had been *three* boys that day at the pond. How could she be sure that the other two might not try to continue the mischief they had started?

As Lily tossed on her cot at night, she admitted to herself that it was not just the boy's mischief she feared. There were even worse dangers in the world beyond Whistler's Woods. Love, for example, could lead to a hurt that was much deeper than hurts caused by hate. She had learned that long ago.

"Shall we gather reeds for some baskets?" she asked her daughter brightly at the noon meal several days after their trip to the market. Daphne had seemed particularly distant all morning. "I'm thinking we should make some special ones for the Christmas festivities. With the extra money, we could buy some cloth to make you a couple of new frocks. You're growing so fast, you're sprouting right out of the ones you have."

"I'd thought to go fishing this afternoon," Daphne answered with a shrug.

"Very well. We could go to the fishing hole together, then walk upstream for the reeds. 'Twould make a nice excursion."

"I was planning to go by myself."

"Oh." Lily struggled to keep her voice even. "Then perhaps you should fish today, and we can do the reeds tomorrow."

Daphne appeared to notice the disappointment in her mother's expression. Her own tight features softened. "Ah, Mummy, I'm sorry to be such an old grump. We can go together. Aye, I'd like you to come. We've not been fishing together in a long time."

"Are you sure—" Lily began, but Daphne had already jumped up from the table and was beginning to clear the dishes.

"We'd best hurry if we're to do both things in one

afternoon," the girl said, now sounding genuinely enthusiastic about the plan.

Lily felt a surge of warmth. Though it was difficult to deal with her daughter's changing moods these days, she was not going to spoil the day by questioning the sudden good humor. "Leave the dishes for later," she said happily. "You get the fishing poles ready, and I'll get out the reed carriers."

Daphne smiled at her. "If I get a new dress from the basket money, can we go to Christmas Night services at St. Martin's?"

Lily hesitated, reluctant to spoil her daughter's good mood. Finally she said, "We'll see," then turned to busy herself pulling out the large linen slings with wooden handles that they used to bring reeds up from the stream.

Growing up in Lymond Castle, she'd attended mass only occasionally. Nonetheless, Lily had then considered herself a good Catholic. It had only been since Daphne's birth that her faith had wavered. She and her sister-in-law, Maired, had found a priest to baptize her daughter, though it hadn't been easy. Since that time, she'd taken Daphne to the big stone church in Banburn only on rare occasions, usually an early morning service where there was little risk she would encounter anyone she had known in her other life.

She hoped her brother was still in London, but if the family had returned, they might be at St. Martin's on Christmas Night.

"Mummy, you're not answering me," Daphne said with impatience.

"Forgive me, Sweetcakes, I didn't hear."

"I asked if we could use some of the bacon in the cellar to bait the hooks?"

"Mmm? Aye, of course. Shall I fetch it?" Sometimes it was difficult for Daphne to manage the steep earthen steps down to the little storage room behind the house.

"Nay. I'll get it." She went out the door humming and doing the half-skip she sometimes used to move quickly.

Lily watched her go, her heart full, then went back to folding the reed carriers. When the front door creaked, she looked up, thinking that Daphne had changed her mind about going down to the cellar. But the person who was pushing on the door was not her daughter. It was John Black.

She jumped up in surprise. "What are you doing here?"

For a moment he looked as if he didn't know how to answer her question, then he smiled and said, "I was passing by and decided I should check on my patient."

Lily reached up and tucked a stray wisp of hair into her cap. It was her old cap. And she was wearing her oldest dress, the one she usually chose for the dirty job of wading through the mud along the stream to collect reeds.

"I—Daphne's fine," she said. "You really shouldn't trouble yourself—"

He stopped her words with an upheld hand. "'Tis never a trouble to pay a visit on two lovely ladies."

His tone was light, his grin engaging, and suddenly Lily felt as if she were a girl again, filled with the exuberation she'd always had when the rare visitor had called at Lymond Castle. Even when she was a young girl her father's guests had always paid her attention—the pretty little daughter of the household with sparkling blue eyes and blond hair. Her hair was darker now, and she wondered how long it had been since her eyes had sparkled.

"Daphne is here, I trust?" Their visitor looked around the room.

"She's in the cellar cutting some bacon for . . . for—" It sounded ridiculous suddenly, as if fishing was not a respectable occupation for two ladies on an autumn afternoon. "We're going fishing. She's getting some bits of bacon for bait," she finished, tipping her head with a touch of defiance.

His grin grew wider. "Fishing? The ladies are not only beautiful, but resourceful, as well. Do you think to catch the evening's supper?"

"Aye, if we're lucky, and some to salt."

John turned as Daphne came up behind him, her hand cupped to hold several pieces of fat. "Dr. Black!" she exclaimed. Her daughter's eyes did sparkle, Lily noted.

John bowed at the waist. "Good afternoon, fair lady," he said to her. "I would kiss your hand in greeting, but I think 'twould be a messy proposition at the moment."

Daphne giggled and held out the bacon. "It's for bait. It works ever so well. My mother's brother taught it to her when she was little."

John gave Lily a glance as if curious to hear more about this brother, but Lily stayed silent.

"Interesting," he said, turning back to Daphne. "I've always used worms or grubs."

"Do you like to fish?" the girl asked.

John nodded. "When I was a boy, my brother and I fished nearly every lake in Killarney."

"Do you and your brother still fish here?"

He shook his head. "My brother's dead, lass. I lost him a long time ago. But I reckon the long, lazy afternoons fishing with him will live in my memory for the rest of my days."

"My father's dead, too," Daphne volunteered.

John looked over at Lily again. She glanced away from him.

"My sympathies," he said.

Daphne shrugged. "He died before I was born. I never knew him." She turned to her mother with a smile. "Could Dr. Black come fishing with us today? We have an extra pole."

When John had begun to talk about fishing, Lily had had the same thought, but had dismissed the idea as ridiculous. "I'm sure Dr. Black has many more important things to do than to spend the afternoon fishing," she said.

John looked up at the whitewashed ceiling, then down at Daphne with a wink. "I can't think of a single one," he said.

Daphne gave a little jump. "May he, Mummy?" she said. "We could look for some grubs and have a contest—see who catches the first fish."

"What about the reeds?" Lily asked.

"We can do them tomorrow. Morning is better, in any event. Then they have the day to dry. Please say aye, Mummy. I'd like it ever so much."

There was no way Lily could refuse, seeing the eagerness in Daphne's face. "Are you sure you care to come?" she asked John quietly.

"Aye," he said. "I do."

Seven

John couldn't remember the last time he'd been fishing. When he'd been living in rebel camps over the years of fighting, sometimes contingents had been assigned to bring back fresh fish for their meals, but John himself had always been too busy strategizing with the other leaders to go.

But he'd never quite forgotten the luxury of relaxing in forced stillness beside a body of gently flowing water. As he sat next to Daphne at the edge of the small stream that flowed through Whistler's Wood, that peculiar feeling of peace came upon him almost immediately. He sensed that Lily felt it, too. Daphne was the least transformed of the trio. In spite of the incident with the boys, she had had little experience with turmoil in her life, and therefore had less contrast with the tranquility of their current occupation.

Daphne and Lily had led him directly to their favorite fishing hole—a spot where the stream took a turn in the woods and appeared to slow down to form a deep round pool before speeding up again on the other side to resume its journey through the hills. Daphne and John were seated directly on the grass at the edge of the water. Lily had taken a somewhat more dignified perch on an old log a few steps down from them. The first strike of the day had been Daphne's—a fat little trout. John had given a low whistle of admiration and declared that he would not even attempt to compete with grub worms against the girl's miraculous bacon.

Within an hour they had pulled in two fish each. Daphne had caught three, but had thrown one back, deciding that it was too small.

"How many people know about this place?" John asked when the girl got her fourth bite of the day. "I'm surprised you don't have the whole village here."

"I'm not sure who knows about it, but they'd likely not come in any event. Not too many people venture into Whistler's Woods," Daphne explained.

John listened for sadness or resentment in her tone, but couldn't find it. "Then I'd say they are missing the best fishing in Killarney."

"Aye," Daphne agreed with a grin.

"Do you think we have enough for today?" Lily asked.

"Oh, let's not stop yet," Daphne said.

John added his own protest. "Daphne's had four and I but two. I need more time to redeem myself."

"I'm in no hurry," Lily agreed with a smile. She looked as if the tranquility of the place had worked its magic on her, much as it had on John.

"I'm going to try down at the Faerie Bridge," Daphne said, standing and gathering in her pole.

"Have a care," Lily cautioned.

"What's the Faerie Bridge?" John asked.

Daphne pointed to the bottom end of the pool. "'Tis there at the bend of the stream where the water swirls. It's not a bridge, really, just a series of rocks, before the water deepens here in the hole. Sometimes there are good fish just on the other side."

"Would you like to try it with me?"

"I'll keep your mother company, but I'll watch you from here."

Daphne nodded and started to pick her way along the water's edge, humming as she went. John smiled after her, then lifted his own pole and stood. "May I join you?" he asked Lily, pointing to her log seat. As he walked over to her, he grimaced and gave an exaggerated twist to his back. "These old bones do not rest as easily on the hard ground as once they did."

Lily chuckled. "I'm sure I know not to what old bones you refer, Dr. Black." She shifted her seat slightly to give him room beside her.

They both turned to watch as Daphne reached the far end of the pond and began studying the rocks to find the best spot to set up operations. "You were right about one thing, Mistress Lily," John said softly.

Lily looked surprised. "About what?"

"She is a happy child. I never would have believed it possible considering—" He paused to measure his words so that he wouldn't offend her. "My first encounter with her was to rescue her from a pond where she'd been callously thrown by mean-spirited boys. Then I learned that she lived in the forest, in isolation, and has a handicap that prevents her from running and playing like other children. Yet, you speak true—she's happy."

He turned his gaze away from Daphne and looked at Lily.

She smiled at him. "Aye, she is. I only hope I can keep her that way."

There was a hint of worry in her eyes. "Do you doubt it?" he asked.

"She's been a little different lately. 'Tis the age, I

warrant. Yet I have to consider it. When she was a child, she was content with our little house and her garden and the birds in her aviary. She loved to read the books we have."

"It appears to be a wonderful collection," he interjected.

"Aye." She nodded without offering any explanation as to where they came from. "But lately I've noticed some changes. I think she'd like to have more to do with other people, but she doesn't want to hurt me by telling me so."

"She appeared to enjoy the little Riordan boys the day we brought you home."

"Aye, she did."

"Perhaps she's right, then. You should do more to join the world—both of you."

Lily stiffened. He was sure that if there had been more space on the log, she would have moved away from him. When she spoke, her voice had grown colder. "I find myself wanting to tell her that for every joy to be discovered in the outside world, there are an equal number of hurts."

She looked directly at him as she said it, and for a moment he felt as if he could read every one of those hurts in her face. What had been done to her? he wondered.

Without thinking, he reached over and took her hand. "You're wrong," he said gently. "I'll admit that I've seen many bad things in my life, especially on the battlefield. But for every bad thing, there are a hundred wondrous ones. I experience them daily here living with the Riordans."

"They appear to be a happy family," she acknowledged.

"Aye. The boys laugh often and are secure and confident in their home and parents. And Cat and Niall have such a strong love for each other. 'Tis a pleasure to witness."

Lily gave a sad smile. "True love is a rare thing."

He studied her face. "Have you felt it?" he asked softly. Normally he would never have dreamed of posing such a question after such short acquaintance, but things had never been normal between him and these two since the dire circumstances of their first meeting. Still, he wondered if she would answer.

She shook her head. "I felt what I believed to be true love, but it turned out to be nothing of the kind."

She seemed to be talking more to the water than to him, so he pushed further. "What happened?"

Her slender shoulders gave a shrug, that turned into more of a shake. "I was mistaken, that's all," she said.

"Was it Lily's father?"

She turned to look at him. In spite of the sunlight of the afternoon, her eyes were dark. "Aye," she answered. "Daphne told you he was dead since I've not yet had the heart to tell her the true story."

"Which is . . ." he prompted.

"Which is that he was betrothed to another back in England. He left the country before he even knew that I was with child."

Bile rose in John's throat. "What a bloody fool," he said. "To have lost not one treasure, but two."

His words brought a smile to her lips. "I've often had the same thought myself," she said.

He wanted to ask her more, to ask what had happened to her when her contemptible lover had abandoned her, but he had the feeling that she had revealed all she would for one day. Instead, he lightened his tone. "You lost a suitor, but gained a daughter. Surely you would agree that the daughter has brought joys a thousandfold to make up for the loss of the poor miserable wretch who must have been witless, not to mention blind, to let one such as you go."

Her smile deepened. "Aye, Daphne has brought me more joy than I would ever have believed possible."

"But you're worried that you might lose her, just as you once lost your lover."

"Nay," she said quickly. "I'll never lose her. 'Tis just that—" She stopped and bit her lip. For the first time her eyes misted over with tears.

She appeared to be unaware that he was still holding her hand. He, however, was highly aware of the touch. He rubbed his thumb over the back of the hand. Her skin was smooth, though he knew that she had no servant for the rough tasks of the household. The light motion turned the handholding into something more intimate. Lily looked up at him in surprise, then slowly pulled her hand out of his grasp.

"I have a suggestion," he said briskly.

She was blushing. The color in her cheeks made her look younger. "A suggestion?"

"Aye. You're worried about Daphne's desire for something beyond Whistler's Woods, yet you're reluctant to expose her to the wicked world. I suggest you come to O'Malley House for a visit. You will encounter nothing wicked there, I assure you—only good-humor and pleasant times."

She shook her head. "I don't know the Riordans. They would have no reason to offer their hospitality to someone like me."

"They have a reason now," John argued. "Cat will do anything to please me, and it would please me to have you there as our guests."

Lily looked across the water at Daphne, who had just hauled up a wriggling fish. "We should be getting back," she said, standing. "It will be twilight soon."

"Say you'll come," John insisted, reluctantly getting

to his feet. "This Friday. I'll pick you both up in the Riordan's little cart."

"I just don't think—"

"It would be a good diversion for Daphne. Remember how she enjoyed Lorcan and Paddy. It would be a way for her to see a bit of this outside world you fear without running any risk of harm. It just might be the answer to your worries about her."

Lily looked at him. The doubt in her eyes was joined by a touch of hope. "Why are you doing this for us?" she asked.

He grinned. "They say when you save a life, that person will always belong to you, in a sense. I reckon I have that feeling about Daphne. I'd like to see her happy."

This time Lily reached out and brushed his hand with hers. It was so brief he could scarcely feel it, yet the touch lingered. "I thank you," she said softly. "If it is agreeable to Lady Riordan, we'll accept your invitation."

"It will be more than agreeable to Cat, I can assure you," he said. He tried not to think about why Lily's agreement sent a surge of feeling through his midsection. The invitation had been merely a gesture of kindness, he told himself. A good neighbor concerning himself with the well-being of two females who had no protector. There was no reason for him to be so unreasonably pleased at the thought of it. There was *absolutely* no reason for him to feel the familiar tingling in the lower portion of his anatomy as Lily turned to walk along the edge of the pond and he noticed that her frock clung to her shapely bottom where the log had wet her skirt.

With a shake of his head, he sighed and followed her along the water toward her daughter.

• • •

As John had predicted, Daphne had been delighted by his invitation. She talked of little else all evening. "Will there be servants at O'Malley House, Mummy? Will they eat at table with us? What shall I talk about? Shall I wear my green frock? It's my prettiest, but Lady Riordan already saw it that day in the market. She'll think I have but the one."

Lily patiently answered all her questions, often pausing to think back to the days when *she* had lived in a grand house with servants, days when she'd changed her dress several times a day, if she chose. Now she found herself with the same dilemma as Daphne. The money she could afford for clothes had usually gone for Daphne's things. She only had one serviceable dress, and it was the same one that she had worn to the market that day. It would look drab and plain among the grandeur of O'Malley House.

"Are we going to collect the reeds today?" Daphne asked the next morning after they had broken their fast with a bowl of porridge.

"We might postpone yet another day. I have another project in mind," Lily told her with a secret smile.

Daphne seemed to catch her mother's excitement. "What is it, Mummy?" she asked, jumping up from the bench.

"Come with me."

Lily led the way into their shared bedroom, and Daphne waited with impatience as she kneeled beside their big bed and pulled a trunk out from underneath. "Are you going to open it, Mummy?" Daphne asked with a gasp.

Daphne had seen the trunk before on several occasions when they'd given the room a thorough cleaning, but when she'd asked what it contained, Lily had always answered, "The past," and that had been the end of it.

"Aye, we're going to open it," Lily said, "though I've no idea what we'll find. There may be nothing more than the remains of many good moth suppers."

Daphne kneeled beside her mother. "Where did it come from?"

"Aunt Maired brought it here after I left Lymond Castle." Daphne knew the story of her flight from her brother's cruelty. She just didn't know the whole truth about what had brought on the family crisis.

"Does it have your things?"

"Aye." She wrestled with the iron latch, which was nearly rusted shut, but finally it popped open, allowing her to lift the top of the box. The first thing she saw was a blue silk gown. Memories flooded into her like cold air.

Daphne laid her hand gently on the fine cloth. "What a beautiful color. It shimmers like the water in Cotter's Pond when the sun shines."

Lily lifted the dress carefully. It had been packed away for nearly a dozen years, but it looked as fresh as if she had worn it dancing only yesterday. "I was once told the color matched my eyes," she said softly.

She remembered the night exactly. She remembered Philip's tone of voice when he had said those words. She remembered the feel of his lips on hers. She closed her eyes and tried to remember his face, but to her horror, the face she saw was not Philip's at all. It was John Black's.

She dropped the dress as if it were hot.

"Is something amiss, Mummy?" Daphne asked, concerned.

Lily gave herself a little shake. "Nay, I'm fine. Let's see what else is in here. I'm looking for something we could alter for you to wear to O'Malley House, since there's no time for a new dress."

"Will you wear this one?" Daphne asked, smoothing her hand over the blue silk.

"I—I'm not sure. It may not even fit me anymore. Women's bodies change as they grow older, you know, especially after they've had a baby."

Daphne seemed to accept her explanation and dropped the subject as they began to look through the other things in the chest. Each garment brought back memories of its own, but nothing hit her as sharply as had the blue dress. She carefully avoided thinking about Philip and *tried* to avoid thinking about John Black, though this was proving increasingly difficult.

She'd thought about him often during another restless night. Half of her was embarrassed that she had told him so much about herself as they sat by the pond. The other half wanted to tell him even more and to hear more about his life. That was the half that had put his face in her mind when she had thought about kissing Philip. It was the half that couldn't wait until Friday.

"It's the most beautiful thing I've ever seen," Daphne said, pulling out another silk dress, this one a shimmering silver. Her voice was reverent.

Lily put aside her own thoughts and smiled at her daughter's pleasure. "I think this could be cut down to fit you in no time."

"Truly?"

"Let's just see." Lily stood and held out a hand to help Daphne to her feet. Then she held the dress up against her daughter. "It's very fine for just a dinner invitation," she said. "It's really more of a dress for a dance."

Daphne's eyes filled with tears as she glanced down at her leg. Lily felt as if she had just stabbed her own daughter. "I shan't ever go to a dance, Mummy," she said.

Swallowing a lump in her own throat, Lily busied

herself measuring the dress to her daughter's much more slender body. "Why, some day you may go to a dance. Who knows? And in the meantime, this dress would be just lovely for a dinner at O'Malley House, I'm thinking. 'Tis a very, very fine place and worthy of such a dress."

The tears had already dried in Daphne's eyes. She gave a little jump of excitement and smoothed the shining silver fabric against her front. "It's much too big, Mummy. Can we make it work?"

"Aye, Sweetcakes," Lily said. "We'll make it fit. By the time John Black comes for us on Friday, you're going to look like a princess."

"So we're to have the company of the Witch of Whistler's Woods," Niall observed with a grin.

John was breakfasting with his hosts before leaving to pick up Daphne and Lily. He looked up at Niall with a frown, but Catriona spoke before he had a chance.

"Niall Riordan, if I hear that ridiculous phrase come out of your mouth again, you'll be moving out to the barn for the rest of the winter."

Niall did not look the least worried over the threat, but he turned to John and said, "I apologize. You know 'twas said in jest. I promise you I'll be on good behavior today when you bring us your new lady."

"She's not my new lady. She's just my friend. She and her daughter."

Niall and Catriona exchanged a glance.

"I mean it," John insisted. "You two lovebirds are always trying to paint everyone else with your cloth. Not everything is a romance. I've told you often enough—I'm too old for such nonsense."

Catriona pushed a platter toward him. "Have another biscuit, John. 'Tis a cold morning for a journey, and you need food against your ribs."

"Will you listen to me?" he asked, growing impatient with the younger couple's smug expressions. "I asked Lily to come because they have lived in such isolation that her daughter has seen little of society. She needs to meet some people. 'Tis for the daughter's sake, nothing more."

"We believe you, John," Niall said, but there was an annoying twinkle in his eye.

John shook his head. Normally he wouldn't be irritated by Niall and Catriona's good-natured teasing. He suspected the irritation might be partly due to his own doubt about the impulse he'd had to invite Lily and Daphne to O'Malley House. While it was true that he had made the invitation for Daphne's sake, it was not the idea of seeing Daphne that had had him awake since before dawn.

"I should go," he said, pushing away his plate and standing.

" 'Tis early yet," Catriona objected.

"Aye, but I thought I'd just clean the cart up a bit before I leave."

Catriona and John exchanged another smug smile. John turned with a snort and left the room, heading toward the stables.

Eight

As maddening as it was to be teased by his hosts about his motives for inviting Lily and Daphne to O'Malley House, John knew that their suspicions were not totally unfounded. He'd already admitted to himself that he was drawn to Lily in a way that he had seldom experienced.

The reasons for his attraction were still a mystery. It wasn't because she was a helpless female who needed his protection. Though she appeared to be alone and defenseless, she gave the impression that she was not afraid to face adversity. The only time he'd seen her truly at a loss was when she revealed her worry about Daphne. She didn't seem to have any fears about her own safety or her ability to continue her strange and independent existence.

Niall and Catriona had been correct. He was looking forward to spending the day with her. She intrigued him, and that was more than he had been able to say about any woman for a very long time.

By cart the trip to the little cottage in Whistler's Woods was under an hour, and, as Catriona had predicted, he arrived earlier than he had intended. For a moment he wondered if he should linger in the woods for a while, but finally decided that he would go on ahead. If the ladies were not ready for their outing, he would spend the time enjoying Daphne's garden.

The little path to their home looked more inviting each time he visited. Today for the first time he noticed that tiny fall marigolds were poking up around the primrose bushes, adding bright splotches of color as if someone had flicked a paint brush along the way.

A silent approach was impossible with the rickety cart, so he wasn't surprised to see the front door open as he climbed down. The surprise came when his two guests for the day emerged.

Daphne was wearing a silver dress that caught the sunlight as she stepped through the threshold. Her curly black hair was tied up on top of her head with matching silver ribbons. Light shone from her dark blue eyes like new stars on a twilight sky.

Behind her came Lily. For the first time since he'd known her, she wasn't wearing a cap. Her rich honey hair was somehow pulled back, then allowed to tumble down around shoulders that were left half-bare by the deep round neck of her blue gown. The dress itself appeared to be silk. It skimmed sleekly over her soft curves. The bodice was tight, perhaps even a bit too tight where it pushed against the full mounds of her breasts. John felt a pulse beat at the edge of his throat.

"I'm early," he called, embarrassed to note that his voice was raspy. "I thought you might not be ready," he said, walking toward them.

Lily laughed. It was a younger laugh than he had heard from her. "I trow Daphne's been ready since before dawn. I'm not sure she even slept last night."

"I did so," the girl protested, then she remembered her manners and gave a little curtsy. "Good morrow, Dr. Black."

"You look beautiful, lass," he told her quite honestly, and was rewarded with a brilliant smile.

"It was my mother's dress," she said with her typical directness. "But we've made it fit."

"It looks as if it were made just for you," he assured her.

Daphne giggled. "Mummy says it makes me look like a princess."

"That's not the dress, lass," John said softly. " 'Tis your smile and winsome beauty. I daresay you'd outshine any princess I could think of."

Behind her daughter, Lily was beaming. John had the feeling that she knew how important it was for Daphne to feel special and pretty today. But when he tried to compliment her gown, as well, she brushed off his words.

" 'Tis a wonder the old thing still holds together," she said, stepping out of the doorway and starting up the path. "I've not worn it in years, and it doesn't even fit right."

She held a basket in her hand. John reached out to take it. "May I?" It was crescent shaped and a unique green color interwoven with reeds of red. He'd never seen anything like it.

" 'Tis a gift for Lady Riordan," Lily explained, "for the holiday season. Perhaps she'd care to use it for boughs or holly."

"It's magnificent," John praised. "Catriona said that you were an artist."

Lily flushed. "She said that?"

"Aye. She showed me the black swan basket you made for her and told me that she thought it was truly a work of art."

"That was kind of her. I'm glad that I'm bringing her a new one." Though she'd rejected the compliment to her appearance, she seemed genuinely pleased at the one to her work.

"Mummy is an artist," Daphne said firmly. "She paints, as well."

John looked at her in surprise. "I'd like to see some of your work."

Lily gave a vague wave and reached to take the basket back from John. "'Tis a pastime. Shall we be going? I'd not keep Lord and Lady Riordan waiting for their dinner."

Once again, John wished he could ask more about her. Where did she come from? How had she learned to make baskets and paint? From where had she obtained her enviable collection of manuscripts?

He stepped aside to allow her and Daphne to walk before him along the path. In their shiny dresses they managed to make the flowers look drab. Who were they? he wondered again. Before, it had been curiosity, but somehow his desire to know had become more compelling. He mocked himself with a half-smile. Never in his life had anyone accused John Black of diffidence. He wanted to know who she was and he was about to spend the day with her. At some point, he decided, he would simply ask her.

It was not at all as difficult as Lily had feared. She'd felt immediately at home sitting at the grand Riordan table, as if the years since she'd last dined in such a fashion never existed. The odd thing was that Daphne, who—except for a few picnics or bites at the market—had eaten every meal of her life in their modest cottage, seemed equally at ease.

Much of it was due to the warmth of their hosts, Lord and Lady Riordan. Lady Riordan had greeted her at the door to O'Malley House with a warm embrace and had whispered that Lily was to call her Catriona.

She'd offered effusive thanks for the basket Lily had brought her, and she'd given Daphne a hug, as well. Niall had bowed over Lily's hand as if she were the finest nobility and had nodded gravely to Daphne and asked with a wink if she'd come to steal away the hearts of his poor sons.

The boys' presence added to the ease of the gathering. Lorcan and little Padraic were with them at table during the meal and were allowed to talk as much as they liked, which was considerable. It was a totally different atmosphere from the meals Lily remembered at Lymond Castle, where children had only been permitted on the most special days, and had been required to remain silent.

The best part of the meal was watching Daphne's face as she looked around the table at the gathering. She was so excited that she forgot to eat until Lily gently prompted her not to waste Lady Riordan's delicious food.

"Try the plum pudding," Lorcan urged his new friend. "Mama makes it herself and only for special 'casions 'cause it needs a long time to plum."

"To plump," Catriona corrected with a smile. "The raisins and currants have to plump."

"Then why don't they call it plump pudding?" the boy asked, then seemed not the least offended when his question caused general laughter.

"I do believe you're right, Lorcan," John said. He was seated next to the boy and leaned over to give an affectionate ruffle of Lorcan's dark hair. "Plump pudding, it is."

John had done his best to be sure the visitors were comfortable. He'd been kind and attentive to both her and Daphne during the trip in the cart. At O'Malley House he'd offered his arm formally to Daphne in the manner of a fine gentleman escorting a lady, and thus had been able to help her up the steps to the front door without putting any attention on her bad leg.

Lily knew that Daphne was taken with him, and she had to admit that she herself found it heady to once again have a man offering attentions. She warned herself not to get used to the feeling. Dr. Black had saved her daughter's life, which had given him some kind of obligation to see to her well-being. But he was just a visitor to Killarney. Soon he would be heading back to whatever life he had beyond their little valley. She wanted Daphne to enjoy herself, but she didn't want her to get too attached to Dr. Black or to any man.

She'd do well to remember the lesson herself, she thought as she watched him across the table laughing with Lorcan. When he was with the two little boys he took on a whole different demeanor, sometimes seeming like a little boy himself. His face, so darkly handsome, brightened in a grin. His gray eyes, which she'd seen grave and serious, danced.

The boys obviously loved him.

"Which one of you young gentlemen is going to offer Daphne a ride on your pony?" he asked now.

"I shall!" Lorcan cried, and was immediately echoed by Padraic.

Daphne's expression was a mixture of excitement and doubt. "I've never ridden a pony," she said.

"Sunshine is easy to ride," Lorcan told her. "I've trained her very well." He glanced at his father. "Papa helped," he added.

"I'm not sure that I—" Daphne hesitated. "Might I have trouble staying on with—"

"I'm sure 'twill be no problem," Niall assured her kindly. "I'll just help you adjust the stirrups. You'll be fine. That is, if you want to give it a try."

"Oh, please, I should like it ever so much. May I, Mummy?"

Lily smiled and nodded. In the reduced world she had fashioned for herself and Daphne, there had been no need for a horse, but she herself had loved riding when she was young. She was pleased that her daughter would have the experience. " 'Tis kind of you," she told Niall.

Once the plan had been made, the boys were restless to leave the table, and in just a few minutes Catriona stood, signaling an end to the meal. "Would you care to see the O'Malley gardens while the boys and Niall take Daphne to the stables?" she asked. "You may join them later to see her progress."

"Will you mind going with Lorcan and Paddy?" Lily turned to ask Daphne, but the question appeared to be unnecessary. The children were already out the dining room door. "I would love to see the gardens," she said to Catriona.

"Perhaps you could wait in the front salon while I check with the kitchen about the cleanup and a small supper. The riders might be hungry later."

"I can't imagine anyone being hungry soon after such a meal," Lily protested. "But let me go with you and help, if I may. The gardens can wait."

"Nay, you're our guest. I'd not put you to work. Truly, I shan't be long."

John stood listening to the exchange. He had not gone along with Niall and the children. "Let me show Mistress Lily the gardens," he suggested.

Catriona looked pleased. "Why, that would be an excellent plan, John. I don't know why I didn't think of it." There was a teasing gleam in her eye as she looked at her friend. John appeared to be slightly uncomfortable, and Lily would have refused his invitation if she could have thought of a graceful way to do so.

"Shall we?" he asked, offering an arm.

"Are you sure I can't be of some help?" she asked her hostess one more time.

Catriona shook her head and made a waving motion with her hands. "Nay, get along, the two of you. I'll join you shortly at the stables, and we'll see how your lovely little girl is enjoying her riding lessons."

In the days before the English troops had burned the original O'Malley House to the ground, the estate had been known for its gardens. Catriona's father had never taken another bride after her mother had died giving birth to her. Instead, he'd poured his love and attention on his daughter and on his beloved roses. Since returning to Killarney, Catriona had tried to rekindle her father's efforts.

John knew little about flowers, but he had spent enough time in the gardens with his hostess to be able to appreciate her labors. Lily, too, seemed impressed, especially by the rose garden, which had a few lingering blooms, in spite of the lateness of the season.

"This must be spectacular in the summer," she observed.

"I daresay," John answered. He was having trouble concentrating on the flowers. Lily's hand was still tucked in his arm. He could feel the warmth of it pressed against his side. Unlike most women, who barely reached to his shoulder, she was tall enough to be almost level with him. Her face was mere inches from his when he turned his head to speak to her. He could see every one of her thick dark lashes.

"You seem very close to the Riordans," Lily observed as they continued to stroll slowly along the path. "The boys call you uncle."

"Aye. Cat is like a daughter to me, and I love her sons dearly. Niall and I have been good friends since our days working together under Shane O'Neill."

"Have you no family of your own left in Killarney?"

"Nay. It was only my parents and my brother, and they've all been gone for many years."

"Then 'tis a marvelous thing that you have the Riordans."

"Aye, no family of my own could be any dearer." He stopped walking and turned to her. "Now I've shared my story. Will you not tell me more of yours? You've never given me your surname. I feel silly calling you Mistress Lily."

She flushed. "You may call me Lily, if you prefer."

"What I'd prefer is to know more about you. Where did you come from? Where were you raised?"

"Not far from here."

They'd left the rose garden and headed down a bush-lined path. He motioned to an alcove with a small bench. "Is it too chilly for you to sit for a spell?" he asked.

"Nay, I find the air marvelously fresh."

She let him lead her to the bench and seat her, then pulled her hand away from him.

"Is your family gone, as well?" he asked, still determined to learn more about her.

"They're not all dead," she said carefully, "but they are not part of our lives."

"So you were left by Daphne's father and you have no association with your family. Forgive me, but it sounds like a lonely existence." He could see that she was still reluctant to reveal her background, and he was unsure why he was pressuring her on the issue. After all, it was none of his concern.

"Lonely?" She looked thoughtful. "Aye, I suppose it would seem that way to some. But I have Daphne. She's all I really need."

"And you intend to keep her there with you for the rest of your life?"

Her slight frown put a crease in the smooth skin between her eyes. "I used to think so. I've always told myself that if I kept her there with me, she would be protected from the cruelties that the world sometimes inflicts on people who are . . . different."

"You said you used to think this. Does that mean you've changed your mind?"

She looked up at him. "I don't know what to think anymore. What happened the other day proved that the cruelties can find her, even in Whistler's Woods."

"You mean the incident at the pond?"

"Aye, but the true reason I'm changing my mind is Daphne herself. She wants to know more of life. I've taught her everything I know with the books we have, but it's not the same as seeing it for herself. I'm afraid . . . I fear she'll continue to venture out alone. One of these days she may want to leave altogether."

Her eyes misted with tears. Without thinking, John put an arm around her shoulders and drew her close. "Which is why you are here with us today, remember? To allow Daphne some of that world she is craving."

He could feel her nod against his neck. "Aye, 'twas a kind thing for you to suggest. I think it will help for a time, but soon you'll be leaving Killarney, and then we shall be alone again."

She made no objection as he continued to hold her. Of course, he told himself, she was occupied with thoughts of her daughter and the changes happening in her life. No doubt she was scarcely aware that her firm breast was pressed against his side. She most certainly was unaware that the vague sweet scent of her hair was tantalizing his senses.

He tried to turn his thoughts back to the subject of her current worries. "I've said nothing about leaving," he objected.

"Nay, but 'tis obvious. You're not a man to spend

long without activity. Soon you'll be chafing at the life of a houseguest, even a beloved one."

He chuckled. "I tried to tell Niall as much the other day, but he convinced me that I must stay through the holidays."

At this she pulled away and looked at him, surprised. "So soon?" At his confused look, she clarified her question. "Does that mean you intend to leave after Christmas?"

Was it his imagination that the idea distressed her? he wondered. "Not immediately after," he answered slowly, watching her face. "I might stay through the winter. I've made no plans to go anywhere."

Now there was no mistaking the relief in her expression. She was glad that he was staying. The notion set up a kind of humming in his midsection.

"Then perhaps we shall see you again," she said, glancing away.

He took hold of the tip of her chin and turned her face back toward him. "Do you want to see me again, Lily?"

Her tears had stopped, but her eyes were still moist, her lips slightly swollen. She looked at him for a long moment, then gave an almost imperceptible nod.

He continued holding her chin as he leaned forward to kiss her. It was meant to be a light caress, but the minute their lips touched, a wave of desire surged through him. He dropped his hold on her face and reached to gather her into his arms.

Nine

It had been many years, but Lily didn't think it had ever felt quite like this with Philip. She would have remembered.

Her memory was that lovemaking with Philip had been quick and fumbled. John's kiss was slow and practiced. It briefly entered her head that John Black had intimately known many women over the course of his life. But the thought fled along with every other one in her head as she gave herself up to the sensations of his mouth on hers.

He pressed her gently against the bench, his arm cushioning her back. With his free hand he loosened her long hair, then threaded his fingers through the strands and held her head steady while he continued his soft kisses.

It had been twelve years since she'd been touched by a man, and it seemed as if her body was waking up from a long sleep. The tips of her breasts tingled, and heat pooled at the base of her stomach. Her breath caught in a little murmur at the back of her throat.

At the sound, John pulled abruptly away. "Forgive

me," he said, his voice husky. "I didn't mean to take advantage."

Perhaps he had taken advantage, Lily thought ruefully, but her immediate reaction was disappointment that he had found his noble side. "I forgive you," she said, still breathless.

He pulled his arm from behind her and sat back, studying her expression. "Truly," he said. "You have my apologies."

She gave half a smile. "*Truly*," she replied, gently teasing. "No apologies are necessary. I rather liked it."

He looked surprised for a moment, then grinned. "In that case, perhaps I should not have stopped."

"Perhaps, but you did stop, and after all, I think 'tis for the best."

He shook his head and asked ruefully, "Now, why would that be, lass?"

She straightened up and smoothed out her skirts. "Precisely because I'm no longer a lass. I'm middle-aged and a mother. I've no business to be . . . to be engaging in such behavior."

"'Twas more in the way of pleasure than business, if you ask me."

John's smile was flirtatious, and once again she was reminded that he had had many years of bachelorhood to learn how to beguile women. The kiss had felt good, she'd not deny it. But she'd be foolish to succumb to this man's charm. By his own admission, his stay here was temporary. It would be the height of folly to let her heart become tangled up with him.

"We should be getting over to the stables," she told him, standing. "I thought it would be good for Daphne to have some time alone with the boys and Niall, but I don't want to miss out on the riding session entirely."

John looked as if he was going to argue, but finally

he stood as well. "First you must promise me that you're telling the truth. You weren't offended."

"Aye," she said. "That is, nay—I wasn't offended."

There was a mischievous gleam in his eyes. "And you must promise not to be offended the next time."

She couldn't help but laugh at his audacity. "I'll promise no such thing, Dr. Black."

"Ah, well, then. I'll just have to take my chances."

This was less dangerous. Though it had been years ago, she remembered this kind of banter from her youth. Lymond Castle had not had many visitors, but the ones who had come had often teased her with flirtatious talk. This she could handle. It was the rest of it that was dangerous. The look in his eyes when she had begun to confide in him about her past. The concern in his voice whenever they talked about Daphne. The sudden, plunging want at the pit of her stomach when he had kissed her. These were the dangerous things.

"Aye, take your chances, Dr. Black," she forced herself to reply lightly. "Next time I'll be forewarned."

She began to walk out of the alcove, but he grabbed her elbow and pulled her back. "Hold a moment," he said. "Now that we've kissed, will you at least tell me your real name?"

She hesitated, then said, "My name is Lily O'Farrell." She'd said her surname so little over the years that it sounded odd coming out of her mouth, as if it were some alien word that no longer belonged to her.

"O'Farrell? The O'Farrells of Lymond Castle?"

Instantly she regretted her impulse to tell him. He was a visitor. She hadn't thought he would know her family. Now there was no help for it. "Aye. The Earl of Lymond is my brother."

His jaw dropped. She smiled faintly and added, "I've not spoken to him since before Daphne was born."

"But . . . he's your brother?" he asked, sounding incredulous.

"Aye."

John looked away from her, lost in thought. Lily waited. Finally he turned back to her and said, "Lily, I have something grave to tell you. I fear that one of the boys who threw Daphne into the water that day was none other than the son of the Earl of Lymond."

Lily nodded. "I suspected as much. I've seen him and his friends watching her when we've gone to the village."

"Her own cousin? Does Daphne know?"

"Nay. I'll give my child no more cause for heartache."

For some reason, her answer appeared to anger him. His voice rose as he spoke. "Don't you realize that by trying to protect her from this outside world you're so afraid of, you may be actually putting her in greater danger? What if your nephew should try to seize her again? What if next time there's no stranger to come along and rescue her?"

His anger stung. "She's my daughter. I have no intention of letting anything happen to her."

"Yet you've done nothing against the culprits who caught her that day."

On the defensive, Lily suddenly found herself telling him the story of her trip to Lymond Castle. She somehow wanted to show him that she was doing all she could to ensure her daughter's safety. But the story only seemed to make him angrier.

"You went to Lymond Castle alone? How did you get there?"

"I walked."

John was shaking his head in exasperation. "How far is it? Over half a day's walk, I should say."

By now her own temper was rising. She faced him,

her hands on her hips. "I'm sorry, Dr. Black, but my horse and carriage were unavailable that day."

His expression softened. "You could have asked for help, Lily. I would have gone with you."

"I managed."

"Aye, I'm sure you did. I know you've been managing things by yourself for years, and I admire you for it, but a wise person knows that sometimes we need to call on friends."

"I have no friends." He stiffened, and she realized that she had hurt him, but the argument simply reinforced the fact that she was better off not getting involved with him.

"You may not consider me a friend, Lily, but I am one. So are Cat and Niall. I believe you could have many friends in the county if you allowed yourself. And your friends would be Daphne's friends, as well. You might want to think about that when she finally realizes that 'tis more fun to talk with a person than with a bird."

He was only saying the same things she had been saying to herself over the past few days, but hearing him say them in that accusatory tone, when only minutes before he'd been kissing her, made her temper finally break.

"Dr. Black, it's becoming clear to me that Daphne and I were happier before you stepped into our lives that rainy afternoon. I thank you for the invitation today, but now I'd like to ask you to take us home."

He waited a long moment, then nodded. "Very well," he said softly.

She turned to leave, and he fell in step beside her. This time they walked along the path side by side, not touching.

• • •

"Forgive me, John," Niall said, "but I'm afraid if the woman is determined to handle her own problems, there's nothing you can do about it. And, to be candid, if she's Lymond's sister, you're well out of the bargain."

The rest of the household had sought their beds, but Niall and John were still at the table, finishing a bottle of contraband brandy that Niall had obtained on his last visit to Dublin. "Why?" John asked. "What difference does it make that she's his sister?"

Niall rolled his eyes. "God's blood, John. She's the sister of an earl. You can't simply diddle her in the garden like a parlor maid and then ride back north to the wars."

John reddened. "I have no intention of doing anything of the sort."

"Ah," Niall said with a knowing nod. "So you'll try to tell me that nothing happened between you two this afternoon before you emerged from the arbor with flushed faces and hardly speaking a word to each other."

"I kissed her," he admitted. " 'Twas a brief impulse."

"Fine. Brief impulses lead to more prolonged ones. Before you know it, you've filled her belly and have one of the most powerful earls in southern Ireland hunting for your hide."

"The way I understand it, Lily's brother seems little inclined to protect her honor or, indeed, to do anything on her behalf. She says they've not spoken since before Daphne's birth." He emptied his glass in one gulp and reached for the brandy bottle.

Niall looked thoughtful. "I've never met Lymond, but the old-timers in the neighborhood say he's a thoroughly disagreeable fellow, and many call him a traitor, outright."

"Because he helped the English?"

"There's no proof, but 'tis said he had a secret pact with the late Lord Wolverton to help him take over Cat's family lands in the Valley of Mor."

"And now he's in London."

Niall nodded. "Brewing who-knows-what mischief with his English friends."

John took another long swallow of the fiery liquor. He'd already drunk too much, but he had yet to feel any of the comforting oblivion the habit had often brought him in the painful days following the death of Catriona's mother. "None of this concerns Lily," he said. "She only went to visit her brother because of what his son did to Daphne. I don't think she has any intention of establishing relations with him."

"Not with him, nor with anyone, apparently," Niall said pointedly. "Don't misunderstand me, John. She's a lovely woman and has raised an enchanting child, against incredible odds, but if she says she wants to be left alone, then so be it."

"She said she has no fren-sshh . . . friends," John pronounced carefully. He was drunk after all, he realized with surprise. Yet still the liquor had not dulled the disappointment of the day.

"Forget about her, John," Niall advised one last time, getting to his feet none too steadily. "You'd be better advised to let Cat continue her parade of eligible candidates."

John groaned. "God save me."

Niall grinned at his friend and extended a hand. "Come, I'll help you to bed."

John waved him away. "You go on ahead. I'll just see that the wee dram left in this bottle doesn't go to waste."

Niall studied him for a moment, then shook his head and turned to leave.

● ● ●

Lily sat on the edge of the bed and watched as her daughter lifted garments out of the old trunk from Lymond Castle. Daphne carefully studied each new offering and divided them into neat piles.

"With just a slight alteration, these will still work for you, Mummy," the girl said with the confidence of an expert tailor. "And this pile looks too small, so we should try to make them over for me. They are beautiful things! I can't understand how you could have left them shut up in a box all these years."

Lily had no answer. How could she explain to her daughter that after being turned away from her own home, she had been so ill in spirit that she wanted to obliterate all traces of Lymond Castle? It was a wonder that she hadn't thrown the contents of the chest into the fire. Now, of course, she was glad that she had not, since Daphne was so delighted with them.

The dresses they had altered for the trip to O'Malley House had been just the beginning. When they had returned, Daphne had gone immediately to the trunk to begin to search for something to wear on the next visit. If she'd noticed her mother's subdued manner, she made no comment on it.

"We can work on the dresses, Sweetcakes," Lily told her. "But I'd not set my heart on wearing them to O'Malley House any time soon."

Daphne turned to her in surprise. She was holding up a pretty pink frock that Lily distinctly remembered wearing the summer she turned fifteen. "The Riordans have already invited us back, Mummy. 'Twas the last thing Lady Riordan said to me when we bid them goodbye. 'Come soon,' she said. Do you think she didn't truly mean it?"

Lily glanced up at the familiar ceiling of their bedroom sanctuary. "I'm sure she meant it, Daphne, but sometimes people get busy about their lives and forget the things they say."

"Dr. Black won't forget," Daphne said firmly.

"I doubt Dr. Black will be around much longer. And once he's gone, I can't imagine the Riordans will think about asking us to call. We're not exactly in their circle of friends."

For the first time since they'd arrived home, Daphne's bright expression dimmed. "Oh," she said. "I suppose not. Truly, we're not in anyone's circle, are we, Mummy?"

Lily slipped from the bed to kneel beside her daughter on the floor. "We make our own circle, Sweetcakes." She took the pink dress from her daughter's hands. "And you shall look beautiful in this next spring sitting among our roses."

"But no one will see me."

"I shall see you . . . and your animal friends."

"It's not the same." Daphne's tone was uncharacteristically dull.

What will happen when she realizes 'tis more fun to talk with a person than a bird? John Black had asked. Lily tried to push aside the memory of his words.

"Perhaps we can get the pink dress finished in time for Christmas," she said with sudden resolution.

"To go to church service in the village?"

"Aye."

Daphne's face brightened. "Do you suppose the Riordans will go, too?"

"I don't know. Perhaps."

"If we see them, it might remind Lady Riordan to invite us again."

"As I said, 'tis not likely—"

Daphne held up her hand to stop her mother's words. Her lower lip trembled and tears gathered in her eyes. "You don't have to say it. I already know." She took the pink dress back from Lily and threw it down on top of the garments still in the trunk, then slammed the lid.

"You know what?" Lily asked, concerned at the sudden tears and rare show of temper.

"I know why we can't ever see anyone or go any-where."

Her small shoulders began to shake with sobs. Lily's heart sank. She knew? Had the children of the village, with the careless cruelty of youth, called her a bastard?

Guilt flooded through her. She should have talked to Daphne about the circumstances of her birth long before this. She should have told her that if there was shame, it was the mother's shame, not the innocent child's. She took in a deep breath. They'd had a long day, and she could tell Daphne was tired, but with her daughter's heartrending sobs unabated, Lily decided she could put off the conversation no longer. She slid over next to Daphne and put an arm around her.

"What do you mean, Sweetcakes?" she asked gently. "What have you heard in the village?"

"In the v-village?" Daphne asked between jerky breaths. "I d-don't understand."

Lily frowned. "Have some of the village children said horrible things to you?"

Daphne shook her head. The streams of tears down her cheeks were finally slowing. "Only those boys. They said I was a witch. But 'twas because they were foolish and wicked. Dr. Black said as much."

"And he was right. So what did you mean earlier when you said you know why we don't go anywhere?"

Daphne looked up at her mother in surprise. "You know, Mummy. It's my leg."

"Your leg?" Lily was dumbfounded. Daphne rarely made any mention of her leg, and from an early age had seemed to be totally at ease with her deformity. Suddenly Lily felt a lump of dread at the base of her throat. "What about your leg, Sweetcakes?"

"Why, 'tis a monster's leg. That's why we can't live out in the world like the rest of the people."

The blood rushed out of Lily's head, and she was afraid she was going to be sick. Struggling for control, she took Daphne firmly by both shoulders. "I've never heard anything so foolish in my life," she said. "Your foot was twisted when you were born, an accident of birth, nothing more. You are no more a monster than I or anyone else in Banburn."

Daphne had stopped crying, but her mother's words seemed to have little effect. "Don't shout, Mummy," she said. "I don't mind so awfully much, truly. Most of the time I'm happy here, and if we can't go back to O'Malley House, I'll be fine with my garden and my animals. 'Tis just—" Her face grew wistful—"I did like the pony very much, and it was fun to be with Lorcan and Paddy."

Lily was so distressed to hear her daughter call herself a monster that she could hardly speak, but for Daphne's sake, she tried to calm herself. "Perhaps we will see them again, Daphne. I only said not to count on it so."

The girl tilted her head, thinking. "It's strange. Lorcan and Paddy think my foot is funny, but I don't feel that it makes them see me differently. 'Tis more the adults who think me a monster. I can tell by the way they watch me when we go into town."

Lily was still fighting the waves of nausea. "Daphne, listen to me, because this is important. You are *not* a monster, and no one thinks you are."

Daphne just looked at her with a sad smile. Finally she said. "May I go to bed now, Mummy? I'm very tired."

Lily, feeling more helpless than she ever had in her life, gave her daughter a quick, hard hug. Then she let her go and sat back. Daphne did her one-legged hop to her feet and limped out of the bedroom.

The morning after Lily and Daphne's visit, Catriona enlisted both Niall and John to help decorate the manor for Christmas with cuttings of pine and holly. The warm fall season had left the greenery healthy and fragrant, and soon the entire house was filled with the clean odor of cut boughs. The boys were so excited at this first sign of the approaching holiday that they became quite wild, dashing about like little hedgehogs, knocking down decorations as soon as they were hung. Finally, Catriona threw up her hands in exasperation and marched them off for a nap. Niall had accounts to review in his office, which left John on his own for the afternoon.

He decided to take Greybolt out for an overdue run. It would do the horse good to take a hard ride over the hills, and it might help clear John's head from the previous evening's excesses. The liquor had given him a vague headache all day, which had not been helped by the pungent pine smell, nor by the antics of his friends' youngsters.

It felt good to breathe fresh air and feel the sunshine on his face. He saddled Greybolt and led him out of the stable. The horse appeared to be appreciating the sunshine, as well.

John turned to look down the road, wondering which direction he should take, then straightened up in surprise as he spied a solitary figure coming toward O'Malley House on foot. It was a woman, and, even from this distance, he knew instantly that it was Lily.

His body knew instantly, too. He muttered a low curse. He'd only kissed the woman, he told himself. And she'd basically rejected him. Now the mere sight of her walking along the road was enough to make his hose bulge? What was wrong with him? he asked with a snort of self-disgust.

He stood for a moment, wondering what to do, then swung himself up on Greybolt's back and began riding toward her. She stopped walking and waited for his approach.

"Good afternoon, Mistress O'Farrell," he said, pulling his mount to a halt and jumping down from his back.

She frowned. "I don't use that name any longer. I'd ask you to call me Lily or nothing at all."

He nodded agreement. "Very well. I must say I'm surprised to see you." He risked a small smile. "Were your horse and carriage unavailable again today?"

She smiled back, though he could tell she was tense, perhaps even more so than after their kiss the previous day.

"Is anything amiss?" he asked, suddenly alarmed. "Has something happened to Daphne?"

She shook her head. "Nay, I've left her at home. With my brother and his son in England, I feel safe enough leaving her. She's promised not to venture away from the cottage."

She was twisting her hands together as she spoke. Studying her face, he noticed dark shadows under her eyes. Her skin looked pale, in spite of the long walk she'd just had. He took a step closer. "What's wrong, Lily? Why have you come here?"

She looked up at him, no longer hiding the misery in her expression. "I've come to tell you that I've changed my mind."

The unruly state of his body wanted to put a provocative interpretation on her words, but John was more or less certain that her reason for coming had nothing to do with anything physical between them. Fi-

nally another possibility came to mind. "Have you decided to accept my help talking to your brother?" he
asked.

She looked confused for a moment, then shook her
head. "Nay, I've changed my mind about Daphne's . . .
condition. You once offered to help her. I came to tell
you I'm accepting the offer."

Ten

Lily was exhausted. She'd slept little two nights ago in anticipation of the visit to O'Malley House. Then the previous evening, after Daphne's heartbreaking words, she hadn't slept at all. Instead, she'd gotten up from her bed early, and by the time Daphne awoke, she had prepared the morning meal and had four loaves of bread rising. She'd asked Daphne to take charge of the baking while Lily went on some errands. Then she'd begun the long walk to the other end of the Valley of Mor where O'Malley House was nestled in the crook of the hills.

By the time she saw John Black riding toward her, she had started to wonder if she would actually make it as far as the house. Her feet seemed heavier with each step.

Seeing John had given her a short burst of strength, but now that she had told him her mission, a wave of weariness overtook her. Her thick linen dress seemed to soak in every ray of the hot sun, making her skin prickle. Beads of sweat seeped from underneath her cap. She blinked hard. Spots of light danced at the top of her eyes.

"You want me to help Daphne?" John confirmed. He looked troubled.

"Aye. You said you might be able to do something about her bad foot."

"Well, I—I'd be willing to try. I can't make any promises, and I wouldn't want her to set her hopes too high."

The prickling across her back intensified. It was incredibly hot, she decided. "Do you think we might continue the discussion inside?" she asked him.

John bent to look at her eyes. "You're flushed, Lily," he said. "Do you feel all right?"

"Aye . . . nay, 'tis beastly hot, isn't it?" She felt herself swaying, and then being lifted in John's arms and carried across the road to the shade of a grove of oak trees. It was an odd sensation, as though it were someone else's body he carried. Her head rolled back as if she were a rag doll and someone had suddenly taken the stuffing out of her neck.

"Lily!"

John's voice sounded blurry.

"Lily," he said again. "Come on, sweetheart, open your eyes."

She was vaguely aware that he had called her sweetheart, and that the word seemed to thaw something inside her. She opened her eyes and saw the spreading branches of a huge oak above her, blotting out the sky. She was sitting on the grass, propped against the trunk of the tree. John was rubbing her right wrist between his hands.

"Are you ill?" he asked, his voice tight with concern.

She shook her head. "It was just that the sun seemed so hot." The words sounded thick.

He sat back on his knees and observed her. "Have you eaten today? Drunk anything?"

She shook her head.

He stood and walked quickly back to his horse, who had stood without moving in the middle of the path where John had left him. He pulled a flask from the saddle, then came back to her and offered it. "Cider," he said. "Don't drink it too fast."

She took several sips of the sweet beverage, then handed it back to him. "I feel better now. I'm sorry for the trouble."

He looked angry with her, and for the dozenth time she wondered if she had done the right thing in coming to him. Then she remembered Daphne's taut face when she had called herself a monster, and she knew that she'd had no choice. If there were any chance that John Black could help her daughter, she had to let him try.

"So will you do it?" she asked him.

He was studying her face so intently, for a moment she wondered if he remembered her request, but finally he said, "I would give everything I own to help her, Lily, but before you agree to my care, I need to tell you a story."

"Tell me a story?" She wondered if the sun was still affecting her.

"Aye. But first we must get you some food."

"I'm fine, truly. There's no need."

He ignored her. "We'll go get something from the kitchen at O'Malley House."

She pushed herself up straighter against the tree and adjusted her cap. "I must be a sight," she said. "Lady Riordan will think—"

He shook his head. "Don't worry. There's no need for a social call. We won't even go into the house. Niall's busy with his books and Cat and the boys are sleeping." He stroked a finger along the top of her cheek. "I should say that it looks as if you could use some sleep yourself."

"I daresay," Lily answered, "but there will be time for that later. First I want to discuss Daphne."

"Fair enough." He stood, and, to her surprise, lifted her from the ground.

"I can walk now," she protested.

"You've walked a great plenty for today, I should say. I'm putting you on Greybolt's back. It's not a sidesaddle, but if you just hook your knee over the pommel—"

Now it was her turn to interrupt. "It's been many years, Dr. Black, but I can still sit a saddle—any saddle."

He smiled. "You're sounding recovered."

"I told you, I'm fine. I can't imagine what came over me." But she let him lift her up on the big stallion's back.

"Just hold on and I'll lead him." John said, gathering the reins.

It wasn't a true ride, but it felt wonderful to be on a horse again. As a child, she'd spent half her days galloping over the countryside. It had been her one way to escape from the oppressive atmosphere of Lymond Castle.

John led her directly to the low brick building behind the house that served as the estate kitchens. "Stay there," he told her. "Greybolt won't move." Then he disappeared into the building, emerging moments later with a small jug and a wrapped package.

Lily was still feeling slightly dazed from her fainting spell, so she made no protest as he tucked the items into a bag at the back of Greybolt's saddle.

"So you can ride?" he asked her. At her nod he added, "Shall we fetch a horse for you from the stables? Are you feeling up to it?"

Her smile must have been enough answer. She jumped nimbly down from the stallion's back, and together they walked the short distance to the Riordan stables, where John asked a stable boy to put a sidesaddle on a pretty brown mare.

Before she knew it, she was mounted on the horse's back, giving the animal free rein to follow Greybolt up into the hills behind O'Malley House.

John had at first planned to take Lily inside O'Malley House, but the ale had seemed to revive her. There was once again color in her face, and the pallor around her mouth was gone. She looked eager to ride, and it would mean they could seek out a place for an uninterrupted conversation. Still, he didn't want to push her. After only a few minutes riding along the stream up into the hills, he stopped and pointed to some rocks at the water's edge.

"This would be a good spot to sit while you eat something," he told her.

They dismounted and he held out his hand to help her climb over a large flat boulder to the side of the stream. She sank down, not appearing to care that her seat was covered with moss and dried leaves. He dropped the package he'd taken from his saddlebag into her lap. "You're to eat every morsel," he told her, taking a seat at her side.

She opened the cloth and obediently began munching at a piece of cheese. John nodded approval and waited to speak until she had finished the entire piece and had started nibbling on the edge of a cold meat pie. "If you insist on traipsing around the countryside on foot," he chided, "I hope you'll at least remember that the exertion requires food and drink. The next time you faint dead away in the middle of the road, I might not be around to catch you." He smiled at her. "It appears I'm beginning to make a habit of rescuing O'Farrell women in distress."

Lily frowned. "I told you—I don't use that name."

"If your daughter is to begin to go about in society, people will want to know her name. It seems a shame not to let her use it, especially when she is by rights the niece of an earl."

"The illegitimate niece of an earl," Lily corrected, "who will never recognize her as such."

"She could as well use her father's name. 'Tis common enough practice, though you never said the vows."

Lily shuddered. The meat pie sat in her fingers, apparently forgotten. "Never. She doesn't even know it, since I've not uttered that name since the day he left me to my brother's tender mercy."

John sighed and leaned over to raise her hand with the food to her mouth. "Mayhap the name can come later. First, I gather, you are wanting to do something about her foot."

Lily nodded, obediently chewing the corner of the pie. "Were you speaking true? Is there a way to help her?"

John looked into the rushing water of the little stream. Sunlight bounced from rock to rock. "Lily, I need to tell you that, though I used to be a doctor, I left the profession over twenty years ago."

He turned back to see her reaction. She was listening to him intently, but did not seem shocked by his revelation. "Why?" she asked simply.

"Back then, with the conceit of youth, I thought I could do anything—cure anyone. But the day came when my skill failed." He held his hands up, palms open. "These failed."

"No doctor can save everyone."

He lowered his hands to his lap. "I know. But this was . . . this was a person I cared about very much. She'd been in labor for two days, and the baby was not going to come out. In my arrogance, I thought my skill with the knife would save her. Instead, it killed her." He looked down at his hands as if they were enemies.

"If you had not tried, she may have died anyway," Lily argued.

"Aye, but in the end 'twas not the babe that killed her, it was I."

"But you saved her child."

John looked at her in surprise. "Aye. How did you know?"

"The babe was Catriona."

"How did you—"

"Lady Riordan and I had a brief chance to talk alone yesterday. She told me of your love for her mother. I believe she considers you as dear as an uncle, or even a father, perhaps."

John smiled briefly. "It always amazes me that women seem to be able to learn a person's life history within moments of meeting one another."

"Catriona owes you her life. You must not blame yourself. She would have died along with her mother if you had not intervened."

He'd given himself the same argument for over twenty years, but it didn't get any more convincing.

"In any event," he said, "you need to understand that when I say I am a doctor, 'tis not strictly true. I will never again take a knife to any living soul, but I still may be able to provide some help to Daphne. Hers is not a case for surgery."

"What can help her?"

"Though I no longer practice, I've never lost my interest in the healing arts. I seek information whenever I can, and a couple of years ago I first heard of the work of a French physician named Ambroise Pare. He has devised a boot for just such cases as Daphne's."

"A boot?"

"Aye. It will stabilize her foot and help her to walk more easily. It may even gradually correct some of the twisting."

Lily's eyes grew wide. "You mean that her foot could be normal again?"

"Nay, not normal, but much better, and with time, her limp will become less pronounced."

"Some days her leg gets so tired that I see her rubbing it at night. When she was little, I used to rub it myself, but she won't let me anymore."

"Straightening her walk should help," he told her.

"How would we get such a boot?"

"I have some drawings of the design. I would have to enlist the help of a couple of the tradesfolk in the village—the leather worker and the blacksmith. The boot will be heavy," he warned. "Perhaps Daphne won't want to wear it."

"I think she'll be willing to try. Especially if you tell her that it may help. She's grown fond of you." She'd moved her hands against her chest, still clutching the uneaten pastry.

"I've grown fond of her, too. Are you going to eat that pie?"

Lily looked at it in surprise, then shook her head and set it back on the oilcloth it had been wrapped in. "The cheese and ale were sufficient. I feel fine now, and, honestly, I've no appetite. All I can think about is my beautiful little girl." Her lip began to tremble. "Oh, John," she said, her voice breaking, "last night after returning from our visit to your friends' house, she called herself a monster."

John's throat tightened. "Surely 'twas nothing—I thought she had *enjoyed* the visit."

"Oh, aye, she did, ever so much, but when I said she shouldn't count on receiving another invitation soon, she told me that the reason we never associated with people was her bad foot." Noiseless tears started running down her cheeks, and she brushed them angrily away. "I had no idea she felt that way."

Almost without thinking, John put his arm around her and drew her close. The gesture had nothing to do with desire. He simply wanted to comfort a mother who was in anguish over her child. "I've none of my own, but from what I've seen of children, they often get odd ideas in their heads. The good thing is that they can shift easily from one mood to the next. Daphne may have been overly tired last night."

Lily had gone into his arms without protest. "Nay, once she said it, I could tell that 'twas a belief of long standing. I blame myself for not seeing it before this."

John pulled slightly back so that he could look down into her wet eyes. "Weren't you telling me not moments ago not to blame myself? Now I'll give you the same advice. Lily, we all make mistakes, but I believe most of us go through this life trying to do the best we know how, especially for the people we hold dearest."

"I've tried to keep her safe and happy."

"Of course you have, and I believe you've done just that. She's a sweet, natural child, and a happy one."

Lily's tears had stopped. She slumped against him with a weary sigh. "She wasn't happy last night."

"None of us can be happy all the time. But if it's true that her foot is causing her distress, then we'll see what we can do about that."

Her eyes closed, as she rested her head against his chest. "I've not asked anyone for help in a dozen years."

"Then it's about time you did," John replied with a chuckle.

"Somehow it's not as difficult as I thought. . . ." Her voice had grown slurred.

He held her for several moments without speaking. The fainting had not been just from the walk and lack of food, he realized. The worry over Daphne and over her own guilt had utterly exhausted her. After a few moments her mouth fell slightly open and her breathing became regularly. Gently he laid her back on the mossy bank and let her sleep.

She'd been dreaming. It was a dance at Lymond Castle, a rare enough occurrence in her youth, but in the dream it seemed perfectly normal. Philip had been there, and though all the young ladies in the ballroom had hovered around him, he kept coming back to Lily. At the end of the evening, everyone else in the room had faded away and only she and Philip remained, dancing alone in the middle of the gilded hall. Even the musicians were gone, though there was still music, somehow, and she was in Philip's arms. "I'll love you always, my darling," he was telling her. "Promise me that you'll be mine, and I'll take care of you forever and ever. . . ."

The smells were not right. It wasn't the candle wax of an overheated ballroom she smelled, but fresh earth and green moss. The only music was the sound of a mountain stream. She opened her eyes. John was looking down at her, his kind, gray eyes narrowed with concern.

"The sleeping beauty awakens," he teased.

"I fell asleep," she said, her voice thick.

"Aye. I suspect 'twas long overdue. You were exhausted when you came here today." He leaned over her. "Are you feeling better?"

She felt as if she'd been asleep for centuries. Her head was still fuzzy. "Aye," she said. "I've kept you here. My apologies—"

He interrupted her with a shake of his head. "I've enjoyed watching you."

Something in the way he said the words made her cheeks feel hot. The concern had left his eyes, replaced by something more primitive. The eyes of a wolf, hunting. She knew that he wanted to kiss her, and she knew in the same instant that she wanted him to.

He gave a slow, knowing smile. "So that's the way of things, is it?" he asked softly. Then he bent to press his lips on hers.

When he'd kissed her the previous day in the garden, she'd been unprepared. It had been brief, over before she hardly had time to realize what had happened. This was different. John had seen something in her expression that told him she was willing. She had the feeling that he had no intention of hurrying.

He started by kissing her mouth, lightly, then the tip of her nose, her chin, and finally back to her mouth, teasing open her lips with his tongue to enter her in warm, languid strokes. She lay sleepy and relaxed on the ground and let him slowly arouse her. After several long moments, she lifted her arms around his neck, and he responded by shifting his kisses to a sensitive spot just under her right ear.

"You smell of violets," he murmured. "But you taste sweet, like candied fruit."

He had a flavor as well, she realized. A manly kind of taste and scent that reminded her of forests and smoky campfires.

He'd shifted back to her mouth, and she found herself participating in the kiss, entwining her tongue with his, seeking the depths of his mouth, as her relaxed body slowly began to tense with wanting. Her arms tightened around his neck. She was suddenly aware of her breasts, pushing against the fabric of her gown.

She loosened her hold on him and reached for his hand, then pressed it against one peaking globe. He obliged by caressing her, through the cloth, finding her nipple and teasing it with gentle fingers. After a moment he switched attentions to the other breast until it was also taut and quivery.

After all those years. It felt so good. He grinned down at her. "It appears you are almost as quick to desire as I, sweetheart," he said.

"Almost?"

He nodded, then guided her hand to his stiffened penis. "This one has been ready this hour past while I watched you sleep."

She gave him a sensual smile and stroked the hard length of him, letting the unfamiliar touch heighten her own arousal.

Suddenly the meaning of his words reached her. "Hour?" she said, pushing him away and sitting up. For the first time she noticed that the sky had turned orange over the hills across the stream. "How long did I sleep?" she asked in alarm. "Merciful saints, 'tis almost twilight."

John released her with obvious reluctance. She shot him a look of apology. "Daphne's alone," she explained.

He nodded, but didn't speak.

"I'm not going to get back before dark. She'll be worried."

He took in a long, ragged breath. "Aye."

"Don't be angry."

He smiled then. "I'm not angry, lass." He jumped up and reached a hand out to her. "Come on. We'll ride over to Whistler's Woods and see what your little lady thinks about the idea of a new pair of shoes."

Lily took his hand and let him pull her up. "Thank you," she said, flooded with a different kind of warmth than that she had felt when he had been kissing her.

He nodded, then led her up the bank toward the horses.

Eleven

"Will it hurt?"

John sat back on his haunches and looked up at Daphne's face. Her expression was a poignant mixture of hope and fear. Once her mother had given a nod of approval, she had sat immediately down on the bench by the fireplace and put out her foot for John to examine.

"I just need to look at it, lass. If anything is uncomfortable, just tell me. Or you can kick me," he added with a wink.

She sat still as one of the little sparrows in her garden as he slowly unwrapped the rags that wound around her bad foot. The foot itself was smaller than her other foot and thicker, but he was pleased to see that all five toes were in place and looked almost normal. The most difficult thing to see was the angle. The foot itself veered out from the ankle at an angle that would cause great pain for a normally constructed person.

Gently he rotated it, noting that it did have a wide range of motion. From what he remembered of Dr. Pare's writings, all this was a good sign. Engrossed in his study, he'd almost forgotten about his little patient until one final twist elicited a quiet murmur.

He looked up at her with a smile. "You did very well, Princess," he told her. "I believe I've seen enough."

"Will Dr. Pare's boot fit me? Do you think it will work?" she asked. She seemed to be holding in a breath.

"I have to be honest, Daphne. I know about Dr. Pare's treatment only from writings. I've never seen it work. But my thought is that it is certainly worth trying. Your foot is not so much misshapen as it is simply twisted the wrong direction."

"But won't it hurt to twist it back?"

"I don't think it would be truly painful, though it might tire you."

"Sometimes my leg aches if I've walked a long ways," Daphne told him. "Mummy makes me feverfew tea."

"You might experience something similar with the boot, especially at the beginning." He glanced over at Lily, who stood in the doorway to the bedroom, watching them. Her hands were clasped at her throat in the way he'd come to recognize when she was worried. "Feverfew would be just the thing," he told her with a smile. She nodded, but her hands remained tightly clasped.

John stood, and Daphne rearranged her skirt to hide all traces of her still bare foot. "You'd be a brave lass to try it," he told her. "I'd not have suggested it if I hadn't already learned what a courageous girl you are."

Daphne looked over at her mother, who smiled agreement, then she turned back to John. "I don't feel the least brave, Dr. Black, but all I know is that if your French doctor's treatment can help me walk better, I'd be a fool not to give it a try."

Her words sounded so adult that it seemed almost impossible that they were coming from the mouth of a young girl. He looked at Lily again and could see the pride shining in her eyes.

"Then we're all agreed," he said. "I'll find my drawings and come back tomorrow to take measurements. Then we'll have to make arrangements with a good cobbler and a blacksmith."

Lily spoke for the first time. "Will you be able to finish it before you have to leave?"

Daphne looked up sharply. "Are you going away, Dr. Black?" she asked.

Something in the girl's voice made John's heart give a lurch. Was he leaving? Of course he was. He couldn't stay in Killarney forever. But just how did he say that to the sweet girl who was looking up at him with something akin to reverence in her big eyes.

"I won't be leaving before I'm sure we're making progress on that new walk of yours," he told her.

"But then you're leaving?" she persisted.

He put a hand lightly on her hair. "Now, Princess, you know I'm just a visitor here with the Riordans. They'll get tired of me eventually."

"Lorcan and Paddy would never get tired of you," Daphne argued.

"I'd not want to risk it," he answered with a grin. "And I'll need to be getting back to my own duties. But it won't be for a good while yet, so let's not have more talk about leaving."

She nodded agreement, but there was a flicker of doubt in her eyes that had not been there earlier when she had so trustingly allowed him to look at the part of her she had all her life taken pains to hide from the rest of the world.

• • •

By the time John got back to O'Malley House, the headache that had gently nagged him all day after his drinking bout the previous evening had turned into a hammering throb. He'd ridden home in the beginning of a light drizzle, leading behind him the horse Lily had used. The entire ride, he'd relived the scene in the cottage—Daphne trustingly allowing him to take her poor little foot in his hands, Lily watching from the doorway with such hopeful anguish, Daphne's doubtful gaze following him as he left the house.

All of it had left him with knots in his gut such as he hadn't felt through all the years of battle. How had this happened? he asked himself. After Rhea's death he'd sworn to never again risk getting involved in such a fashion. For over twenty years Dr. John Black had been a man who got things done and solved problems, quickly and dispassionately, and never got hurt in the process.

Suddenly, somehow, these two females living their independent lives hidden away from the rest of the world had become *important* to him in a way that was simply unacceptable. Simply foolish.

"Where the devil have you been?" Niall asked with unaccustomed irritation as John walked in the front hall after stabling the horses.

"I went for a ride."

"And return at this hour? It's well after dark."

John frowned. With the state of his head, he was in no mood for his young friend to turn nagging nanny. "The stable boy knew we were riding. You could have asked him."

"We?"

"Lily and I."

Niall ran his hand through his hair—the dark tangled curls that were identical to his two Riordan brothers and had now been passed on to his own sons. "Mistress O'Farrell? Where did *she* come from?"

John looked at his friend in surprise. He knew that Niall had doubts about John's growing friendship with Lily, but his tone told John that something else was wrong. "What's amiss?" he asked. "Why were you waiting for me?"

Niall nodded his head toward the front parlor. "You're wet. Go warm yourself by the fire while I tell Cat that you're back. You look like you need food, as well."

John walked into the parlor, pulled a chair close to the fire, and sat down wearily. What he needed was his bed, he thought grumpily, not food. But when Niall came back carrying a tray, he found himself devouring one of the same meat pasties that Lily had ignored that afternoon. The pie brought a brief memory of what had transpired on the bank of the stream. He took a deep drink of the ale Niall had brought. Then he leaned back in the chair and turned to his host. "Now, tell me," he said simply.

Niall stood by the fireplace, drumming his fingers on the mantel in impatience as he waited for his friend to take some refreshment. "We've had news from Cormac," he said.

John sat up. "Is anything amiss?" he asked. "Has there been a problem with Maura's baby?" Maura, the wife of the middle Riordan brother, Eamon, was with child. Though the family had now thoroughly disproved the old curse about Riordan brides dying within a year of the wedding, each Riordan pregnancy was greeted with wariness.

"Nay, 'tis none of the family. Both my brothers and their beautiful wives are just fine."

"Then 'tis news of the war."

Niall nodded his head gravely. "Not of the war precisely, for the rebels have still not united enough to represent a threat to the queen's forces. That's the problem. She and her ministers are so confident of their rule that they've begun to seize Irish estates as rewards for their favorites."

John shook his head. "Once the precedent has been established, where is it to stop? Soon we'll be a country of disenfranchised landowners."

Niall turned from the fireplace and paced to the far end of the room and back. "Aye, and the devil of it is, they seem to want to start with Killarney."

"You can hardly blame them. 'Tis the jewel of the country."

"Not only that, it has been the most peaceful. Most of the fighting up to now has been in the Midlands and the North. The landowners here know nothing about defending themselves against invaders. Our tenants are farmers, not fighters."

"I should ride north and see if I can get some of the rebel soldiers to come help out here."

Niall paced across the room again, then finally took the seat across from John. "According to Cormac, the rebels are too busy fighting among themselves to be able to help anyone."

John closed his eyes for a minute to try to stop the pounding in his head. He would be able to think about this more clearly in the morning. Opening his eyes, he said, "Let me sleep on it. Tomorrow you and I can go meet with some of your neighbors and make plans."

"From Cormac's letter, it appears that one of my neighbors is taking an active part in seeing Killarney turned over to the English."

John's damp tunic gave him a sudden shiver. "The Earl of Lymond?" he asked, already knowing what Niall's answer would be.

"Aye, the traitor is none other than Nevin O'Farrell,

the brother of the lady you went riding with this afternoon."

He'd think about that in the morning, too, John decided, standing. "I've already told you, Lily has nothing to do with her brother."

"Perhaps not now, but if it comes to a fight, blood will usually tell. I'd stay away from her, John. Before my warning was for your sake alone, now it's for all our sakes."

John's head throbbed and his stomach was threatening to reject the cold pasty he'd gulped. "We'll discuss it all in the morning," he said again.

"Just promise me that you'll stay away from the woman," Niall persisted.

"I can't do that," he said quietly. Then he turned to seek the comfort of his own chamber.

"The woman said she was yer sister, milord," the servant said without raising his eyes to look at his irate master. "I did disbelieve the story, of course, but"—he dared to raise his eyes for the briefest instant—"beggin' Yer Lordship's pardon, she did have that sort of *air* about her, if ye do know what I mean. She stood so tall and puffed up. High and mighty, she was, that was it. High and mighty."

"Stop babbling, you addlepated fool." The Earl of Lymond lowered his voice. "What did she say she wanted?"

The man's legs began to shake. "Why, er, she didn't rightly say. 'Tell him his sister come to see him.' That was it. She didn't rightly say anything more."

"We must send for her," said a female voice. Lymond looked up. A small, slender woman dressed entirely in gray stood in the doorway to his office. Lymond's thick eyebrow rose in surprise. "I didn't hear you knock, my dear," he said.

"I didn't knock," she said. "I learned from the servants that Lily had been here. Something must be wrong or she wouldn't have come."

"No doubt 'tis something for that brat of hers. She'd never come for herself."

"That brat is your niece," she said evenly.

Maired O'Farrell had long ago resigned herself to the life fate had cast her. She stayed mostly in her own quarters, rarely appearing even to take meals in the big Lymond Castle dining hall. But even with her lonely life, she had retained a serenity and a quiet dignity that her overbearing husband had never been able to break.

Lymond looked over at the servant, who stood listening to the rare exchange between master and mistress with a fascinated expression. "Leave us," he told the man.

Reluctantly the retainer turned to go. Maired stepped inside the office to allow the servant to pass. "Close the door," Lymond told her.

Maired did so, then turned back, her hands folded in front of her. "Her name is Daphne," she continued.

"I don't give a damn what her name is. She's Lily's bastard, and I washed my hands of both of them long ago."

Maired nodded. "I shall go to them myself, then."

Lymond rose to his feet and planted his hands on the desk in front of him. Leaning toward his wife, he said firmly, "You shall do no such thing, especially not now."

Maired's dull hazel eyes brightened slightly. "Lily is your sister and my friend. If she needs something, I intend to help her."

Lymond's knuckles grew white where they rested on the desk, but his voice was conciliatory. "My dear, there are plans afoot that you can't be expected to understand. This is not the time to be running around the countryside on missions of mercy. I'm afraid I must forbid you from leaving the castle grounds."

"I'm to be a prisoner now?"

"Nay, of course not. I'm merely trying to protect you. Changes will be taking place in this area, and it's likely not to be safe travel for a time."

"What about Lily?"

"I'm sure if Lily truly needs something, she'll make a return visit."

Maired stood watching her husband for a long moment. Her expression had not changed during the entire conversation. "If she comes here again, will you help her?"

Lymond took in a long breath that closed his nostrils. "Aye," he said finally. "If 'tis money she needs, I'd not see the slut starve."

Maired's eyes narrowed, but she gave a nod and left the room.

"I have a favor to ask you, Cat." John was standing next to the mantelpiece of the big parlor fireplace, repositioning one of the Christmas boughs that had been knocked about by the boys' antics. Catriona was seated across the room, stringing dried apples for a garland. She looked up as he spoke.

"Something tells me this favor is going to concern Mistress Lily O'Farrell."

John finished pinning the branch and walked over to take a seat next to his hostess. "You know that Niall has asked me to stay away from her?"

"Aye. Because of her brother's involvement with the English."

"Lily has not even seen her brother for years. She told me so herself."

"Still, if it comes to fighting—"

"Aye, if it comes to fighting, the divisions will come

soon enough. It's not necessary to begin making them ahead of time."

Catriona smiled and reached out to put her hand on John's knee. "You've grown fond of Mistress O'Farrell, haven't you, my friend?"

"I've promised to help Daphne. We're making a special kind of boot for her."

"For her twisted foot? You think you can help? John, that's wonderful!"

He gave a wave of caution. "We don't know if 'twill produce results. But at least the shoe should allow her to walk more comfortably."

Catriona tipped her head to see his eyes. "So 'tis to help Daphne that you go there? This has nothing to do with Daphne's beautiful mother?"

John smiled. "I'll not deny that Lily's a beautiful woman, but if you could have seen Daphne's hopeful face when I told her about the treatment, you'd not ask the question."

"John, I can't tell you how it pleases me to hear that you've decided to return to your medical profession."

He shook his head. "Nay, Cat. Though I'll admit to a great satisfaction in once again being able to help a patient, I've not gone back to being a doctor."

"But you have. Perhaps 'tis only with Daphne for a start, but this might be the beginning—"

"I shall never again be a true doctor, Cat. I can help Daphne because, in truth, her treatment is more a matter of engineering than of medicine. If this boot works as Dr. Pare has described, the leg will begin to correct itself. I'll have nothing to do with it."

"The treatment will only work if the patient is willing, and 'tis faith in the doctor that makes the patient willing. I should think that makes the doctor the most important ingredient in any cure."

John stood and leaned over to give Catriona a kiss

on the cheek. "Ah, Cat, how did you get to be so wise?"

She looked up at him. "So you do admit that by treating Daphne O'Farrell, you are a doctor once again, if only in this one case?"

"Aye, if you put it that way, but I am a doctor who will never again wield a knife or a saw, which is to say, I am not much of one at all."

She settled back into her chair and resumed threading the dried fruit. " 'Tis a start," she said in the determined voice he had come to know.

He chuckled at her stubbornness. "We've gotten off the subject of my favor," he reminded her.

She continued threading. Before he'd had a chance to make his request, she said, "Of course, Lily and her daughter may share Christmas dinner with us."

John rolled his eyes. Why was it that women always seemed to know every thought in a man's head? "I thought 'twould be a chance for Daphne to try out her new boot in front of a friendly audience."

Catriona looked up at him, her cat's green eyes wide and ingenuous. "Of course you did. 'Tis Daphne you want here and it's sheer courtesy to invite Lily as well."

" 'Twould please me to have them *both* here," he answered a bit testily.

"I'm teasing you, John. They are welcome, truly. Both of them."

He nodded his thanks. "Perhaps you should discuss it with Niall first. He's worried about Lily's relationship to Nevin O'Farrell."

Catriona set aside her garland and stood, shaking the extra bits of apple out of her skirt. "I know. 'Tis a male way to look at things, planning for war instead of building ties for peace."

"So you will ask him?"

"Nay, I shall *tell* him. If he has any objection to Mistress O'Farrell and her daughter joining us at Christmas, I don't think it will take me long to convince him of the worthiness of the plan." She turned toward the door with a swish of her taffeta skirt, giving John a coquettish glance over her shoulder.

Her hips swayed enticingly as she walked out of the room. *Women*, John thought, with another rueful chuckle. *How did we men ever get the notion that we are the ones in control?*

Twelve

John arrived early leading the same brown mare Lily had ridden the other day. Lily could ride the mare, he suggested, and Daphne could ride in front of him on his big stallion. Lily wondered if her daughter would turn shy at the idea, but her daughter seemed perfectly fine with it. Of course, all Daphne had been able to think about this past week was the special boot John had promised her. If she had to ride into Banburn on a squealing pig, she'd probably not have any objection.

As they started along the path out of the woods, Daphne seemed to be settling easily in the saddle. Lily followed behind on the other horse.

John turned back to her. "Do you want to go ahead of me?" he asked.

"Nay, I'll follow you. Your Greybolt appears to be used to taking the lead."

John smiled and turned back to look at the road.

It was odd for Lily to watch them—her daughter perched in front of John, his arms lightly around her, as if they had ridden together this way for years. This is what it would have been like if Daphne had grown up with a father, she realized with a pang.

They reached Banburn in a short time. Lily had almost forgotten how easy it was to cover distances on horseback rather than on foot. Perhaps it had been a mistake to leave behind her horses at Lymond Castle. She and Daphne would enjoy taking an occasional ride. Ride where? she asked herself, and suddenly realized that the destination she had in mind for these rides was O'Malley House.

Careful, Lily, she cautioned. Once before she'd let the casual kisses of a visitor spin her head around and make her abandon good sense. She wasn't about to let it happen again.

John led them past the marketplace and into the center of Banburn before stopping at a small thatched cottage. Lily knew the house belonged to Thaddeus, the cobbler, who had been making shoes for the people in the area since Lily was small. Thaddeus had made the shoes she was wearing and the one shoe Daphne wore on her good foot.

John jumped down and helped Daphne to the ground, then turned and offered his arms to Lily.

"I haven't forgotten that much about horses," she told him. "I can dismount by myself."

But as she swung herself off the saddle, his hands went around her waist, cushioning her drop to the ground. "I'm sure you can," he murmured low enough so that Daphne wouldn't hear. "But I found myself with a sudden desire to touch you."

Lily felt the heat move up her neck as she stepped out of his hold. In just a few words, he'd managed to bring all the memories of that day on the riverbank flooding back. By the time they'd walked the few steps to the cobbler's cottage, she was sure her cheeks were bright scarlet.

Fortunately, Daphne was so excited about the fitting

of her new boots, she didn't seem to notice her mother's discomfiture.

Thaddeus had always been a small man, and now that he was older than anyone in Banburn could remember, he seemed impossibly tiny, but his eyes still sparkled and his smile was merry as he welcomed them inside.

"So someone is to have a new pair of shoes, eh?" he asked Daphne. "And 'tis to be a true *pair* this time."

"Aye," Daphne said proudly. "I'll have two, just like everyone else."

She sat on the stool the old man placed for her next to his workbench. Then he reached behind the bench and pulled out a pair of light brown boots. The leather looked soft and smooth on both, but one of the boots was oddly made with pieces of metal protruding from strange angles. Daphne looked at it warily, and some of the excitement in her eyes dimmed.

"Don't be afraid of it," John told her. "The metal is there to help the foot straighten."

Lily had her doubts as well. The shoe with the metal rods looked heavy. She wondered if Daphne's slender leg could support such a weight.

No one spoke as John knelt in front of Daphne and unwound the rags from her foot. He took the boot from Thaddeus and eased it onto the foot, then began to turn screws that were attached to the metal. Lily watched Daphne's face for any sign of pain, but she merely seemed engrossed in the procedure.

"How does that feel?" John asked.

Cautiously Daphne moved her foot. "It's heavy," she said.

"Aye, I warned you about that, remember? But I think you'll soon get used to the extra weight."

Daphne leaned over and touched one of the screws. "What are these for?"

"To tighten the brace. If your foot begins to grow straighter, we can change the position."

"Can I try walking?"

Thaddeus put the other, normal boot in John's hand. "You should try it with both," the cobbler said.

John helped Daphne with the other shoe, then gave her his hand as she gingerly rose to her feet.

"It feels odd," she said.

"Does it hurt?" John asked.

"Nay, 'tis just odd."

John stood to watch her take her first few steps. "No doubt 'twill feel strange for a spell, and I only want you to wear it for an hour or two at a time until you get used to it."

Daphne was smiling, and Lily could see that already her walk looked more balanced. For one thing, the uneven height of her legs seemed to be corrected. She still dragged the bad foot, but it moved in a straighter line.

Daphne walked to the end of the room and back, then looked down at her two feet, a triumphant expression on her face. "You can hardly notice the difference, Mummy."

Lily felt a lump in her throat. She looked over at John, who was smiling broadly.

The cobbler leaned over the bench and was studying the shoes with a practiced eye. "If the foot begins to turn more," he said, "I'll tighten up the leather on the inside. But you're right, missy, they make a mighty fine pair."

Daphne did a little skip, lifting her skirts higher. "I think I could even dance in these," she said.

"Didn't I tell you we'd have you dancing?" John asked her. "But not today. I want the foot to get used to the weight before you try anything too fancy."

"Can I wear them home?" Daphne pleaded, looking at her mother.

Lily looked at John.

"Aye," he said, "since we'll be on horseback. But when we get back to your house, I want you to take them off until tomorrow morning. When you wake up, try a little walk, then take them off again until afternoon. If everything feels right, you may wear them the day after that to Christmas dinner at the Riordans. That is, if you and your mother will agree to come."

Daphne's reaction left no doubt of her opinion on the subject. Lily, too, felt an odd elation at the thought of spending Christmas with the happy Riordan family. But the notion frightened her, as well. Hadn't she just flushed all the way to her toes at the mere feel of this man's hands at her waist? Hadn't she just been warning herself about getting any closer to John Black and the warm, inviting world of his friends at O'Malley House?

"Of course we'll come, won't we, Mummy?" Daphne urged.

"Seems to me that Christmas would be perfect for the debut of a fine pair of boots like this one," Thaddeus added. "For in truth, what I'm seeing is a kind of Christmas miracle. When Dr. Black first described this shoe to me, I never thought it'd work."

"And much of the credit goes to you, my friend," John told the little cobbler. "Anyone with less skill could not have done it."

The man looked pleased with the praise, and utterly refused to take the extra coins John tried to give him. "We had a fair price set, Doctor," he said firmly. "And my satisfaction is in seeing the young lady so happy."

That was the key, Lily thought as the trio made their way out to the horses, Daphne walking proudly on her new shoes. It wasn't only the new gait it gave her, it was the happiness and the pride. You could see it in her straighter bearing and her smiling, confident face. Whatever happened between her and John Black, he had given her daughter these precious gifts, and she would always be grateful.

"So you will come to O'Malley House for Christmas?" he asked as he helped boost her on the back of the little mare.

"Aye," she said. "We'd be pleased to come."

Before he left them, John Black had showed Lily and Daphne exactly how to fasten the new boot so that Daphne would be able to try it herself the next day. He'd promised to return for them on Christmas morning, and she assumed that she would not see him until then. Even so, when she heard a horse coming through the woods along the path to the cottage, she couldn't help a surge of anticipation that made her drop the knife she'd been using to cut up a kettle full of turnips.

But the rider dismounting outside was not John Black.

"Aunt Maired!" Daphne shouted at the newcomer and went hobbling out of the house to show off her new boots.

Lily pulled off her apron, wiped her hands, and straightened her cap before she followed Daphne out the door. Even though Maired never once mentioned the differences between Lily's current circumstances and her childhood at Lymond Castle, Lily sometimes felt a bit self-conscious around her sister-in-law. Maired's fine clothes and delicate white skin were reminders of a way of life Lily had long ago left behind.

As usual, within a few minutes Maired's unassuming ways allowed Lily to relax. The visitor showered Daphne with compliments over not only the new boots, but her general appearance. "You've grown so tall, child, I'd not have known you. And a beauty! Who'd have thought? Of course, it had to be, looking like your mother, as you do."

Daphne had beamed and paraded for her aunt until Lily had gently reminded her that she had surpassed the time limit Dr. Black had suggested for her first time with the boots.

"It doesn't bother me, Mummy," Daphne had protested, but she'd obediently sat to remove the shoe, and Lily had seen her surreptitiously rubbing her leg as she did when she had overtired herself.

"Lily," Maired said with a glance at Daphne after the three had talked for almost an hour. "Why don't we walk outside so you can show me your garden?"

"Shall I, Mummy?" Daphne asked.

Lily shook her head. Maired obviously had something on her mind that was for Lily's ears alone. "You've had enough walking for this morning, I think. Remember, you want your leg to be in good shape for Christmas at O'Malley House tomorrow."

This argument convinced Daphne immediately, and she sat down by the fire and began to stir the stew.

Maired and Lily went outside. "Are you truly going to spend Christmas with Lord and Lady Riordan?" Maired asked in surprise.

"Aye." Lily didn't elaborate. Maired had been her one true friend during her exile from her family home, but Lily's years of independence had made her lose the custom of sharing confidences.

"I didn't realize that you knew them."

"We've met a few times in Banburn. I sold Lady Riordan a basket."

Maired still looked curious, but when Lily didn't offer any more information, she changed the subject to the purpose of her visit. "The servants told us that you visited Lymond Castle while we were in London."

"Aye," she answered slowly. She'd hoped to talk to her brother about the actions of his son, but she hadn't reckoned on telling Maired. Maired was the boy's mother. If she felt about Desmond the way Lily felt about Daphne, she would not want to hear Lily's charges. She might not even believe them.

"I was afraid"—Maired glanced around the grounds of the cottage, as if looking for some sign of misfortune—"afraid that something had happened to one of you, that you were in need in some way. . . ." Her voice trailed off and she looked embarrassed.

Lily felt a rush of warmth toward her sister-in-law, who had never stopped caring about her in all these years. Impulsively she put an arm around Maired's slender shoulders and gave her a quick hug. "Nay, 'twas nothing like that. I came to talk with my brother."

Maired looked surprised. "I—I'm sorry Lily, but I don't think he has any desire for a reconciliation. In fact, after the way he treated you, I'm surprised that you would want one."

"I don't." They'd reached the end of the cottage path and stopped walking. She turned to face her sister-in-law. "Dearest Maired, I don't want to cause you any hurt, but I came because I fear that your son may have tried to harm Daphne. I was hoping that Nevin would talk to him."

Maired's face went white. "Harm her?"

"Aye. Perhaps they thought it was in jest, but 'twas cruel and dangerous. From Daphne's description it was Desmond and two of his friends."

"The Crawleys."

"Aye."

Maired let out a deep breath. "I don't think I even want to know the details, Lily. But, tell me, she suffered no hurt?"

"No lasting hurt. They did frighten her."

"You will think me a monster and an unnatural mother, Lily, but I have always known that I would live to regret the day a baby from your brother's loins was given life in my body."

Lily had never heard such coldness in Maired's gentle voice. "As I say, they could have considered it a boys' prank."

Maired shook her head. "Today 'tis a boys' prank, but tomorrow it will be something worse. He's his father's son, and though I tried to change that for years, I've now given up hope." A shaft of sunlight through the trees hit her light brown eyes, illuminating the misery there. "I'm a coward, Lily. I've long ago retreated to my own quarters and let evil take over my household."

Lily looked around at the beautiful little world she and Daphne had created for themselves—the cozy cottage, the tidy path and beautiful flowers, all surrounded by the protective warmth of the woods. She'd been right to leave Lymond Castle, she thought to herself. Leaving had saved her. And her daughter.

Once again she put an arm around Maired. "I'm sure you've done the best you can. I can't imagine how you've lived with my brother all these years."

Maired shook off the comforting words. "What I've had with your brother has not been a life, Lily, it's been an existence. If I were as strong as you, I would have left long ago."

Lily did not know how to reply. She'd known that Maired was not happy in her marriage, but she'd never heard her talk like this before. She wished there was something she could do to repay Maired's kindnesses through the years, but she didn't know how. "Just remember that I'm here if you ever need comfort or . . . or even shelter." She looked uncertainly at her tiny house. "We have little room, but you would certainly be welcome—"

Maired cut her off with a bitter laugh. "I thank you, sister, but you don't need to worry about me showing up on your doorstep. I've made my own little world at Lymond Castle and see my husband rarely. But I shall talk to Nevin about Desmond. If our son did anything to hurt Daphne, I'd never forgive myself."

Lily kept her arm linked around Maired's waist as they started back toward the cottage. "I appreciate that, Maired. Did you, at least, enjoy the sights of London?" she asked, trying to raise her sister-in-law's spirits.

Maired stopped abruptly. "Lily, I almost forgot the other thing I came to tell you. 'Tis more of a warning, actually. I'm not sure how to tell you this, but while we were in London, Nevin met with Philip Stratton."

Simply hearing the name made the back of Lily's throat bitter.

Maired studied her face with alarm. "Lily, are you unwell? I'm sorry to blurt it out so directly, but I thought you should know. In fact, he's coming back here to Killarney."

Lily clutched Maired's arm to steady herself. "When?" she asked.

"Any day now. They're working together on something. I'm afraid Nevin might be involved in dealings with the English that will make us even more unpopular in the area. He's forbidden me from riding beyond the castle grounds."

"Yet you are here—"

Maired shrugged. "It's been a long time since I've paid much attention to what my husband says I shall or shall not do."

"Did you—" Lily halted, wondering if she could say the name out loud. "Did you speak with Philip?" she managed finally.

Maired shook her head. "Nay, he spoke only with Nevin. I saw him, though. He's as handsome as ever and no doubt as unprincipled. Forgive me, Lily, but I never could understand what you saw in the man."

"I find it hard to remember, as well." She kept her voice casual, but deep down she knew that she remembered *exactly* what she had "seen" in Philip Stratton. She'd seen the charming, fascinating man she'd dreamed of during her lonely childhood days at Lymond Castle. She'd seen a man who would take her to heights of passion she had not even been able to imagine and who would then rescue her from her brother's dominion and take her away to a lifetime of happiness.

She'd been right about the charm and the passion. It was the lifetime part that had finally smashed the idyll.

"We'll pray you don't have to encounter him if he does come, Lily. He doesn't know, does he?" She lowered her voice. "About Daphne?"

"Only if Nevin has told him."

Maired shook her head. " 'Tis doubtful, knowing Nevin. And knowing men. I'd not be surprised if Nevin scarcely remembers that it was Stratton who . . . who . . ." Her face colored.

"Who seduced his sister while knowing perfectly well that he was betrothed to another," Lily finished for her.

Maired sighed. "Aye. Some men would have challenged the blackguard to a duel. Nevin welcomes the man to our home and joins him in political intrigue."

"I assume Philip is now married?" She knew the answer would hurt, but she somehow had a morbid need to put the question.

"Aye," Maired said gently. "I believe so. At least, I did see a Lady Stratton at one of the soirees, and I assumed it was—"

She stopped as she suddenly seemed to realize that

her sister-in-law was more affected by the topic than she was letting on. "My dear, you shouldn't be wasting a single moment thinking about that snake." She pulled Lily toward the cottage. "Come, I want to spend more time in your sunny cottage with your delightful daughter before I have to return to that gloomy place I call my home."

Thirteen

Lily wore the same blue dress she'd worn her last visit
to O'Malley House, but they had managed to rework
another of the old dresses from her trunk to fashion a
new yellow frock for Daphne. With her new dress and
her new boots, Lily could see that she was practically
glowing with excitement.

Once again she was up and dressed and watching
the road for John to arrive before dawn. Lily herself
was more hesitant. Her talk with Maired the previous
day had brought back all the memories of Philip that
she had tucked away for so many years. It had also
brought back the pain.

She heard Daphne greeting John outside the cottage,
laughing as he teased her about something. She knew
that Daphne was reveling in his attention—something
she'd never experienced in all her life. The problem
was, Lily said to herself as she put on her cloak, she
was reveling in it, too. Though she hoped she looked
properly decorous as she went out the door and walked
down the path toward John and Daphne, she felt as if
her insides were full of buzzing bees.

John had brought the cart today, perhaps anticipating that they would be dressed in their best. He took her hand to help her climb up onto the seat, and she felt the imprint of his thumb in the middle of her palm as though it had been a kiss.

Daphne was talkative and bubbly during the entire ride, while both John and Lily stayed mostly silent. Was he feeling it, too? she wondered. This pull between them. This giddy sensation that she neither wanted nor welcomed?

Once again, Lord and Lady Riordan were the perfect hosts, greeting them on the steps of the manor as if they were long-lost family come to spend the holidays.

Catriona embraced her and whispered, "I'm so glad you've come."

"Do you have bags?" Lord Riordan asked, looking out at the empty cart.

Lily frowned. "Bags? Why, nay."

"But you are staying the night, surely? Did you not tell them, John?" Catriona asked.

John looked uncomfortable. "I didn't think about it," he admitted.

At the same time Lily clarified, "Nay, we're not planning to stay."

Daphne looked from one adult to another, her face hopeful.

Catriona put her hands on her hips. "This is what I get when I leave the details to the men. Of course you are staying. We always go into Banburn for mass on Christmas night, and it will be entirely too late for you to think about returning home afterward."

Lily's hands flew to her throat. Mass? When she'd promised Daphne that they could attend church, she had thought she would be brave enough to face her brother, but now with the possibility that Philip Stratton might be with him, there was no way she was going to go.

"Er, you have my apologies, Lady Riordan, but I'm afraid we'll have to be leaving before you go into the village. I—I won't be going to evening mass. Forgive me, but I have my reasons."

Catriona tipped her head, thinking. "I see." She looked at Daphne, whose disappointment was easily read on her face. "Would you have any objection to Daphne going with us? You could stay here at the house and have a relaxing drink by the fire while we go. We shan't be long."

Christmas night mass. She remembered it from her childhood as a magical time—candles creating dancing shadows everywhere on the carved stonework of the old church. Should she deprive her daughter of the experience? Most likely Stratton had not yet arrived at Lymond Castle.

"May I, Mummy?" Daphne appeared to be holding her breath, waiting for an answer.

"We have none of our things. . . ." Lily said slowly.

Catriona acted like the matter was already decided. "I have nightrails you both can use, and I'm sure we can find anything else you might need."

"Then, aye, we shall stay, and Daphne may go to church with you, providing you have no objection to my waiting for you here."

"Perhaps I should stay, too," Catriona said with a slight frown.

"I'll stay at home with Lily," John volunteered quickly.

His hostess's face brightened. "Ah, that's set, then. Shall we go inside?"

As she turned to leave, Lily had the feeling that Catriona had known all along that things would turn out the way they did, and that she was pleased with the plan.

• • •

Dinner had been another triumph of Catriona's efficient household management and her cook's skills, but John had eaten less than normal of the sumptuous feast. He was having trouble focusing on food when all he could think about was that he and Lily were to be virtually alone in the house for a good portion of the evening.

Lily was wearing the dress he'd seen her in once before—blue, slightly worn silk molded closely over her breasts and bodice before it tucked into her narrow waist. Though she was tall, he could practically span that waist with his two hands. He remembered the feel of her when he'd lifted her down from his horse.

"Uncle John, you're not paying attention." Lorcan's insistent voice forced him out of his reverie.

"What is it, Sprout?" he asked, trying to look normal and ignore the fact that the entire lower portion of his body was aching.

When in blazes did the mass begin? he wondered. One more hour? Two? Lily had seemed slightly more distant today. Did she know he intended to resume their lovemaking where they had left off the other day at the river?

"We asked if we could go ride the ponies, and can Daphne ride with us?" Lorcan repeated.

John looked around the parlor where the group had retired following dinner. Niall and Catriona had both excused themselves to attend to household duties, leaving John and Lily with the three children. "Aye, we may go out to the ponies, but there'll be no wrestling in the mud, you two," he cautioned the boys. "You must look presentable for church."

Neither of the two youngsters looked too enthusiastic at the reminder of their evening duties, but Daphne smiled happily. "We'll be careful, Dr. Black," she said. "May I wear my boots to church?"

John felt a flush of guilt. He'd been so busy thinking about kissing her mother that he'd given little thought to Daphne's new brace. He walked over to where she was sitting and kneeled. He grasped her ankle just above the boot to be sure the leg was not swollen. "Does it tire you, lass?" he asked,

He was sure that it must, but she answered quickly, "Nay."

He looked over at Lily, who was watching them with her usual intent expression. "Has she had any unusual aches or fever?" he asked her. "Have the boots slowed her down?"

Lily shook her head. "Nay, I believe she would sleep in them if I let her."

John released his hold on Daphne's foot and stood. "Then, aye, wear them to the church this evening. If they cause you any difficulty, you can get help from Lord or Lady Riordan."

"You haven't changed your mind, Daphne?" Lily asked. "You are sure you want to go?"

John realized that he was waiting like an eager schoolboy for Daphne's answer. If she chose not to go with the Riordans, that would mean he wouldn't have the time alone with Lily that he had been anticipating all day.

"Of course I am, Mummy," she said.

John let out a breath of relief. Still, the afternoon seemed to move slowly. Niall joined them again as they went out to the stables, and the three adults watched while the children rode their ponies. Daphne was beginning to get the feel of the saddle, and John promised her that next time she could ride a regular-sized mount.

Catriona had hot cider and Christmas cakes waiting for them in the parlor when they returned. She complimented the boys on having maintained their tidy appearance, and bestowed a hug on each of them along with their cake.

Finally it was time for the family to leave for the village in order to arrive in time for the evening mass. John watched them all climb up into the Riordan cart, masking his impatience. Lily's face was unreadable as she stood beside him in the doorway and waved good-bye to her daughter.

"She'll be fine," he told her. "The Riordans will take good care of her."

She smiled up at him. "I know. 'Tis just that we've been apart so little."

"Shall we go back to the fire?"

He offered his hand and she took it. "It's kind of you to stay with me," she said.

"Aye, that it was," he agreed gravely as they made their way back into the warm parlor. "I must be the most noble man in Killarney tonight. I've given up the privilege of spending the evening kneeling on the cold stone of St. Martin's Church listening to the Latin drone of a company of doddering prelates. Instead, I must suffer here by the warm fire, drinking mulled ale in the company of a beautiful woman."

She laughed at his teasing, but argued, "You might be more comfortable here, but you're missing out on the nourishment for your soul."

Something in her voice made him look at her sharply. "Is that how you feel?" he asked gently. "Do you think you are missing it, too?"

She shrugged. "I've made my peace with the church. After Daphne was born, I took her to be baptized and gave my confession."

"Yet you refuse to go to mass." He pulled her down on the bench beside him.

She shook her head. "Nay, I go. I've taken Daphne.

But only to early morning matins where I can be sure no one from Lymond Castle will be in attendance."

John felt a surge of anger. "Surely your brother would not be so spiteful that he would object to you being at church."

"You've not met my brother, Dr. Black," she said dryly. "But 'tis not that I fear his objections, I just wouldn't want to subject Daphne to such a scene, so I've preferred to avoid it over the years."

"I heard that your brother and his family are back from England. What if Daphne should encounter them tonight?"

"My brother has never seen Daphne. I doubt he'd notice her. And if he did, I rather think he'd do nothing when she's there under the protection of Lord and Lady Riordan. 'Twas part of the reason I agreed to let her go."

The conversation had taken a more sober turn than he had expected. Such talk was hardly conducive to the lovemaking he'd had in mind when he'd thought of their evening together. "I'm glad you did," he said, slipping his left arm behind her along the back of the bench. Suddenly he felt as awkward as a young swain courting his first girl, but Lily seemed unaware of his befuddlement.

She smiled up at him. "I'm glad I did, too. Daphne's wanted to go to mass for a long time, and I've put it off." She sighed, and leaned back against his arm. He wasn't sure if her movement had been deliberate or if she was unaware of the proximity. "Perhaps I should just have said a pox on my brother and gone with her," she added after a moment.

He let his left hand wander to her shoulder. "Nay, she's growing up. It's good for her to be on her own."

"Aye. And she's so proud of her new boots. Truly,

I'll never be able to thank you for what you've done for her."

He looked into her eyes and saw the gratitude shining out of them. Appreciation, gratefulness . . . respect, perhaps. He didn't see that other thing he sought—invitation.

He moved imperceptibly closer to her on the bench, wondering why this was so difficult. For years his dealings with women had been easy and quick. He'd chosen the kind of women who could make him laugh and fill his physical urges without engaging his heart. They'd served his needs and he'd served theirs, and the partings had always been amicable. Now, when he'd found a woman he wanted more than any he could remember for a very long time, he felt like a bumbling novice.

"There's no need for thanks," he said. "I'm fond of Daphne, as you know. I'm fond of her mother, as well."

Her eyes darkened and her mouth opened slightly. He gave a slow smile of approval. This was more like what he'd been looking for. "So fond of her," he drawled, "that all day long I've been able to think of little else but the moment that I would be alone with her and could do this. . . ."

He pulled her toward him and lowered his mouth to hers, his right hand cupping her face to hold her steady as he tenderly kissed her mouth. After the first kiss he paused to give her a chance to protest, but instead, she seemed to melt against him and offered her lips again.

He obliged, all hesitation now gone. He'd been right, he thought. This wasn't like the casual loves of recent years. The pounding in his loins was stronger, and the feeling of tears in his throat told him that this time the engagement would be neither quick nor easy.

"I want you, Lily," he whispered. She pulled away in surprise, and he cursed himself for moving too fast.

Her face was grave and pale, but there was no fear in her expression, only deliberation. "I want you, as well, John Black," she said after a long moment. "And I'd thought never to say that again to any man."

His heart was now pounding as urgently as the lower portion of his anatomy. The circumstances were not ideal, but the woman was willing, and his body was demanding that he make this work. He gave her a hard kiss, then swiftly stood and went to close the big double doors of the parlor. He knew that most of the Riordan servants had gone into the village. He and Lily should be undisturbed. He walked across the room and swept up an armful of pillows from the window seat, then dumped them on the floor in front of the fireplace.

"Our bower, milady," he said, noting that his voice was altered.

He took her hand and pulled her from the bench, then pushed it out of the way with his foot while he folded her in his arms.

"I—I've not done this in a long time," Lily began, sounding slightly less certain than she had a moment ago. "I scarce remember—"

"There's nothing to remember, my love. Everything is new." He pulled her down on the pillows. "This is the first time for me and the first time for you."

She looked amused. "Then Daphne is an even more miraculous child than I've always considered her to be."

He chuckled and put his arm around her again. This was the first time for neither of them, yet he almost felt as if what he'd told her was true. The insistent throb in his hose certainly made him feel like an untried virgin, ready to spill his seed at the first touch of a woman's hand. He took a deep breath, trying to gain control.

"At least," he insisted, "'twill be the first time for

us. Are you truly willing, sweetheart, for I fear once 'tis begun, I'll be hard pressed to stop."

As an answer, she took his hand and placed it on her breast, which was already swollen and hard, the nipple standing erect. He pushed her back against the pillow and began to unlace her bodice. "I'd see thee naked in the firelight," he told her, his voice hoarse.

She seemed as eager as he to be rid of their encumbering garments, and soon they both lay bare, illuminated by the flickering flames in front of them. He propped himself on one elbow and studied her. Her body was long and slender, with full breasts and a hollowed stomach. He ran his hand from one nipple to the other, then along her middle down to the soft, curling hair protecting her private woman's place. His penis flared to life. Slow, he told himself. She's little enough used to this sport.

Moving over her, he massaged her breasts while he took her mouth in another long series of deep, wet kisses. Both their bodies grew warm where their legs joined. He was more than ready to make their union complete, but he forced himself to wait, kissing, touching, kneading, stroking, until finally he felt the telltale moisture against his hardened member. He moved his hand to part her feminine folds, wet his finger there, then brought it to his mouth and licked the musky slickness.

"You feel ready, Sweetheart," he murmured.

Her eyes were wide, her cheeks flushed. She gave a nod of permission. Positioning himself above her, he eased his way into her warm body. He worried about hurting her as he stretched her tight passage, but she put her arms around his back and gave a moan of obvious satisfaction. Reassured, he began to move in the age-old rhythm. He braced himself on his arms so that he could look down at her face and her body. Her hands gripped the pillows beside her and she undulated her hips to meet his thrusts.

"Open your eyes," he rasped.

They fluttered open just in time for him to see them widen as she convulsed around him. The sensation was too much for his overeager body. Before he could pull out of her, he came in a shattering climax.

For several long moments the only sound was the fire crackling in front of them. Finally John moved to one side on the pillows and gathered her into his arms. "Verily, Sweetheart, I think I was speaking the truth about this being the first time, for I swear I never felt the like."

She looked up at him with a sleepy smile. "I believe you. And you were right—there was nothing to re-member." She stroked her hand down his side. "This is entirely new." She sounded incredulous.

For several moments they lay silent in each other's arms, the only sound the crackling of the fire. As the sweat dried on his body, John felt himself growing hard again where his penis pressed against her soft bottom. "Of course," he teased. "The next time it won't be so new. It might even be better."

"The next time?" she asked archly.

He moved against her, showing her how quickly he'd grown ready for her again. "Next time I intend to make it last," he said in her ear. "Until you are aching for me." He reached his hand down to begin a slow massage, felt the moisture there, and frowned. "Perhaps you need to—" He paused, searching for the words. "Do you want to . . . *see* to yourself first?"

"See to what?"

Lord. "I—forgive me, Sweetheart, but surely you are aware that I wasn't . . . careful that first time. I didn't mean to do it that way."

She lifted her head to look at him, confused. "It certainly appeared that you meant to do it."

He grinned. "Aye, well, I meant to . . . you know. I meant to do this. I just didn't mean to compromise you, to put you at risk."

She still looked confused, and he had to remind himself that Lily was no tavern wench. She'd not been with many men. She had, however, given birth. Surely she knew very well the consequences of lovemaking? He kissed the tip of her nose. "I'm afraid I didn't pull away in time."

"Pull away?" She sat up and hugged her arms around herself as if she were cold.

He sat up alongside her and reached for his tunic to use as a blanket around her shoulders. "I know 'tis not romantic after the wondrous thing that just happened to us, Sweetheart, but there could be results of this night's work if we're not careful. We'd not want that to happen."

She was shivering, in spite of the wool tunic around her. "Nay," she said dully. "We'd not want that."

"Can you, er, do you know how to deal with this?" he asked. Suddenly he felt cold, too.

"Deal with it?"

"A sponge," he said, "with some vinegar." Weren't women supposed to know these things? he thought desperately.

She turned her face away toward the fire. Her cheeks were flaming. "If I'd known of such things, no doubt I would never have had an illegitimate child."

He had no answer to that. He tried to take her in his arms again, but she pulled away. "I should get dressed," she said, hugging the tunic around her as she stood. "They might be returning from the village soon."

John got reluctantly to his feet. "Nay, we have

plenty of time." He realized that he had said the wrong thing, but he wasn't sure how to make it right. "Let me hold you," he said.

She shook her head. "Could you—" She paused, still not meeting his gaze. "Do you think you could find me the items you spoke of? A sponge and some vinegar? I'd like to—as you said—*deal* with this."

"There's no hurry," he told her. "Later tonight will be—"

"Later tonight I'll be with my daughter, Dr. Black," she said, and now there was no doubt about the ice in her tone. "And although she's growing up fast, I'd not like to have to explain"—she swept out her arm to indicate the pillows at their feet—"all this."

"Lily, forgive me. I can see that I've hurt you somehow, when all I wanted to do was to protect you. What we had here tonight was wondrous. We did nothing that should cause you shame."

Her expression seemed to soften slightly. "I'm sorry, too, John. But, please, I'm tired, and I'd like to be by myself now. If you could get me those items, I'll retire to my bedchamber."

He looked at her for a long moment, wondering if anything he could say would make things better. Finally he took in a deep, frustrated breath and turned to go to the Riordan kitchens for some vinegar.

Fourteen

Lily swallowed hard, trying to keep down the cider and Christmas cakes her hostess had served with such pride. The heavy feeling in her stomach matched the heaviness of her heart. How had she let this happen? she asked herself. Had she learned *nothing* all those years ago? Had the life of an outcast taught her no lesson about life?

She lay on the soft bed she and Daphne had been given in a chamber in the north wing of O'Malley House and let the tears roll slowly down her cheeks.

She blamed herself, not John. He had merely acted as males act when given the opportunity—a willing woman. And she had been willing, eager even. From the minute he'd begun looking at her early in the day with that special light in his gray eyes, she'd felt the pull. Only yesterday she'd been remembering her association with Philip and swearing that she would not let this thing with John Black turn into another disastrous misstep. Yet as the afternoon wore on, she could think of little else but the fact that she and John would be alone together all evening. When he'd kissed her, all rational thought had fled.

But as with all men, once John had had his way with her, he'd been in a great hurry to make it plain that he cared for no lasting attachment to come from this night's encounter. At least he'd had the decency to apologize for putting her at risk. It was more than Philip had ever done. Philip had sown his seed, then ridden back to his London fiancée without a second thought. If he'd ever wondered about a child, he'd shown no signs of it.

Of course, John Black was a doctor, she thought with a touch of irony. If she'd had to be foolish enough to lie with a man, she'd picked a good type.

And at least the kisses had been wondrous. The kisses and what had followed them. She lay back with a deep sigh. The tears had dried and her stomach had begun to settle. In some ways she didn't regret it. She'd thought that she would go the rest of her life without ever having those feelings again, without ever feeling a man's body against her. She'd been wrong. She'd had one more night. One *final* night.

Tomorrow she and Daphne would return to Whistler's Woods where they belonged. And John Black would be one more memory to tuck away in the old trunks under her bed.

"So that's the devil-spawned brat?" The Earl of Lymond leaned back against the hard pew, turning his head toward the party who had just entered at the back of the church. "Is her mother with them, too?"

His son stood to get a better view. "So that cripple is truly my cousin? Why have I never heard anything about that? I've seen her in the village off and on for years, but I had no idea she was related to us."

"Sit down, Desmond," Maired O'Farrell chided. "It's unseemly to be gawking in the sanctuary."

"I don't see the girl's mother," Desmond said, taking a seat. "But why is she with Lord and Lady Riordan?"

"I'd like to know that myself," Lymond muttered.

The priest had begun the opening prayers. His sonorous voice seemed to float out from the altar and reverberate around the cavernous old church. Lymond continued to watch as the newcomers walked down the aisle to take seats toward the front. "She's not as crippled as I thought," he said, not bothering to lower his voice.

"Aye, but she is, Father," Desmond corrected. "Her right foot's crooked as a stile."

"Hush, both of you," Maired urged. "We are in a holy place."

Lymond ignored his wife. "Is she dimwitted, as well?" he asked Desmond, idly curious.

His son shook his head. "I don't think so. Anyway, she seems bright enough when I've seen her in the village with her mother. With my *aunt*," he added with a sly glance at his father.

"You're no relation to that woman." Lymond bristled as he said the words, which seemed to broaden his son's smile.

"Of course he is," Maired said in a undertone. "Lily is your sister, which makes her Desmond's aunt, whether you like that fact or not. Now, if the two of you don't stop talking, I'm going to stand up in front of God and everyone and walk out of this church."

Both Desmond and his father gave her a look of surprise, then lapsed into silence.

"Are you well, Daphne?" Catriona whispered as they took seats side by side in the narrow pew. "Your foot's not bothering you?"

Daphne's gaze was on a row at the front of the church, but at her hostess's question, she turned to her with a smile. "I'm fine. 'Tis so kind of you and Lord

Riordan to agree to bring me. I've never been in the church at night." The sanctuary seemed to have candles glowing in every nook.

Catriona nodded. "There's something special about Christmas night mass. I've always loved it myself." She nodded toward the people Daphne had been looking at. "Would you like to greet them after the services?"

"Greet them?"

"Your aunt and uncle and cousin. We can stay a moment to talk, if you like."

Daphne's face went white. "That is Lord Lymond? And the boy with them is their son?"

"Aye, 'tis Desmond, their only son. Have you never met him?"

Daphne shook her head slowly. "Nay," she said. "Nor my uncle. I've met only my aunt."

"Perhaps your mother would prefer you not speak to them, then," Catriona said quickly as the priest's chanting became louder and more insistent.

Daphne reached down to rub her leg where the new boot chafed. "Perhaps," she said.

The ceremony lasted a long time with the priest's extra Christmas message, and by the time the congregation began filing out of the church, Lorcan and Padraic were drooping. Niall picked his younger son up in his arms, and the boy immediately went to sleep on his shoulder.

Daphne's leg ached, but she forced herself to keep her walk as normal as possible. She was keenly aware of the Lymond family, walking just behind them. She could still hardly believe that the boy who had thrown her into Cotter's Pond was her cousin. She wondered if her mother knew, and suspected she did.

"Look, the cripple's wearing shoes!" someone said from just behind her.

Daphne recognized the voice immediately. Hunching her shoulders, she tried to walk faster. She'd almost reached the end of the aisle, when she could feel him come up next to her. "Show us your new shoes," Desmond O'Farrell taunted, pulling up the skirt of her new yellow dress.

Daphne clutched at her leg to pull herself out of the older boy's grasp. Catriona and Niall turned around to see what was happening, and at the same moment Desmond's father reached him and hauled him back by the collar of his cloak. "What in the name of hell do you think you're doing, you brainless boy?" he said to his son in a deadly undertone.

Daphne didn't wait to hear Desmond's answer. Taking Catriona's outstretched hand, she hurried away from the church.

"What was that boy doing to you, Daphne?" Lorcan asked as they reached the Riordan's cart.

Niall deposited Padraic in the cart and reached to lift Daphne. "Are you all right, lass?"

"Aye," she said.

"Did he want to see your new boots?" Lorcan persisted.

Daphne smiled at the young boy. "I reckon he did," she said. Then she settled back into the bed of the cart and tried to stop shaking.

Even Daphne had little to say the following morning as John drove her and Lily back home after their stay at O'Malley House. John supposed that the girl was tired from her late night in the village. At least she had smiled at him. Lily had been not only silent, but frosty, and had refused all his attempts to lighten the mood with humor.

John noticed that Daphne was strongly favoring her good foot as he helped her from the cart and she started down the path to their cottage. "Is the boot bothering you today?" he asked.

She turned back to him and smiled. "'Tis nothing. I wore it all day yesterday, you know," she added proudly.

"Aye, but mayhap it was too long. I suggest you take it off for the rest of the day, and if your leg is chafed, have your mother rub it with a bit of bacon grease."

He turned to help Lily jump from the cart, but she had already climbed down without assistance. "Please give my thanks once again to the Riordans," she said in obvious dismissal.

He frowned and called to Daphne. "Lass, do you mind if I speak with your mother alone for a moment?"

Daphne gave a cheery wave and disappeared inside the house.

"I don't really have anything to say," Lily protested.

John walked around the front of the cart to tie up the horse, trying to control his mixture of temper and confusion. "You may not, but I do," he said, moving back to her and seizing her hand. "We'll take a walk."

She let him lead her around the house and along the path to the stream. "Now tell me what's wrong," he said after a moment.

She didn't pretend not to understand him. "I'm merely trying to get this over with as soon as possible. If I hadn't seen that Daphne was limping this morning, I'd have suggested that we walk home to save you the trouble of coming all this way."

Her face looked severe and stern. It was almost impossible to believe that only hours ago he'd seen those same eyes flare with passion as he'd entered her body. "Lily," he said, "I'm not sure what happened to you between last night and this morning, but I suspect 'tis some wrong-headed mixture of guilt and fear. You should have neither."

He pulled her down on the bank and was relieved that she put up no resistance. She would, at least, listen to him. "If 'tis guilt you're feeling, then I apologize. But we're neither one of us a virgin. We're middle-aged adults who have known the pleasures of a lover's body, and I see no reason why we should feel remorse about that. If 'tis fear, be reassured. If there are results of our coming together, I swear I'll stand by you."

"I once was foolish enough to believe that about another man," she said.

John muttered a curse. "You have a right to your bitterness, Lily. Whoever the man was, he was a blackguard and a coward. But don't make me his equal."

Her face softened slightly, and he felt a glimmer of hope. "I don't believe you are like him," she said softly. "And I'll never forget what you've done for Daphne. But what happened last night made me realize that I'm weak. I can't afford to let my heart begin to soften, because I know the results."

"I thought the results were rather amazing," he said with a smile, trying to find a way to lighten the heaviness in her voice.

Tears trembled on her lower eyelids. He reached to take her in his arms, but she pulled away. "Nay," she said firmly. "I don't want you to touch me. I don't want any man to touch me ever again."

"Ah, Lily," he said, aching, "don't think that way. Perhaps I'm not the right man to convince you that it's normal and good to share these things, but don't shut yourself away from the idea forever. You've devoted years to raising a beautiful daughter, and the bitterness you harbor may have been part of what kept you strong. But Daphne is nearly a woman now, and it's time you admitted that you are still one, too."

She turned her head away from him and remained silent, but he could see her shoulders shake with sobs.

"If I could meet the man who hurt you so, I'd skewer him straight through his black heart," he said finally.

Lily wiped her eyes with the back of her hand and turned around. "You've been a good friend to us, John Black. I won't forget you. But I hadn't expected that things would"—She paused, looking for the words—"would take the turn they did. Now I must ask you to stay away. For my sake. I'm sorry, but I can't see you again."

"I still want to help Daphne—" he began, but she interrupted him.

"I shall help her. I promise. Your efforts won't be in vain. We'll continue to use your miraculous boot, and I'll turn the screws the way you taught me if her foot begins to straighten."

John was surprised at how much it hurt to think of not seeing either of the O'Farrells again. "What will you tell her?" he asked, his throat dry.

"She already knows that your stay here is temporary. I'll just explain that you've left, gone about your business."

Her tears had dried as quickly as they had begun. She was smiling and seemed to be much more in control than he was feeling. "I'd like to come back to check Daphne's foot one last time before I leave Killarney. If you agree." He stood and extended his hand to her.

She ignored it and jumped to her feet. "Very well. One last visit. I'll let Daphne know to expect you." Then she smiled again and turned to walk up the path.

Catriona met him at the stables when he returned from taking Lily and Daphne back to Whistler's Woods.

"Are you going to tell me what happened between you and Lily?" Catriona asked.

Her hands were on her hips, and she looked determined. Just what he needed today. Another stubborn woman to deal with.

"Why do you say something happened?" he asked her.

Catriona threw up her hands. "Good lord, John, the woman hardly said a word this morning. She didn't touch a bite of breakfast. She was obviously wanting to be on her way home from the moment she came out of her room."

"Yesterday was a full day. We were all tired."

Catriona raised an eyebrow. "What happened, John?"

He, at least, was tired, he thought with a touch of irritation. "Cat, I'm not entirely sure what the problem is. If I knew, perhaps I could have done something about it. I won't lie to you. There was something between us last night, and it seems that whatever it was did not meet with Mistress O'Farrell's approval. So that's the end of it."

He'd finished unhitching the horse from the cart and released the animal into the corral. Catriona reached out her hand. "You didn't eat much this morning, either, John," she said. "Come with me to the kitchens and I'll find you some food."

He smiled and took the proffered hand as they began strolling together toward the house. He hoped the subject of his dealings with Lily would be dropped, but, knowing Catriona, he was not optimistic.

"Was Lily as quiet during the ride home?" she asked.

"I reckon."

Catriona sighed. "What did you do, John? It must have been something. You men say we women are capricious, but it usually turns out that we have good reasons for our humors."

John chuckled. "I'll not argue with you, Catriona. But neither will I discuss my dealings with Mistress O'Farrell. Forgive me, my sweet girl, but 'tis none of your business."

John had always found Catriona to have extraordinarily good sense. She seemed to know when to leave a battle for another day. "Very well," she said breezily. "You *do* look tired, John. I'm going to see that you eat some of my cook's famous berry tarts and then send you off for a nap."

Her tone made him feel like a child being sent off to bed, but he obediently let her lead him around the back of the house to the big stone kitchen. The Riordan cook, a large, shy woman who said little but produced wonderful dishes, was working on the midday meal. She bobbed her head in acknowledgement, but didn't speak as Catriona directed John to a stool in the corner of the kitchen and put a flaky pastry in his hand.

"Eat," she said.

She stood watching him as he obliged her, downing the pie without enthusiasm. In his mind he was going over the events of the past day, wondering what had gone so dreadfully wrong. The only conclusion he could reach was that the whole thing had been wrong from the beginning. As Niall had warned him, Lily was not a tavern wench to be tumbled in the hayrick and discarded. He'd known that, yet it had been as if he couldn't help himself. As if some unseen force had pushed them both to the inevitable conclusion they'd reached last night in front of the fire.

Now he had to worry about the consequences. With her icy attitude that morning, he'd been unable to bring himself to ask her if she had used the method he had suggested to prevent a possible pregnancy. When he'd given her the vinegar the previous evening, she'd looked at it as if he'd been giving her a vile of poison.

Even if she had used it, there was no guarantee that the remedy would be effective.

He jammed the last piece of tart into his mouth. He had no idea what flavor it had been.

"Now for the nap," Catriona said firmly.

"I told Niall I'd ride rounds with him."

Catriona pulled him up from the stool and reached to brush a pastry crumb from his cheek. "I'll make your excuses," she said. "You need some sleep."

John smiled in spite of himself and didn't argue, though he knew sleep would not heal this particular ache. "Aye, milady," he said.

"Why didn't you tell me, Mummy?" Daphne's lower lip trembled.

Lily sighed and put down the towel she'd been using to polish the pewter plates that had been another gift from her sister-in-law. Lily had long ago stopped feeling guilty about the gifts. She'd decided that in an odd way it was Maired's way of exacting some kind of private revenge against her husband.

"Sweetcakes, you know that I prefer not to talk about Lymond Castle or the people in it."

"Aye, and I understand that when your brother turned you out, it must have been a terrible thing, but that was years ago. This is now, and you didn't tell me that one of the boys who did that thing to me was my own cousin. I didn't even know that Aunt Maired had a son. She never speaks of him."

Lily picked up one of the plates and stared into its reflective surface. The face looking back at her was no longer the innocent young girl who had fallen so disastrously in love with Philip Stratton. Life had begun to etch fine lines on both her face and her once-pretty sister-in-law's. Though Maired's life would appear more traditional to an outsider, in many ways, it had been as twisted by circumstances as Lily's. She'd been forced to marry Nevin in order to pay off the family debts, and soon after, her own parents had died, leaving her with nothing. She was married, but she was as alone in the world as Lily. More alone, really, for Lily had not been forced to live side by side with a person who treated her with contempt.

How did Lily explain all this to the child she had tried to raise to believe in a sunny world? "Aunt Maired has not been as lucky as I have in my offspring," she began carefully. "Desmond has always been a difficult child."

"Doesn't she love him?" Daphne's expression was vaguely accusatory.

"I believe she has tried to love him. Undoubtedly, she does love him in a way, but I'm afraid Desmond has turned out to be more like his father than his mother."

Daphne was silent a moment, digesting the information. "Does Desmond hate me?" she asked.

"I can't imagine that Desmond would have any reason to hate you."

"Then why did he and his friends throw me into the water?"

Lily shook her head. "I don't know. As I say, I don't believe Desmond is a very nice boy. I'm afraid that's why you don't hear Aunt Maired talk about him."

Daphne was silent for another long moment, then she said wistfully, "It would have been nice to have a cousin to play with."

Lily felt the familiar wave of guilt. "Aye, but I don't think you would have enjoyed playing with Desmond."

Daphne smiled. "Now I have Lorcan and Paddy to play with. They're good boys, even if their father calls them rascals sometimes."

"Aye, they are good boys," Lily agreed, "with good parents. That makes a lot of the difference."

"Can we invite the Riordans and Dr. Black here, Mummy?" Daphne asked. "I've been thinking that I'd like to show Lorcan and Paddy my garden and my aviary."

This was not the moment to tell Daphne about her conversation with John Black. There would be time tomorrow when they weren't so tired.

"Perhaps we can invite the Riordans in the spring, Sweetcakes. 'Twill be prettier then with the flowers blooming." And John Black would be gone.

"Spring?" Daphne's eager expression dimmed. "That seems a long time away."

"It will be here before you know it," she said. Then she picked up her towel and resumed polishing the plates.

"I need to have you prepare for a number of visitors," the Earl of Lymond told his wife curtly.

Maired was making one of her rare appearances at dinner with her husband and son. "Visitors?"

"Aye, Philip Stratton will be arriving shortly from England along with a number of English soldiers. They'll be staying here at Lymond Castle."

"English soldiers? Why is he bringing soldiers?" Maired set down her fork in surprise.

"We may have need of them."

Maired sat for a long moment, staring straight ahead, breathing deeply. Finally she said, "I can't understand how you are receiving that man in our house."

Lymond cast a glance at Desmond, who sat sullenly between them, pushing his food around his plate with the tip of a knife. "Philip Stratton is to be made welcome," he said slowly, "along with his men. I'll not

have my careful politicking ruined by minor grievances from the past."

Maired's eyes showed a rare flash of anger, but neither her husband nor son seemed to notice. "Minor
grievances?" she repeated. "You think destroying the
life of your sister a minor grievance?"

At this, Desmond straightened up and began to listen.

"We'll discuss this later," Lymond said.

"Nay, we'll discuss it now. I'll not play the friendly
hostess to that man."

Lymond threw down the piece of bread he'd been
about to lift to his mouth. It bounced off his plate and
skittered across the table. "I'll remind you, madam,
that this is your house only as long as I suffer you to be
here. You'll receive whom I tell you to receive."

Desmond's face had a half smile as he looked to the
end of the table to see his mother's response.

Maired stood and put both her hands on the table in
front of her. "You may bring whom you choose into my
house, but you will not force me to receive him. If you
require my attendance during the man's visit, you may
be sure that I'll mince no words in telling him my exact
opinion of him. I care not whether that fits your *politicking*."

Lymond kept his voice even. "Madam, if I have to
chain you to your bed, you'll not bring up the past to
Philip Stratton. His visit here has nothing to do with—
with past dalliances. I'm sure His Lordship has forgotten all about them."

"No doubt. But what will happen, pray tell, when he
goes about the neighborhood and encounters Lily in
the village. Or encounters *his own daughter* at evening
mass, as we did the other day?"

There was a devilish spark in Desmond's black eyes

as his gaze darted back and forth between his father and his mother.

"He doesn't know the chit's his daughter," Lymond answered. "And there's no reason for him to find out. Nor is it likely that he'll encounter Lily, since she hides away in the woods like a lowly tree frog."

Maired straightened up and looked down the table at her husband. "Your sister might not be as helpless as you think, Nevin. She's found some powerful friends— the Riordans. If she hears that Philip has returned to Killarney, there's no telling what she might do."

At this, Lymond looked thoughtful. "You may have a point," he said with a frown. For the first time he seemed to notice his son listening with avid attention. "You are to speak nothing of this to anyone, boy. Do you understand me?"

Desmond gave a dutiful nod.

Maired rolled her eyes. "There are few secrets in this valley, husband. If we have English soldiers staying at Lymond Castle, you can be sure the neighborhood will know of it soon enough."

Lymond reached for his cup and took a long drink of ale. Then he stood, wiping his mouth with the back of his hand. "For once, wife, you have the right of it. People will know of Philip Stratton's visit."

"So what about your sister?" Maired asked.

Lymond pushed back his chair. "My sister? Aye, I believe 'tis time I paid the whore a visit."

Fifteen

"You are my uncle," Daphne said, looking up at the richly dressed man on the big horse.

For a moment he looked taken aback, then he swung out of the saddle and said gruffly, "Take my horse, girl. I've business with your mother."

"I saw you in church on Christmas," Daphne continued, walking toward him. His gaze was on her bad foot. She took the reins he was holding. "We've no stable," she said.

Lymond was looking around the clearing with distaste. "No stable, nor much of a house, either, from what it appears. Is this all? This is where you live?"

Daphne smiled agreeably. " 'Tis quite enough for two ladies by themselves. Of course, I've lots of animal friends that come to visit." As if to prove her words, a small squirrel chose that moment to jump up on a rock in the middle of the flower garden. Daphne laughed, but the merry sound didn't scare the little animal away. "I call him Turnip," she explained to the visitor, "because he pops up so sudden like."

"Where is she?" Lymond said, turning away from

Daphne's sunny expression. "Your mother. Is she inside?"

Lily answered the question by opening the cottage door. "Welcome to Whistler's Woods, brother," she said, her voice thick with irony.

If Lymond noted the tone, it was not apparent. Leaving his horse with Daphne, he stalked down the path. "I've come to speak with you," he said.

Lily stepped back and allowed him to enter her house. She gave Daphne a reassuring glance. "Just tie Lord Lymond's horse to the tree, Sweetcakes. He'll be fine."

"May I bring him some water?"

"Aye. Just be careful not to walk too close behind those rear hooves."

She closed the door, then turned to face the man she'd last seen twelve years before in the front hall of Lymond Castle as she left the only home she'd ever known. She'd been young and pregnant, and more scared than she'd ever been in her life, but her brother had stood watching her with a grim smile. She could still remember his face that day.

He'd aged. There was now considerable gray in his dark brown hair. The lines around his mouth that had once made his countenance look strong, now made it look harsh. Yet his stern face intimidated her far less than it had before she'd left home. She'd aged, too.

"To what do I owe the honor of this visit?" she asked him.

He was looking at her intently. "You've changed, Lily," he said slowly.

"I'm twelve years older."

"Quite. But 'tis more than age. You've grown beautiful, for one thing. Who would have thought my awkward, gangly sister would have grown into such a swan?"

Though the words were complimentary, the way he said them, examining her as if she were a piece of meat on the butcher table, made Lily shiver.

"Is that why you came? To see how I look after all these years?"

"Nay." Nevin looked around the room with a grimace of distaste. "Where do you sit in this place?" he asked.

She pointed to the bench by the fireplace. "The bench there or here at the table. 'Tis your choice."

With ill-concealed disgust, he sat on the bench. "I came to tell you that I'm expecting a visit from Philip Stratton."

Lily was glad that Maired's warning allowed her to greet this news without emotion. "I'm sure you will give him my regards," she said coolly.

"Nay, I'd not thought to mention you. No doubt he's long ago forgotten your existence."

The man who had utterly changed her entire life had forgotten her existence? Lily was pleased that the idea caused her little more than a twinge.

"I came to tell you to stay out of sight for a few weeks while he's here," Lymond continued. He was still studying her in that disturbing way, his eyes roving over the length of her body. She pulled a chair from the table and sat, folding her arms in front of her. "However, I might be rethinking the matter," he ended.

"What do you mean?"

"Perhaps you could be useful to me, for once in your life. It's possible that Philip has not totally forgotten you after all. He might find it *amusing* to have some entertainment during his stay here. It would make him even more amenable to our cause."

As she began to realize the import of his words, Lily could feel the rage bubbling up inside her. "You would have me sleep with the man in order to gain you his political favors?"

Lymond shrugged. "You did it before."

Lily stood with such abruptness that the chair fell over behind her. "I foolishly believed myself in *love* with Philip, Nevin. I realize 'tis a concept you know nothing about, but I can assure you that it is a powerful feeling. And it's the only thing in this world that would make me give my body to any man."

Lymond smiled and stood up from the bench. "Quite," he drawled. "In any event, I may not need you. Stratton would no doubt prefer a younger woman from the village. And 'twould be less complicated to keep you out of it, what with the brat and all. She's a pleasant surprise, by the way. I thought she'd surely be an idiot."

Lily bit the side of her mouth to keep from screaming.

"As I say," he continued, "my original reason for coming was to warn you. The area will soon be crawling with Englishmen, Philip Stratton among them. If you're wise, you'll stay tucked away in this mole's den you've built for yourself and not come out for air in several months."

"Daphne and I go where we please," she said through tight lips.

"Suit yourself. If I change my mind and decide that you can be useful, I shall send for you." He gave her one last head-to-toe survey, and added, "Remarkable. Who would have thought it?" Then he turned and stalked out of the cottage.

Lily was left standing in the middle of the room, hugging her arms tight around herself.

Niall ushered the three newcomers through the front door and into the formal front parlor of O'Malley House. "Sir Thomas, you and Dr. Black are already acquainted. Have you other gentlemen met John?"

The leader of the delegation stepped forward and offered John his hand. "Cedric McDougall, at your service, Dr. Black. I've heard a lot about you over the years, but I've not had the honor of making your acquaintance." He gestured to the two men with him. "You know Sir Thomas Barton and this is Red Donovan, Baron of Tidewater."

"I trust your lovely daughter is well," John said to Sir Thomas politely, though he knew that today's gathering had nothing to do with matchmaking.

The men shook hands all around then settled into the seats Niall had placed in a semicircle around the fireplace in anticipation of the meeting. They'd received word the previous day that the three barons from the south would be arriving. Catriona had spent the day frantically airing linens and preparing rooms for the guests, though they had had no indication whether the three would seek lodging with them.

"We understand you were Shane O'Neill's closest associate." Red Donovan had obviously garnered his name from a thatch of hair as thick as a hayfield that seemed to cover not only the top of his head, but all other visible parts of his body. "'Twas a sad day for Ireland when we lost him."

The others nodded agreement, but John said, "O'Neill always knew that he was not destined to live to old age. He did what he had to for the sake of his country. But you are right, if he were still around today, we may by now have a lasting peace with England."

The first speaker, Cedric McDougall, shook his head. "We'll never have a lasting peace until they agree to get out of our country and leave us the bloody hell alone."

John's wearying years of fighting and negotiating had forced him to much the same conclusion, but it was an assessment that left no room for hope, since he knew that the English had no intention of leaving. "Why have you gentleman come here today?" he asked. Unlike the English, who seemed to love talking round in circles without coming to the point, he knew that Irishmen preferred directness.

McDougall leaned forward. "We've come because it's started again. The English courts have begun drumming up their false charges in order to force honest landowners out of their rightful estates. It's just happened to Red, here."

John and Niall both turned to look at Donovan. The little bit of skin that showed around his bushy beard had grown as red as his hair. "Aye, they've taken my home and given it over to one of the bloody queen's lapdogs. Word is, they intend to do the same thing with various estates all across the south."

"Red has had to move his family and all his belongings to my estate," McDougall explained. "We've started procedures to sue for redressal of rights, but the process could take months, years even."

"In the meantime, the buggers are planning the same treatment for the rest of us," added Sir Thomas. "I've armed men right now back at Barton Hall protecting my daughter and the others, but we'd be of little resistance to trained English troops."

All five men turned toward the door, then stood, as Catriona entered the room. "Gentlemen, may I present my wife?" Niall announced with a touch of pride.

Catriona gave a gracious curtsy as the three southerners bowed. "Shall I send in refreshments?" she asked.

Niall nodded. "Aye, then join us, my dear. These gentlemen have come with news that concerns all of us."

While the food was brought in, the conversation turned to more general matters, but finally, when Niall had pulled a chair close for Catriona and the group was once again settled, talk returned to the key topic.

"The English are being more clever this time than they were in O'Neill's day," McDougall continued. "Instead of wresting estates away by force, they're doing it through the courts, which is harder to fight. They've sent a number of officious lackeys to handle the details, along with one of the queen's most powerful nobles."

"Who's that?" Niall asked.

"Philip Stratton. His family estates cover practically half of Yorkshire," McDougall answered. "He has an ally here in Killarney—the Earl of Lymond. We understand he's already arrived and is staying at Lymond Castle."

John frowned. "Has anyone tried talking with Lymond? Tried to get him on our side?"

"Nay, 'twould be a lost cause. The man's totally without loyalties," Red Donovan said with a rasp of disgust. "He'd sell his own mother for a guinea. Threw his own sister out years ago, according to rumor. She was with child, poor girl, and he tossed her out without a qualm."

John took in a long breath, and he noticed that Catriona was watching him. "Aye, well if there's no hope to reach Lymond, we need to plan other strategies."

"We were hoping you'd help us," McDougall said

with a satisfied smile. "With John Black working for
our cause, things look less bleak."

John made no response to the tribute. "I may be
able to do more good in London than here," he said.
"I know you gentlemen would probably like to hear
me talking about arms and fighting, but the truth is,
more can usually be accomplished at the bargaining
table, if you're willing to be patient."

"We don't have the time to be patient," Red Donovan said nearly coming up out of his seat. "If we wait,
every estate in the south will be swallowed up by
these vultures."

John had heard the same tone from many of the
landowners he'd dealt with other the years. It was
hard to tell a man to wait and negotiate when his family and his land were being threatened. "Yet as you
gentlemen yourself are admitting, we don't have the
forces to go up against seasoned English soldiers, if it
should come to that."

Red Donovan sat heavily back in his chair. "Nay,
we don't."

"If it comes to that, we'll need help from the north.
The rebel forces there are organizing again under
Shane O'Neill's cousin, Tyrone." John felt a heaviness in his midsection at the thought of the fighting
starting up again, but he tried to keep his tone calm
and businesslike—the voice of reason, as Shane
O'Neill had liked to call him.

"Do you know Tyrone?" McDougall asked.

John nodded. "Aye, he grew up in England, and
has had some dealings with the queen, but he's now
returned to assume his grandfather's title. He's a good
man, and a strong one. If you need to fight here in
Killarney, you want Tyrone on your side."

"Will you go see him on our behalf?"

John glanced at Catriona, whose eyes were troubled. She didn't want him to leave Killarney, particularly not if it was to get back into fighting, but her home was at risk, as well. Her sons' heritage was at stake. The English had taken the O'Malley estates once, and they could do it again. "I'll go to Tyrone if necessary," he said. "But first there is one other person I want to meet."

"Who's that?" McDougall asked.

"I intend to have a private conversation with the Englishman who's come to visit our fair Killarney. This Lord Stratton."

"You'll go to Lymond Castle?" Catriona sounded troubled.

"Aye," John answered. "I'll go on the morrow."

In the end, the three visitors did not spend the night. Though it meant riding in the darkness to reach their homes, they left late in the afternoon. John and Niall were content to continue sitting by the fire nursing their brandies, but Catriona had insisted that they come into the dining hall for some supper. "If you're to be up riding before dawn, John," she said, "I'd like to think you had a hot meal in you tonight." As usual, his hostess's plan was wise. After an afternoon of bad news and drinking, the plain fare settled his stomach.

"If you'll excuse me, I should seek my bed if I'm to be off early," he said, standing, when they had finished eating.

Catriona stopped him from leaving with a question. "When do you intend to go tell Lily that her brother is harboring an English leader? I mislike the thought of her there all alone in the woods when troops are prowling about and fighting may start at any moment. At the very least she should return to her brother's protection, though I'd not like to see her sided against the rest of us."

John had been thinking of little else all afternoon. "I'm almost certain she'll not want to seek protection from her brother." He sat back down at the table and looked at his two hosts. "'Tis much to ask you, but I wondered if you would be willing to offer Lily and Daphne shelter here while the danger persists."

"Of course," Catriona said at once.

"Coming here would put her in direct opposition to her brother," Niall pointed out.

"I don't think she'll care. He treated her cruelly, and she has had no contact with him in years. Even so, it will take some persuading to convince her to come."

"Why? Daphne gets along famously with the boys," Catriona argued, "and I got the impression that Lily enjoys my company."

"I know she does," John agreed. It was *his* company that would cause the objection, he thought ruefully. The shelter of O'Malley House would keep Lily safe from the English, but would throw her into direct proximity with the man she had professed not to want to see again.

"If she's willing to go so openly against her brother, by all means, bring her here," Niall said after a moment. "Cat's right. One can't be too careful with soldiers wandering the neighborhood. Even though we're still officially at peace, soldiers are soldiers. Lily's a beautiful woman and even young Daphne—" He stopped as the unspeakable possibilities entered their heads.

John stood up again. "I'll go to Whistler's Woods in the morning to tell them to ready their things. Then I'll pick them up on my return from Lymond Castle."

"And if Lily says she doesn't want to come?" Catriona asked.

John turned toward the door, his expression sober. "Then I'll just have to convince her."

John had left before much of the household was awake, yet Daphne was already up and working out in her aviary when he reached the cottage in Whistler's Wood. She walked out to greet him with a big smile.

"I swear, lass, you've grown a foot taller since you started wearing those shoes," he told her. "You're all of a lady now."

" 'Tis the extra sole," she said, but she straightened up even further and looked pleased.

"How are your little friends this morning?" he asked.

"Cheery. I believe they know that Twelfth Night means winter is over half done. Spring won't be long."

John had forgotten all about the traditional holiday festivities. " 'Tis tomorrow, is it not?"

Daphne nodded. "My mother and I usually make an oyster stew, but this year we haven't been into market to get the oysters. Perhaps we'll go today."

"I have a better idea," John told her. "Why don't you and your mother come to O'Malley House again?"

"For Twelfth Night?"

"For Twelfth Night and to stay for a while. Perhaps for several weeks."

"Several weeks?" Her eyes grew round.

"Aye, would you like that? You would be almost like a big sister to Lorcan and Paddy."

"Do the Riordans want us to come?"

"Aye."

Daphne looked back at her aviary with a slight frown of worry. "My birds would miss me."

"We could ride over and put out some seed for them. You can come here as often as you like."

Her expression cleared. "Then 'twould be wonderful. Would I be able to ride?"

"Every day," John said. He pointed to the end of the path. "I've brought the cart so you can put your things in the back."

"You've brought Greybolt, too," Daphne noted, looking over at the cart and John's stallion tied to the back.

"Aye, I'll leave the cart here for you to load while Greybolt takes me on another errand." He looked at the old gelding at the front of the cart. "Will you take care of Rags for me while I'm gone?"

Daphne nodded. "Shall I feed him some carrots? We still have some in the cellar."

"He'd like that," John agreed.

"Does he have to stay tied to the wagon?"

"Nay, you can unhitch him if you can make out how to do it."

"I can. I've seen how you do it."

He watched as she walked past him toward the cart and the two horses. She went around the front of the cart to Rags and rubbed the animal's nose as if she'd been around horses all her life. The animal tossed his head in pleasure.

Daphne, at least, seemed pleased with the notion of spending some time at O'Malley House. Once she'd known that she could still tend to her birds, the idea had met with no opposition. He hoped her mother would be as easy to convince.

The cottage door had been closed, but Lily must still have been able to hear their conversation. The door opened as he walked toward it. She stood regarding him, her face troubled. "What is this nonsense, John?" she asked in a low voice.

"I want you and Daphne to come back with me to O'Malley House." He'd expected anger at his suggestion. What he saw was more like . . . fear.

Lily's hands went to her throat. "I'm sorry you bothered to come all this way," she said. "But, nay, we can't go with you."

Sixteen

From the moment she'd seen John pull up in front of the cottage with the cart, Lily had known he'd come for more than just a goodbye. And somehow she suspected that his mission was connected to the unexpected visit from her brother. She wasn't sure what was happening, but she knew that things hadn't changed. The mere sight of John through the cottage window talking with Daphne had her heart racing. She'd turned John away, telling herself that she would not risk the same kind of heartache she'd had with Philip, but the truth was, it was too late. The heartache was already there.

"I have no intention of going to O'Malley House," she repeated after clearing her throat to make her voice sound more firm.

John glanced out at Daphne, who was leading Rags away from the wagon. The girl and the horse already seemed to have developed a bond. "Then I'm going to have to change your mind," he said calmly.

Lily took her hands down from her throat and smoothed the apron she'd decided not to remove. "You'd have a difficult time doing that," she said.

The determination in his expression matched her

own. He had also, she thought ruefully, never looked
more handsome. He smiled, and she felt it as a plunge
in her stomach. "Not that difficult," he said. "I know
the exact way to convince you."

Her palms began to sweat. If he had reached for her
at that moment, she believed she would have gone will-
ingly into his arms, in spite of her resolutions and the
fact that they were in plain sight of her daughter.

Nevertheless, she put her chin up and said with
some bravado, "I doubt that, Dr. Black. I'm done being
convinced by you."

He shook his head. "What's between us is not over,
Lily. You made your feelings plain, and I'd thought I
could ride away and forget about what happened the
other night, but the minute I saw you today, I knew that
this business is not finished."

"I told you—" she began.

He interrupted her putting his fingertips gently on
her lips. "But that has nothing to do with the reason
I've come for you today. We've received information
that English troops have ridden into the area. The Valley of Mor is no longer safe for two females living
alone, and while you may not care for your own safety,
I know you care very much for Daphne's. That's what
I meant when I said I knew how to convince you."

"English troops?" she asked, trying to focus on his
words instead of the lingering warmth of the touch of
his fingers.

"Aye, and I'm sorry to have to tell you, but I fear
your brother has allied himself with them, against his
neighbors."

"He has always been a friend to the English," she
acknowledged.

"Aye." He paused. "Perhaps your sympathies lie
with them, as well, in which case, I suggest you go to
Lymond Castle and—"

"Nay!" Lily blurted before he could finish. "I'll never seek anything from my brother."

He seemed pleased. "Good. Then the only course is O'Malley House. Unless you want to risk Daphne being captured, not by three foolish boys, but by a whole dragoon of English troops."

She could feel the blood drain from her face.

"I'm sorry to speak plainly, Lily, but you must see that 'tis only good sense."

"Have the Riordans agreed to this plan?" She was stalling, avoiding the inevitable answer. She knew John would not have issued such an invitation without his hosts' permission.

"Of course. Catriona is waiting to welcome you as part of the household, for as long as necessary until the region is once again safe."

"She's a remarkable lady," Lily observed, still avoiding the inevitable capitulation. For that was what it seemed. Somehow she knew that if she went with John to O'Malley House, her strongest resolutions to stay clear of him would dissolve.

"Aye. I believe she thinks much the same of you. She's worried about you and Daphne. The sooner you get to the safety of the Riordan estate, the better everyone will feel."

" 'Tis hard to turn down such generosity," Lily said finally.

"Aye." John gave a brisk nod. She had the feeling that he'd never considered the outcome of the debate in doubt. "I've brought the cart so that you can bring as many of your things as you like. Of course, we can return for anything more you might need. I've told Daphne we'd make regular trips to tend to her menagerie," he added with a smile.

"Thank you," Lily said. "It would seem that the debts we owe you continue to mount."

John shook off her gratitude. "I'll leave the cart here for you to pack and return this afternoon to ride with you back to O'Malley House."

Lily glanced out at John's stallion. "Will you not stay for midday meal? Are you going somewhere?"

He hesitated, then answered her with obvious reluctance. "I'm going to Lymond Castle."

"But you just said—"

"Aye, that your brother is allied with the English. That's precisely why I'm going there. There may be no way to prevent fighting with talk, but I shall at least make the attempt. I hope to be back by midafternoon."

"You're going to speak with my brother?"

"Aye," he said, "to your brother and to his houseguest, an English lord named Philip Stratton. I believe he's the one I'll have to deal with if there's to be a settlement of this fight."

Lily swayed slightly.

"Is something amiss?" he asked, grasping her elbow to steady her.

"Nay, 'tis just . . . 'tis just the midday sun."

He nodded. "I should be going before it gets any later if I'm to make it to Lymond Castle and back here before dark."

Lily gave a noncommittal murmur. John Black was riding to see Philip? What devil's game were the fates playing with her now? She wondered if she should at least tell John that she knew the man, but before she could decide how to form the words, he leaned over, gave her a quick kiss on the cheek, then turned to leave.

Gaping, Lily watched him walk up the path to his horse and mount.

"I'll see you soon!" he yelled to Daphne with a quick wave, spurring Greybolt to action. Then he disappeared into the woods.

• • •

John's first impression of Nevin O'Farrell, Earl of
Lymond, was that he was a man who would be easy to
underestimate. He looked, in fact, much like his sister,
but the fine features and willowy stature that made her
such a desirable woman made her brother look delicate
and weak. It was Lymond's face that revealed the true
character. The deeply etched lines told a tale of cruelty
and willfulness.

Philip Stratton, on the other hand, proved to be a
surprisingly agreeable fellow. He had thick black hair,
flashing eyes, and an easy smile that John reckoned
had earned him more than a glance or two from the
eager ladies of Queen Elizabeth's court. He'd greeted
John with a hearty handshake and warm words. It was
hard to believe that he'd come on deadly business.

They sat in a drafty room somewhere in the bowels
of Lymond Castle. John had lost track of his bearing
while following his host through the endless dark halls.
The three men sat in big chairs of richly carved oak.
Once they were seated, four men in the uniforms of English soldiers filed into the room and took seats on a
bench against the back wall. Neither Philip nor Lymond bothered to present them to their visitor. Out of
habit from his old days with rebels, John took a quick
inventory of the men's strength and the weapons they
carried, though he had little worry that Lymond would
try anything so bold as to assassinate him right here in
his own home. At least not while fighting had yet to be
openly declared.

"I understand you are staying with the Riordans,"
Stratton observed.

"Aye. I was a long-ago acquaintance of Lady Riordan's mother, and I've been close to all three Riordan
brothers over the years."

"Their reputation is well known in London," Stratton said. "I daresay the trio sent far more than their share of good English souls to their final resting place during the days of fighting." His words were accompanied by a smile that took any menace out of the observation.

"They are good fighters, and more important, good men," John answered evenly.

"Quite." Lymond was obviously not interested in discussing the Riordans. "What's your business here today, Black? Why have you come?"

Stratton's smile turned apologetic, as if to excuse his friend's bluntness.

"I've come to see if we can discuss this matter of confiscation of estates by the Crown, before all of Killarney turns into a battlefield," John answered calmly.

"The estates are being legally seized and transferred," Stratton said. "We want no violence."

"I'm sure you do not," John agreed. "But I'm just as sure that the landowners here are not going to peacefully let their estates be taken."

"Then they are fools." Lymond stood and walked over to the empty fireplace. Dressed all in black, with tight black hose on his long spindly legs, he looked to John like some kind of crafty spider. "They should take what the queen is willing to give them for their poor parcels and be grateful. Most of these men fought against Elizabeth. She could be demanding their heads instead of offering compensation."

Stratton nodded agreement. "I'm afraid my friend Lymond is correct, Black. Most of these lords could have been tried for treason and executed. They should be grateful that Her Majesty is a merciful monarch."

John had come with the intention of trying diplomacy, but he couldn't help his quick retort. "So merciful that instead of taking their lives, she is one by one robbing them of their family heritage and legacy, which is just as dear?"

Lymond kicked at an old piece of blackened wood that lay on the hearth. John wondered how long it had been since a fire had burned there. Or anywhere in Lymond Castle. The place was colder than a dungeon.

"They'll just have to take what the queen, in her benevolence, is willing to give them, and make the best of it," Lymond said.

"Aye," Stratton agreed. "Most of them will receive fair payment."

Though the Englishman's tone was much more pleasant, John had the impression that he would be just as intractable as Lymond on the subject. "And if they refuse to give up their estates?" John asked.

"Then the violence we've tried to avoid will be inevitable," Stratton said gravely.

John turned to look at the earl. "Lymond, how can you support this? You're an Irishman. First it will be your neighbors, then who's to say Lymond Castle itself won't be the next target? Have you no concern for your own family?"

"The fate of Lymond Castle is not in question," Lymond answered with a shrug.

"And what about your sister? Have you no worry for her safety if the region becomes a powder keg?"

John had not expected such a dramatic reaction to his question. Lymond's eyes narrowed dangerously, but it was Stratton who spoke. "Sister?" he asked sharply. "Lily is still here?"

The Englishman's tone told John that his question was not casual. "Are you acquainted with Mistress O'-Farrell?" he asked him.

Stratton took a moment to answer. He looked over at Lymond, then back to John. "I knew her long ago," he said finally. "She was a lovely young woman."

"My sister has nothing to do with any of this," Lymond said harshly, "and, in fact, I believe further discussion here is futile. Dr. Black, I suggest you tell your landowner friends that the best way to ensure their interests is to cooperate with the English in the transfer of these estates. If they are agreeable, they are more likely to receive compensation."

John stood. For once he was willing to agree with Lymond. These men were not interested in negotiating. They had the vast power of the English Crown on their side and the opposition had so far been unable to mount an organized front against it. Why should they compromise?

He had learned one thing. The mention of Lily had given a start to both these men. Lymond had been willing enough to continue talking until her name was mentioned. He wished he knew more about the circumstances of the break between Nevin O'Farrell and his sister.

"Shall I relay a message to your sister?" he asked Lymond as he and Stratton escorted him to the front door.

Lymond looked at him sharply. "How exactly do you know my sister?"

John thought it best not to reveal how exactly he knew Lily. Instead, he said, "We have mutual friends, the Riordans. I shall, in fact, be seeing her today." Let them ponder that, John thought with some satisfaction as both men's eyes widened with surprise. "Shall I tell her you send your regards?"

Lymond's face was a grim mask. "You may tell her anything you like. It matters nothing to me. I no longer consider her part of my family or my responsibility."

"You may give her *my* regards," Stratton said softly.

Something in the way he said it made John curious. "Will she remember you, Lord Stratton?" he asked, studying the man. Stratton was probably ten years younger than he was, John reckoned. And far less worn by life.

Stratton smiled sadly. "Aye, I warrant she'll remember me," he said.

John made his farewells and left, an inexplicable irritation prickling at him as he took Greybolt's reins from a stable boy and began the ride to Whistler's Woods. He should have been considering the next step in the fight to keep the English from overrunning the estates of Killarney. Instead, all he could think about was the look in Philip Stratton's eyes when he had talked about Lily. *I warrant she'll remember me.* The words had been said without arrogance, but with utter certainty. John wasn't sure precisely why, but the idea made him feel slightly sick to his stomach.

"Where is she, Lymond?" Philip Stratton turned on his host with a rare flash of anger as they stood in the castle yard after their visitor left.

"Who?" the earl replied.

"You know who. Lily. Where is she?"

Lymond gave one of his chilly smiles. "It's a bit late to be worrying about that, isn't it, Stratton? After all, it's been fully twelve years since you seduced my sister and then abandoned her."

"What's happened to her? Black said she was still in the neighborhood. Is she married?"

"I haven't spoken to my sister in years, Stratton," he lied coolly. "Black seems to know more about her than I do. You should have asked him."

Stratton turned on his heel and stormed into the castle. As he neared the old stone staircase, a slight figure stepped out of the shadows.

"Do you want information about my father's sister?" It was Lymond's son, Desmond.

Stratton stopped. The odd boy made him feel uneasy, but he might know something useful. "What information?" he asked.

"I know a number of things about my father's sister that you might find interesting, Lord Stratton," the boy said slyly. "And about her daughter, as well."

"Daughter?"

"Aye." The boy looked toward the front door, keeping an eye out for his father. "Let's just step into this side parlor, my lord, and I'll tell you all about it."

Lily lay beside her daughter on the big feather bed in the chamber they'd been given at O'Malley House. Daphne's breathing had been even and peaceful for at least two hours, but Lily's mind continued tumbling and refused to surrender to sleep.

As usual, the Riordans had been warm and welcoming when they had finally arrived at O'Malley House with John. It had been late, but Catriona had insisted on taking them into the dining hall for a hot meal before personally showing them to their room. She had the ability of making guests feel as if they were doing the hostess a favor by being there, and Lily was grateful for her graciousness. She was confused enough by the turn her life had taken.

Tossing from one side to another, she reviewed the events that had transpired since the day last fall when John Black had arrived at her house with her frightened, soggy daughter in his arms. Sometimes it seemed as if the simple, isolated world she had built for herself had begun to dissolve that rainy day.

Daphne had begun to long for the world outside of Whistler's Woods. She'd agreed to treatment for her infirmity. The two of them had been taken into the warm circle of the Riordan family. Her brother had come to see her after twelve long years. Philip was back in Killarney, half a day's walk from the daughter he didn't know he had. And then there were her conflicting feelings about John.

Finally she slid out from the covers, careful not to waken Daphne, and made her way in the dark to the clothes stand where she had left a night robe. If sleep was impossible, she might as well see if she could find her way down to the Riordan library and spend some time reading. Catriona had made it clear that the cozy room lined with books was at Lily's disposal at any time during the duration of her stay.

She grabbed the candle from the nightstand, then went out into the hall, quietly closing the door behind her. The wall sconce at the top of the stairs was lit, giving her a light for her candle so that she could make her way through the darkened house.

All was quiet downstairs. She reckoned it would still be a few hours before the first servants were stirring. Growing up in maze-like Lymond Castle had given her a good sense of direction. She found her way to the library without a problem, but stopped short when she saw a light shining from the doorway. Had the fire been left unbanked? she wondered.

Cautiously she approached the door.

John Black was by the fire, reading. He was comfortably ensconced on pillows—just as the two of them had been on Christmas night. The memory made her cheeks flame. He looked up as the light from her candle made the room slightly brighter.

"Good evening," he said evenly. Then he laid aside his book, but didn't move from his prone position on the pillows.

"Oh, I apologize," she stammered. "I didn't think anyone would be awake and I—"

Now he rolled to his feet and started walking toward her. "Don't apologize," he said. " 'Tis a pleasant surprise. I presume you had as much difficulty sleeping as I."

She nodded. Her heart seemed to beat faster with each step he took toward her. "I warrant 'tis the talk of war," she said.

He stopped close enough to touch her.

"Ah, 'twas not the war that had me tossing on my bed."

"It wasn't?" she asked. Her mouth had gone dry.

"Nay." In the light of her candle, his gray eyes looked like the eyes of a wolf.

"Then what—what was it?" she asked. Everything about the conversation had become dangerous.

"I was kept awake by the notion that you were lying in a bed just at the other end of the hall, probably dressed in something flowing and silky, much like"— he reached out a hand and touched the sleeve of her robe—"much like this."

"I should go," she said, taking a step back.

"Nay," he said. "You shouldn't." Then he calmly took the candlestick from her hand, set it on the nearby bookshelf, and took her into his arms.

Seventeen

This time it was not so much urgency as inevitability. From the moment he began kissing her, Lily knew that she had no desire to stop him. All other considerations of broken hearts and betrayals disappeared as once again John's skilled lips and hands obliterated all rational thought.

She made one attempt to rescue herself when he lifted her to carry her over to the nest of pillows by the fire. "I thought we'd settled this," she murmured. "I can't risk my—"

She'd been going to say "heart," but John misunderstood and whispered, "I'll be careful this time, sweetheart, I swear. Don't worry, don't even think. Just let me make you feel good."

He set her on her feet and pushed the robe down her shoulders, baring the tops of her breasts above her thin nightrail. She could see the sudden flare of his nostrils. She closed her eyes as he traced his fingers along the lace trim, then gently massaged her nipples through the silk.

For a moment, he stopped touching her, and when she opened her eyes, he was naked, the firelight dancing a pattern of shadows over the hard ripples of his body. The light sprinkles of hair along his chest veed at his waist before turning into a thick dark thatch that nestled his erect penis. He stood without moving, watching her, and after a moment, she reached out her hand and stroked the hard muscles of one arm. He smiled. "I like it when you touch me," he said.

Emboldened, she moved her hand to touch him where she knew he was most sensitive, and his quick intake of breath told her that she had reached the right spot.

"Will you lie with me before the fire?" he asked hoarsely.

She nodded. Her legs felt like they were fast turning to liquid. "Shall I take this off?" she asked, beginning to lift her nightgown.

John pulled her hands away. "Leave it," he said. "I want to feel the silk against your soft skin."

They sank to the cushions, and once again, John began to caress her, moving the silk in circles over her breasts and stomach, the tops of her thighs. Lily lay back and gave herself up to the sensation. Finally he pushed the gown aside to lift out her breast and sucked gently at the nipple. At the juncture of her legs she could feel the heat of him through the soft silk.

When he'd taken his mouth from her nipple, she impulsively reached downward and encased his penis in the silk of her nightrail and used the silk to move up and down the length of him. He lay back on the pillows and groaned.

"Does that feel good?" she asked in a seductive voice that she could not even recognize as her own.

"You have no idea," he said again, giving another groan of satisfaction.

She continued her manipulations, watching him and feeling a peculiar and satisfying sense of power. It worked both ways, she realized, this seduction thing. The control could lie with the woman as well as the man. As if to confirm her thoughts, his penis gave a sudden jerk in her hand. Yet as she continued to move the silk along him, she could feel the effect in her own body. She'd grown moist, and the familiar flutters had begun to radiate from her middle down into her legs.

She was almost ready to give the game back over to him when he opened hooded eyes, brushed her hand away, and flipped her back over onto her back. "Little girls shouldn't play with fire," he growled. "Or with silk."

She wanted to make some kind of defiant reply, but by now the clamoring in her own senses had become too insistent. She put her arms around his neck and held on tightly as he slid her gown over her hips, baring her private area. After a quick survey with his fingers which revealed that she was ready, he pushed himself into her with something like a sigh of relief.

He stayed a moment without moving, and Lily felt surprising tears sting her eyes. The thickness of him inside her body felt so good . . . and so *right*. No matter the outcome, she decided, blinking away the annoying tears. This was meant to happen to her. A union so perfect could simply not be wrong.

He began to move then, and once again thinking gave way to feeling. The flutters in the lower part of her body turned into ripples, then broad, crashing waves. Lost in her own climax, she was scarcely aware when John pulled away from her toward the end and held her tightly against him, his seed spilling between their pressed stomachs.

She wasn't sure how long they lay entwined, but the fire had made the silk hot against her back when she finally moved. John sat up, reached for a piece of his clothing, and gently wiped the remaining stickiness from her skin, then rearranged her nightrail to cover her. "I may have to ask you to wear this every time we make love," he said with a grin.

She gave him a lazy smile. She didn't want to think about every time or next time or if there would ever be even one more time. This moment was hers and it was enough.

"Perhaps you should begin wearing silk," she teased. "You seemed to . . . enjoy the texture."

He rolled his eyes. "In London the courtiers wear silk hose, and Niall and I thought them fools. Perhaps they know more than we do."

"'Tis far more pleasurable than linen. We women have always known that." She ran her own hand up and down the silk across her stomach.

He covered her hand with his own. "Don't do that to yourself, sweetheart, or you'll have me on top of you again."

She flipped her hand over his and moved it along her stomach. "Is that against the rules?" she asked. "Doing it again?"

His eyebrow went up. "Not my rules."

She smiled. "Well, then, lad, I don't see anything stoppin' ye." It took him only seconds to take advantage of her invitation. "I like playing by your rules," she murmured as his renewed kisses made the spinning begin again in her head.

They both had dozed briefly, John realized, as he opened his eyes to see that the fire had died down considerably. The front of him, where Lily lay nestled in his arms, was warm, but he could feel the chill of the room across his back.

"Sweetheart," he said softly, nibbling the lobe of her ear. "We must be getting up."

She gave a low moan and shifted in his arms, but

didn't awaken. Sometime during the course of their second bout of lovemaking her silk nightgown had been discarded. He ran his hand along the curve of her bare hip. His body was perfectly ready to begin making love to her all over again, he realized with some surprise, but he figured she would not be too receptive to the idea of being discovered by some early riser.

Gently he pulled himself away from her and rose to don his clothes. When he'd finished, he looked down to find her watching him, her bright blue eyes soft with sleep.

"Good morrow, sweetheart," he said.

"Is it morning?" she asked without any apparent alarm.

"Not yet, but soon. We should probably seek our own chambers lest we scandalize our hosts."

"Not to mention my daughter," Lily agreed, but she did not appear as troubled by the idea as he would have thought. Nor did she seem to mind the fact that he was taking a slow survey of her naked body. In fact, she stretched, voluptuously.

"If ye have in mind to entice me back down there, scamp, 'tis working, but don't blame me when the servant arrives to stoke the fire."

At that she sat up and reached for her nightrail. "Heavens, I have to walk through the house in this, don't I?"

"Unless you want me to carry you," John said with a grin.

She stood and hurriedly donned her gown and robe. "Nay, I'll make my own way, thank you, sir."

John felt an unaccountable surge of happiness. When he'd begun making love to her, he'd been uncertain, remembering how their last encounter had ended. But this time something was different. Lily seemed to be accepting what had happened without the recriminations or whatever it had been that had spoiled things before.

He leaned over to briefly kiss her lips. "'Twas a wondrous night, sweetheart. I fear I'm going to begin to pray that both of us continue to be plagued by insomnia."

She smiled and without the least tone of accusation asked, "How much longer will you be here at O'Malley House?"

He supposed he should not be surprised by the question, but it rankled. It had been asked with entirely too much nonchalance. "I have no immediate plans to leave, if that's what you mean."

"I thought you'd be involved in this fighting you've predicted."

His night with Lily had put all thought of the meeting at Lymond Castle out of his head. He looked out the trio of small leaded windows at the other side of the library. The first rays of dawn were showing in the distance. "I may be."

"When you picked us up yesterday, I refrained from asking you how your appointment with my brother went. I didn't want to alarm Daphne."

He paused. A horrible suspicion was beginning to form. "I would not say that it went well," he answered slowly.

"And did you meet with Philip Stratton, as well?"

"Aye."

"Did he—" She looked down at the expensive woven carpet Catriona had purchased in an attempt to make her home more like the elegant ones she had seen while living in London. "I don't suppose there was mention of me?"

Was this the reason for Lily's change of attitude? Obviously there had once been something between her and Philip Stratton. He could hear it in her voice as she

said the man's name. Had she come here tonight de-
liberately looking for John so that she could get information about him? Would she be capable of sleeping
with one man in order to pursue some ends with another? As soon as the suspicion took form, he discounted it. Lily was simply not that woman. He wasn't
sure if her coming had been an accident, but he was
sure that she wouldn't have acquiesced to his lovemaking if she were in love with another man.

"Aye, you were mentioned," he said.

Her face went white.

"What was Philip Stratton to you, Lily?" he asked.
"What's your connection to this Englishman who has
come to sow havoc among your neighbors?"

She shook her head. "I knew him long ago."

"Knew him well apparently."

"Aye, I knew him well." She lifted her eyes to look
at him directly.

She'd made it clear that there had been no man in
her life since her daughter's birth. Suddenly he felt as
if he didn't have quite enough air to breathe. "Is he
Daphne's father?"

She hesitated a long moment, not taking her gaze
from him, then finally nodded. "Aye."

The moment of breathlessness was replaced by
rage. "Then why in God's name has he left you to fend
for yourself all these years?"

"He didn't know. He still doesn't unless my brother
has told him, which I doubt. Philip was betrothed to
another when he came here all those years ago. I was
young and gullible."

"And innocent," John added. He could picture
Philip's amiable demeanor and pleasant smile. He
wished he'd taken the time to smash the man's handsome face.

"Innocent, aye. I'd lain with no man, but 'twas not

a seduction. I was as eager as he. I loved him very much."

"But when you found out you were with child, surely you thought of telling him. Betrothals can be withdrawn—"

"Nay, Philip knew when he made love to me that the bonds his family had made with the family of his future wife were unbreakable. He just neglected to inform me of that fact. By the time I learned that I was with child, he was back in London, no doubt getting fit for his wedding attire."

John took a step closer to her and pulled her into his arms. "My poor darling," he murmured into her sweet-smelling hair. "I don't understand why your brother didn't call him out."

Lily gave a bitter laugh. "I've come to believe that my dear brother was delighted by the whole proceedings. He was able to get the favor of a powerful Englishman and find an excuse to get rid of his sister, all at the same time."

"Forgive me, since 'tis your blood, but your brother is a monster."

Lily took a step back. "Aye," she agreed without emotion.

"What about now? Do you think to tell Stratton about Daphne?" The idea made bile rise in the back of his throat.

Before she could answer, the library door opened and the little downstairs maid stepped into the room. "Lordy!" she said. "I beg yer pardon!"

Lily pulled her robe more closely around her. "Don't apologize," she said to the girl with a nervous smile. "Dr. Black was just, er, helping me pick out a book. I like to read for a few minutes in bed each morning." Then she snatched a volume from the shelf and fled from the room.

The maid continued gawking at John. "Shall I come back to do the room, sir?" she asked.

John scarcely heard her. His mind was still whirling with the news that Philip Stratton was Daphne's father. And the bastard had left Lily to bear the burden alone.

Lily was trying hard to stay awake through the afternoon of sewing with Catriona and Daphne in the Riordan parlor. She'd managed to get back to her room that morning before Daphne was awake, and as far as she could tell, no one but the maid knew of her nightly wanderings.

She wished she could steal away to her bedchamber. It would be good to have some time by herself to think over what had taken place in the Riordan library. She smiled, remembering. Unlike the first time she and John had come together, this time she was not bothering with recriminations. She'd made love because she had *wanted* it to happen. She'd done it with no expectations for the future. John could ride away tomorrow, but that wouldn't alter what they had had. After twelve years of believing that that part of her life was over for good, last night her body had come alive and told her that she was not only a mother—she was a woman.

"If you'll excuse me, I'll see who the visitor is," Catriona said, standing.

Lily looked up. She'd been so lost in thought that she hadn't even seen the young maid slip into the room to tell her mistress that there was a person waiting in the front hall.

"You seem tired today, Mummy," Daphne said after Catriona had left.

She smiled at her daughter. "I imagine I am. You'll admit 'twas quite a day yesterday—to learn in the morning that you're to move your household that afternoon."

Daphne did not seem entirely satisfied with her mother's explanation, but she said, "Mayhap you should rest before the Twelfth Night supper."

"I might do just that, Sweetcakes."

"I'm to get a riding lesson from Dr. Black if he and Lord Riordan get back in time." John and Niall had ridden off to consult with one of the neighbors about the growing troubles.

"Then I shall stay awake," Lily announced firmly. "I'd like to see that."

The parlor doors opened, and Catriona came back in, her expression sober. She looked first at Lily, then at Daphne. "Daphne, the boys have awakened from their afternoon naps and are up in the nursery with Nanny. Would you like to go up with them for a while?"

"Oh, yes, ma'am," Daphne answered quickly, setting aside her sewing with a sigh of relief. "May I, Mummy?"

At Lily's nod, she walked out of the room, her limp barely noticeable.

Catriona had remained standing. When Daphne had closed the door behind her, she said, "You have a visitor, Lily."

Lily gave a start of surprise. "I do?"

"An Englishman. He says his name is Philip Stratton, and he's come to see you."

Lily's sewing fell to her lap. Catriona nodded, as if confirming something to herself. "He's the father, isn't he?"

"How—how did you know? Did he say—?"

"Nay. 'Twas just the way he looked when he spoke of you just now. I suspect the man's in love with you. Or at least he was once."

Had he been? Lily had thought so at the time, then had discounted it. She'd told herself that no man in love could do what Philip had done to her. Now, with the passage of time, she was no longer so certain.

"You don't have to see him," Catriona said gently, walking over to Lily and putting her hand on her shoulder. "I can send him away."

Philip was here in this very house. He'd come to see her. Oddly, she felt none of the excitement she once would have. "I'll see him," she said, looking up at Catriona.

"Do you want me to stay with you or—?"

"Nay, I'll see him here, by myself, if you don't mind allowing me the room."

"Of course. I'll send him in." She turned to leave, then said. "I'll keep Daphne upstairs with the boys unless you send for her. But I'll be near, in case you need me."

Lily gave her a smile of gratitude.

As soon as she left the room, Lily's heart began to pound. It had been twelve years since she'd seen Philip Stratton. What would he be like? She'd thought that her love for him had long ago died, but what would she feel when she saw him again?

She put her sewing on the floor and smoothed her dress. The wait seemed much longer than the time it should take to walk from the front hall to the parlor. Finally the door opened, and there he was. As simple as that. Philip.

Twelve years had changed him little. He still had the same strapping physique, the same too-perfect features, the same thick black hair that had been a legacy to his daughter. She stood as he approached. There were lines around his eyes, and he appeared more serious than she remembered.

"Lily," he said, reaching out his hands.

She let him take hers, then gave a start of surprise as he bent and kissed her on the lips. The kiss was chaste, but nevertheless, she found herself fighting off the impulse to wipe her mouth. This was good, she decided with grim satisfaction.

"It's wonderful to see you," he said, smiling for the first time.

"You haven't changed, Philip," she said, pulling her hands away from his. Her heartbeat was almost back to normal. "Would you care to sit down?"

He waited until she sat, then pulled a chair close to hers. For a moment, neither spoke, and he appeared to be studying her. "I suppose I should say that you haven't changed, either," he said finally, "but it would not be the truth."

She couldn't imagine that he meant the words to be insulting. Philip had turned out to be a scoundrel, but he'd always been a charming one. "I'm twelve years older," she said.

"Aye. When I knew you back then, you were a girl. Now you've become a stunning woman—full of grace and confidence. The years have favored you." His smile was slightly sad.

She ignored his compliment. "How did you know I was here?" she asked.

"I had my men ask in the village. Banburn is too small for secrets. Yesterday I learned something quite surprising from your nephew."

Lily stiffened. "From Desmond?"

"Aye, he told about your daughter. *Our* daughter," he added, leaning toward her.

Suddenly the room felt too close. "I—I do have a daughter, but—"

"He also told me that his father turned you out of his home while you still were with child, and that your daughter turned out to be a cripple who—"

"*My* daughter is a beautiful child."

Philip leaned back and gave his sad smile once again. "I'm sure she is. She could be no other way since she is your daughter . . . and a product of our love for each other."

"She's my daughter," Lily replied stiffly, "but she is the product of a foolish liaison that should never have happened."

"You don't truly believe that."

Philip continued studying her. She had to admit that she still found him startlingly handsome. His smile still seemed to light the room. His voice sounded utterly familiar, even after all these years. But deep inside the feeling was gone. "It took me a long time, but, aye, 'tis what I believe," she told him. "It was foolish, but I shall never regret it, for it brought me my daughter."

"I want to see her, Lily," he said.

From the moment Catriona had announced his visit, Lily had known it would come to this. Philip was Daphne's father, and he wanted to see her. Perhaps he had a right to see her. It was a question she'd never pondered, for she'd never thought he'd return to Killarney. All she knew was that the idea of letting him see Daphne terrified her.

"She doesn't know who you are," she said after a long moment.

Philip winced. "I suppose not. But don't you think 'tis time she did?"

She glanced at the roaring fire. The room had definitely grown warm. She wanted to be gone from it, to flee upstairs and find Daphne, to hold her daughter in her arms and pretend that Philip Stratton had never come here today.

"I'll speak to her," she said after a long breath. "I'll need some time."

Philip stood. "I'll come tomorrow at this same hour."

Lily nodded, then watched with bleak eyes as he turned and left the room.

Eighteen

On the big Riordan estate in the north near Tara Hill, Twelfth Night had always been a raucous occasion, but Niall and Cat had yet to duplicate the feasting at O'Malley House. The boys were still too young for such revels, they'd decided. This year the supper was especially subdued. The talk of war and the knowledge that English soldiers were already ensconced nearby at Lymond Castle had dampened everyone's spirits.

Even so, Lily had had trouble sitting peacefully through the long meal. Her thoughts were on the conversation she would have to hold that night with Daphne. She tapped her foot nervously as the Twelfth Night cake was served, and watched as Daphne, to her delight, was served the piece with the little doll of the baby Jesus. Then finally, Lily and her daughter were able to bid goodnight to the rest of the household and make their way to their bedchamber.

Lily had spent the evening trying to decide the best way to broach the subject, but in the end, she said simply, "Sweetcakes, I need to talk to you about your father."

"My father?" Daphne had already donned her night-

gown and had been sitting propped against the pillows
of the bed. She sat bolt upright at her mother's words.

Lily was still dressed, and had begun to pace. "Aye,
your father."

"But, my father's"—she hesitated—"my father's
dead. At least, that's what I always thought. You never
wanted to talk about it, but I figured that if he were
alive, surely he would want to see me."

"Nay, he's not dead, and he's here in Killarney."
Keeping her tone as matter-of-fact as possible, Lily
gave Daphne a quick account of the reason she and
Philip had parted all those years ago, and why it had
been impossible for them to ever be together as man
and wife. Surprisingly, Daphne did not seem to be
bothered by the knowledge that her parents had not
been married. Perhaps she had sensed it all along.

"So now he's here staying at Lymond Castle," she
concluded.

"*Has* he come looking for me?" Daphne asked. Her
hopeful smile gave Lily a pang.

Lily forced herself to stop walking and went over to
sit on the bed next to her daughter. "I don't think so,
Sweetcakes. I don't believe he knew about you until he
arrived here in Killarney. He came to stay with your
uncle, and it seems that your cousin Desmond told him
about you."

Her smile evaporated. "If Desmond told him about
me, he probably doesn't want to see me. I'm sure he
told him that I was"—she paused, tears quivering on
her lower eyelids—"was not like other children."

Lily kept her voice steady. "You have to stop thinking about yourself that way, Daphne. Your father *does*
want to see you. His name is Philip, and he came here
today for that precise purpose."

"Does he know about my foot?"

"Aye, he does. Your foot is not going to make any

difference to him. He's going to see at once the beautiful person you are—inside and out. He's going to be enchanted and so proud to think that he has such a daughter."

Daphne didn't look totally convinced, but the tears had disappeared. "I want to wear my boot when I meet him."

"Of course. John says you may begin wearing it whenever you want now." She slid closer on the bed and put her hand against her daughter's cheek. "But I promise you that your father will be looking at this precious face, not at your leg."

"What shall I say to him?"

Lily smiled. "You can say anything you like. I'm sure he'll have plenty of questions to ask you."

Daphne took her mother's hand. "You say he came here today? Did you see him?"

"Aye."

"Oh, Mummy, are you all right? Was it not terribly difficult?" As usual, Daphne had gotten past her personal worries and turned her attention on her mother. She was old enough to be concerned how her mother had been affected by this meeting with the man who had been so important in her life.

Lily smiled. "It was slightly daunting at first, but not as bad as I might have expected."

"Did you feel as if—are you still in love with him?"

"Nay. He's a charming man, as you will see tomorrow, but my feelings for him died a long time ago."

"Tomorrow?"

"He said he'd come in the afternoon. I promised him I'd talk with you before then. Of course, you don't have to see him, if you'd prefer not."

Some part of her hoped Daphne would choose not to see Philip, but she knew her daughter and was not surprised when she said quickly, "Oh, but I *do* want to meet him. My father—after all these years. Just imagine!"

Lily leaned over to kiss the top of her head. "Then it's into bed with you, Sweetcakes," she said, holding up the covers so Daphne could slide under them. "You need your sleep if you're to have such a momentous meeting tomorrow."

"Aren't you coming to bed, Mummy?"

"Shortly. I might see if I can find some milk down on the sideboard. I didn't sleep well last night. I suppose it's hard to sleep in a strange bed."

"I like it," Daphne said with a grin, snuggling into the blankets. "I think it's ever so exciting to do something brand new."

"Sleep tight, then," Lily said.

"I shall, Mummy. Perhaps I shall dream of my father. Does he look like me?"

"You have his black hair. You'll see tomorrow. Now close your eyes."

She waited until Daphne looked settled, then left.

She knew, of course, that it wasn't milk she sought as she made her way down the curved staircase. It was comfort of a different sort. Something told her that John would be in the library again, and he was.

He jumped up with a smile when she appeared. "I was hoping you'd come again," he said. "Though I must say I liked last night's attire better."

She smiled at his teasing, but said, "I didn't come here for you to lure me into scandalizing more of the Riordan servants, Dr. Black."

"Now, that's disappointing news." He moved toward her, grinning. "Of course, 'tis early. I imagine we've hours and hours before dawn."

"Aye, and I imagine much of the household is still awake. Who knows? We might yet be joined by Lord Riordan and Catriona."

"Nay, I bribed Catriona to entice her husband early to bed this night so that you and I could be alone."

"You did no such thing."

"Of course I did. Do you think the notion came as any surprise to her?"

"I should hope it did. What must she think of me?"

"She thinks you're a lovely, capable, worthy woman and that I'm lucky that you have any interest in an old man like me."

Lily couldn't help laughing. "I don't believe a word you say, John Black," she said.

"Ah," he replied with mock remorse. "This is the price I pay for a lifetime of paying false compliments. When I finally need to convey the real thing, I'm not believed."

"Nay, you're not. But at least you make me laugh, which I no doubt need more sorely than compliments at the moment."

He grew serious immediately. "What is it, Lily? What's happened?"

"Did Catriona not tell you of our visitor today?"

"Nay. We arrived just in time for the Twelfth Night supper, and afterward, Cat spirited Niall off to their bedchamber. Who was the visitor?"

"Philip Stratton."

"He came here? To O'Malley House?" John sounded upset. "Was he looking for me?"

"Nay, he was looking for me. And for his daughter."

John was silent for a moment, then he took Lily's hand and began to lead her to the bench across from the fireplace. "Sit down here and tell me about it," he said.

His voice had become reassuringly calm. Lily found it was easy to give him a full account of her meeting that afternoon, including the fears she had about introducing Philip to Daphne. He held her hand while she talked, but made no other move to touch her. When she had finished, it felt as if the weight she'd been carrying since she'd heard Philip's name that afternoon had lightened.

"What is it you're afraid of exactly?" he asked.

Leave it to John to get right to the heart of the matter. "I'm not sure."

"Perhaps you think Daphne will be fascinated by this new parent, which will lessen your place in her life?"

"I believe she already is rather fascinated by him, or at least incredibly curious."

"Which is only natural," John pointed out.

"Aye, but I don't think that's what's making me afraid. The bond Daphne and I have is so strong, nothing will ever weaken that. But I'm worried. . . ." She bit her lip and gripped his hand more tightly. "Oh, John, what if he tries to take her away?"

"That won't happen, Lily. I promise you that." He put his arm around her and let her head rest against his shoulder. "Philip Stratton will never take your child while I or any of my friends are around to prevent it. Put the thought out of your head."

The words gave her some comfort, but a niggling worry persisted. She let herself be comforted by the warmth of his arm for several minutes without speaking. Then she sat up straight and smiled at him. "You've been a good friend to us, John."

He looked a little surprised, and she decided that she hadn't fully conveyed the gratitude she'd meant by the words, but she was too exhausted to improve on them. "I should go back up to my chamber. For some reason, I didn't get much sleep last night," she added, trying to lighten her voice.

His smile looked forced. "Aye, we're both tired. Sleep well, sweetheart, and don't worry further about that English scoundrel. If he makes one move out of place tomorrow, Niall and I will see that he's run clear across the Channel."

She leaned to kiss his bristly cheek, then went to seek her bed.

"They've been talking almost two hours," Lily said, rising to pace the room one more time. She, John, Catriona, and Niall were waiting in the front parlor while Philip Stratton met privately with Daphne in the Riordan's cozy solar at the back of the house. Lily felt as if they'd been there a fortnight.

"I think that's a good sign, Lily," Catriona said. "They must be getting along well."

Lily looked at John, who gave her a nod of reassurance. "It won't change her, Lily. She's had two hours with him, but a lifetime with you."

"Would you like me to go get them?" Niall asked. "The blackguard's already had more time than he deserves with the girl, if you ask me."

"I appreciate the offer, Lord Riordan," Lily answered, "but I told Daphne she could feel free to end the conversation at any time, so I'll leave it up to her."

He smiled sympathetically. "Aye, but 'tis you I'm thinking of now, lass. I swear you've worn an entire path in Cat's new rug. And you'd best call me Niall, since you're family now, after a fashion."

Lily felt a swelling of gratitude for the three good friends who had become a dear part of her life in such a short time.

All four turned as the door opened and Daphne came in with Philip Stratton. His arm was around her lightly, his hand resting on her shoulder. She was smiling.

"Have you all met my father?" she asked. There was a touch of pride in her tone.

Niall crossed the room to shake hands with the

newcomer. John and Catriona remained seated. Lily was searching her daughter's face looking for any sign that she'd been upset or altered by the encounter, but she seemed to be her usual sunny self.

"It's impossible to make up twelve years in a couple of hours, but it's a start," Philip said, giving Daphne's shoulder a pat. To Lily, the words sounded ominous.

"I'm sure you had a lot to discuss," Catriona offered, when the other occupants of the room remained silent.

"That we did, Lady Riordan." Philip looked over at Lily. "Now I'd like to beg your indulgence further, Lily, and ask to meet with you in private. If you will excuse us," he added to the others with a smile that encompassed everyone.

"If you want us here, Lily, we stay," John told her.

The presence of her friends would be comforting, but she'd learned over the years that in the end, it was better to handle things herself. "I shall speak with Philip alone," she said.

"Shall we go to another—?" Philip began, but Niall, Catriona and John were already up and moving toward the door.

"Come with us, Daphne," Catriona said, reaching to take the girl's hand.

With some reluctance, Daphne moved away from her father's arm. "I'll see you again, shall I not?" she asked him anxiously.

"Aye, child. You'll see me again soon."

With that, the group exited, leaving Philip and Lily facing each other across the room. She still hadn't risen from her chair.

"You were right, Lily. She's a beautiful child—inside and out. You've done a wonderful job raising her, considering the circumstances."

The words irked her. "Considering that I raised her in a cottage instead of a palace?" she asked.

"Considering that you raised her *alone*," he corrected gently. He walked toward her and she motioned him to a chair. "I didn't apologize to you the other day when I was here, but I'm doing it now. As I told you at the time, I don't regret making love to you, but I regret that I wasn't as forthcoming as I should have been about my circumstances."

"You never said in so many words that we would marry." She couldn't believe after harboring such anger all these years that she was making excuses for him.

"Nay, but I told you I loved you. I took your virginity. You had a right to expect that, as a gentleman dealing with a gentlewoman, marriage would follow."

"Except for the small detail that you were already betrothed."

He sighed. "I was a foolish young man, Lily. Today I would do things differently. But the past cannot be changed. All I can do is offer you my apologies and hope for forgiveness."

"If I hadn't given myself to you, I wouldn't have Daphne."

He smiled. "Then 'tis my luck, for I can see that she would be enough for you to forgive almost anything."

She smiled back, realizing that it was true. Daphne was enough to forgive anything. She had forgiven Philip, and it made her feel light-headed with relief. In fact, she almost felt sorry for him, because he had not been fortunate enough to bear and raise a child like Daphne.

"Do you and your wife have children?" she asked.

His dark eyes were sad. "Nay, we've not been so blessed."

Lily paused a moment, considering the irony of life, then said gently, "Mayhap they're yet to come."

"Lily, I want you to consider carefully what I'm about to say, because I know 'twill be difficult."

Her momentary feeling of satisfaction over the discovery that she no longer hated Philip disappeared. She knew exactly what Philip was going to say. She'd known it as soon as she'd heard that he was in Killarney.

"I want to take her back with me," he said. "You've done a wonderful job, but she's growing up. She should learn about more than birds and bunnies in the woods—a backwater village. She should be taught by fine tutors and see the streets of London. My wife is a generous person. I know she would help groom her to go out in society. In time she could be presented at court, have a Season."

"She's a bastard, Philip," Lily interjected bitterly. It was the first time she'd ever used the word.

Philip waved off the objection. "As is half London these days, it would seem. Elizabeth herself was called a bastard by many who didn't recognize her father's marriage to Anne Boleyn. You don't hear that much nowadays, of course," he added quickly.

He was obviously enthusiastic about the plan and had put some thought into it. Lily tried to calm both her anger and her fear. "Daphne is perfectly happy here," she said. "She doesn't need tutors or courtiers to make a satisfactory life for herself."

"Perhaps now, Lily, but think of the future. Can you tell me that she will be able to find a worthy husband here in Killarney, considering her, er, background and her disability?"

It was something that Lily herself had only recently begun to consider, and she had no satisfactory answer.

Philip continued pressing his case. "In London I could adopt her and no further questions would be asked."

"She would never be happy there without me, Philip. We have been each other's world for too long."

He was quiet for a long moment. "I've thought about that, too, Lily, which is why I'd like to make this suggestion. You could come to London as well. I could set up a house for you." He did not appear to notice her eyes beginning to widen with outrage. "What is there for you here? You live in the woods, as I understand it. You see no one. In London, at least you and I could spend some time together. You've become an extraordinarily beautiful woman, Lily, and—"

She rose, her hands clenched at her side. "You think the life I have here would be improved by making me into some kind of whore in London?"

He stood as well and made calming motions with his hands. "Nay, Lily, I'd expect nothing of you. The house would be without any conditions. You wouldn't even have to receive me there unless you wished it."

"I think you should leave now, Philip. You've seen your daughter, now please go."

He stepped closer to her, and she had a perverse whiff of memory from the days when such close proximity to him meant an instant awakening of her senses. "It seems to be my lot to apologize to you, Lily. I'm sorry. I meant no insult. Perhaps it was a bad idea, but it was my attempt to find a way to offer Daphne a better life without separating her from the person she most loves in the world."

Once again, his sincerity was convincing. Philip's sincerity had always been convincing, she reminded herself. "I can't let her go," she said in a calmer tone.

"Don't answer me now. I'll be staying at Lymond Castle for a while. I know that you have Daphne's welfare at heart and that you will think of the advantages I could offer her. For one thing, Lily, it would take her away from a territory that may turn bloody before long if the landowners here decide not to be cooperative."

"If they don't agree to be cheated of their lands, you mean."

He shrugged. "However you put it, war is an ugly thing, and no place for children. Think about it, Lily. Daphne could be experiencing many new things in London, and she would also be *safe*."

Lily shook her head. She wanted to get away from Philip and his persuasive words.

"Just promise me that you'll think on it," he urged.

She looked up at him, miserable. "I'll think on it," she said.

Philip looked pleased. "Good. I've bought several horses from your brother that I intend to take back to England with me. One is a little mare that I picked out for Daphne."

"For Daphne?"

"Aye. In London she'll learn to ride properly, of course. May I bring the animal here next week? I would compensate the Riordans for its care."

Lily couldn't think of a gift that would please her daughter more. "Aye," she said. "You may bring it."

"Then it's settled. Please tell Daphne that I shall see her on Monday, and that I have a special surprise for her." Finally he seemed to notice Lily's gloomy expression. "She is truly a lovely child, Lily," he said softly.

She nodded. If she tried to say something, she would cry, and she was determined that would not happen.

Philip waited a moment longer for her to speak, then gave a small bow. "Until Monday, then, Lily. I shall see myself out."

Lily remained standing in the middle of the room for a long time after Philip left.

Nineteen

She found Daphne playing with Lorcan and Paddy in their nursery upstairs. "He was ever so handsome, Mummy," Daphne exclaimed, jumping up. The special glow had not left her face. "And very nice. I'm so relieved. I was afraid I might not like him, and that would have been horrible."

Lily smiled. "I rather suspected that you would like him, Daphne. Remember, I fell in *love* with him."

Daphne frowned. "Aye, that's the one bad thing. I get angry when I remember what he did to you."

Lorcan and Paddy had stopped playing to listen to the exchange. Lily walked over to give her daughter a hug. "I don't want what happened between Philip and me to affect how you see him. If you like him, that makes me happy."

"Truly?"

"Aye."

"What did you two talk about after we left?"

Lily hesitated. She wasn't yet ready to tell Daphne about Philip's offer. "He told me that he was delighted to learn what a bright and lovely daughter he has."

"Did he ask about my foot?"

"Nay, he never mentioned it." Which was to Philip's credit, Lily realized with surprise. In a way, it was unfortunate. If she had detected any sign of reservation about Daphne's affliction, it would have been easier to reject his proposal of taking over her upbringing.

"He asked me about it, but it didn't seem to concern him," Daphne confirmed happily. "I'm ever so grateful to Dr. Black for giving me these boots."

Lorcan, who had been waiting patiently while they talked, finally pulled at Daphne's skirt. "The pirates are coming, Daphne," he said. "We have to finish building the fort."

Lily smiled. "I see you have some important work yet to do before supper," she told her daughter. "We'll talk more tonight before bed."

Daphne nodded agreement and went back to her play as Lily left the nursery and began to walk slowly down the hall. She knew that the Riordans and John would also be interested in hearing what she had talked about with Philip, but her thoughts were still so jumbled in her own mind, she wasn't sure she was ready to share them.

What she could use was a walk in the fresh air, she decided. She went to her room to collect a cloak against the wintry day, then headed downstairs, hoping that she wouldn't encounter anyone on her way out. The front hall was deserted, but as she pulled open the big front door, John was coming up the steps.

"I saw Stratton ride away," he said. "I was coming to look for you."

Suddenly she realized that talking to John was exactly what she needed. "He wants to take her," she blurted out, and the tears that she'd been holding back began streaming down her face.

John grabbed her hand and drew her down the steps and along the path that led around the house. When they were out of sight of the front, he stopped, pulled her into his arms so that the side of her face was against his chest, and demanded, "Tell me."

Amid sobs, she recounted her conversation with Philip, including his final warning about Daphne's safety that had left her in such a quandary. When she was finished, John moved her away and wiped her eyes with the end of his sleeve. "Feel better?" he asked with a smile.

She did. Her tears had stopped. But she still had no idea what she was going to do about Philip's offer. "I'm sorry for crying all over you," she said. "I've soaked your tunic clear through."

"All in a good cause," he assured her. "Now that you're feeling better, are you ready to hear my opinion on your contemptible former lover's suggestion?"

"He's not truly contemptible. That is, what he did was contemptible, but Philip has a good heart."

"As does many a scoundrel, no doubt, but that doesn't alter the fact that he deserves nothing from you or from Daphne. He seduced you, then skipped merrily back to his nuptials in England without a second thought. After losing family support, a less strong woman would likely have died and the child along with her."

"He didn't know that I was with child."

"Stop defending the son of a bitch, Lily."

John's anger surprised her. He looked as if he wanted to ram his fist into the wall behind her. "The truth is," she explained, "this has nothing to do with Philip. It has to do with Daphne and what would be best for her. He might be right in saying that she would have a better life with the things he could give her in London."

John gave a snort of exasperation. "How can you think that she would be better off in some foreign land than here in Killarney, where she has you by her side?"

"Only last night she was telling me how much she enjoys doing new things. Mayhap she'd want to go with him."

At that John smiled. "Then the solution is simple. Ask her. I have no doubt what the answer will be."

Lily was not as certain. "I'll have to talk with her tonight," she agreed. "Philip will be pressuring me for an answer."

"Tell him to come pressure me instead," John said grimly.

Lily smiled. "You're a good friend, John."

He grimaced. Then took her hand to lead her back inside the house.

"I believe she's actually considering letting the bastard have her," John said. He wondered if the steam he felt rising inside him was visible to his listeners. He'd followed Niall and Catriona to their bedroom after supper. It was a rare breach of his host's privacy, but he knew that he'd not be able to sleep until he'd told the whole story to someone who would agree with his opinion.

"Stratton is the girl's father," Niall pointed out. Unmindful of his friend's presence, he'd begun stripping off his clothes. Catriona sat perched on the edge of the bed, obviously preferring privacy before she disrobed.

"I agree it would be a mistake to send Daphne with him," Catriona added, "but Niall's right. A child's upbringing is a matter for her parents to decide. There's very little anyone else can do about it."

"The devil of it is that Lily's so alone. She's always been alone, even when she lived under the dominion of her brother. I'm not sure she will stand up to Stratton if he insists."

"Which is why you intend to step in to give her support," Catriona observed with a knowing smile.

"I—nay, as you say, 'tis an affair between two parents and I have no right—"

"Being in love with her gives you the right, John."

He didn't answer. Niall finished undressing and slid into his bed, then said with a yawn, "When you and Lily are married, you'll be the girl's stepfather with more legal rights than the blackguard who bred her."

John looked from one of his young hosts to the other. "Marriage? Don't be ridiculous. You know I'm destined to go a bachelor to my grave. And Lily thinks of me as a friend, nothing more."

Catriona scowled at him. "John Black, I'd always thought you to be wise, but only a fool could believe that a woman like Lily would lie with a man she didn't love."

He could feel his face grow hot. "How did you—?"

"Servants talk," she said, bouncing on the bed with indignation. "You're in love with Lily and she with you, and it seems to me that both of you have spent so much of your lives running away from happiness that neither one of you knows what to do when it's staring you in the face."

John looked at Niall, who gave a firm nod of agreement. "As usual, old man, Catriona is exactly right. Now perhaps you should go find that lady of yours and leave me some privacy to congratulate my wife for being so wise."

John was still trying to digest what Catriona had said. He had spent his life running from happiness—at least the kind that could be provided by a wife and family. It was easier to stick to the company of old friends and the satisfaction of his work for his country. These were things that wouldn't desert him . . . or die on him.

"So you think I should talk with her?" he asked, feeling oddly like a young man asking advice of his parents instead of the mentor he had been to the young couple up to now.

Catriona gave Niall an exasperated look. "Do we have to start again from the beginning?" she asked.

Niall grinned and looked back at John. "Nay, he understands the message right enough, and he knows that we're speaking the truth. It's just that it sometimes takes longer to change your thinking on things when you're a stubborn old man."

John grinned back. "This old man is going to give you one more chance to beat him in a horse race tomorrow before he gives up on the Riordan stable entirely."

"I can beat you if you're on any horse but Greybolt," Niall retorted.

"Greybolt is my mount," John said with a shrug.

"Gentlemen," Catriona said, standing up from her perch on the bed. "If we're done straightening out John's romance, do you think the horseracing discussion could be put off until tomorrow at breakfast?"

John looked from one of his friends to the other. "I can't tell you how much—" He faltered a little on the words.

"Go!" Niall shouted with a wave of his hands.

John turned to leave, smiling.

•   •   •

"But, Mummy, how could we go to London when my father has, you know—" Daphne stopped and looked down at the bedclothes. "When he has a wife," she finished finally.

"He's not asking both of us to go, Sweetcakes, just you." She would spare her daughter the details of Philip's offer to establish Lily in a house. Perhaps it had been innocently made, but she had seen her former lover looking at her in that certain way that made her believe he would not be averse to resuming their former relationship.

Daphne flopped back into bed. "Well, then, we'll not go, of course. I thought you meant he was inviting both of us."

As John had predicted, she had not even hesitated with her answer. It warmed Lily's heart, but she still was not entirely comfortable with dismissing the idea. Philip had had some good points about Daphne's future and her safety. Points that a child of Daphne's age would not be expected to understand.

"Your father asked us to think about it, Daphne, and that's what we'll do. He would have a great deal to offer you in London."

"I don't need to think about it. I have no desire to leave Killarney," Daphne said firmly.

"Your father might want to talk with you about it. He'll try to persuade you."

"I'll explain it to him, Mummy. I just need to make him understand that I will never live anywhere far away from you. She reached over to take her mother's hand and gave it a squeeze. "Shall we go to Lymond Castle tomorrow to explain it to him?"

Lily shook her head. "Your father said he would be back on Monday. That will be soon enough to tell him your decision."

Daphne snuggled into the covers. "Are you going to sleep now?" she asked.

What Lily wanted to do was to go find John. She wanted to tell him about the conversation with Daphne and thank him for comforting her earlier. She wanted to see his gray eyes warm as he looked at her. She wanted to feel his lips on her again.

John was no doubt discussing political matters with Niall, she told herself sternly. Perhaps even now he was planning his departure. She'd begun to let thoughts of him preoccupy her night and day, and it had to stop. The truth was painful to admit. She'd done the very thing she'd sworn never again to do. She'd fallen in love.

"Aye," she said, slipping in beside Daphne. "I'm going to sleep."

Lily and John had been oddly shy with each other at breakfast. As the rest of the household chattered about the day's activities, neither one had had much to say. When the meal was finished and John asked Lily in an undertone if she would care to go riding with him, it came as something of a relief from the tenseness that had sprung up so suddenly between them.

"I'd like to go visit my house," she told him, "to see that everything's all right. In fact, we should take Daphne with us."

John paused a moment, then shook his head. "I'll take Daphne there tomorrow, if you like. This morning I'd like you to myself."

Lily spent the first part of the ride telling John about her conversation with Daphne and accepting his gentle teasing that he knew her daughter better than she did. "I'm still not totally sure we're making the right decision," she said.

John pulled back on Greybolt's reins so that Lily's horse could keep up with the big stallion's pace. "Put it out of your mind, Lily. Daphne's told you what she wants, and there's an end to it. Tell me the truth, do you really believe she would be happier in a stuffy court gathering full of simpering courtiers than she is in her aviary in Whistler's Woods? Would you be happier there, if you were she?"

She smiled at him. The day was cold, but with bright sun that added to her buoyant mood. It appeared that she was not to lose her daughter after all, and John had asked her to ride with him. Things could change in the future with Daphne, and John would soon be leaving, but at the moment, her world was happy.

"I would never compare the gilded rooms of London with this," she said, throwing her hand up to indicate the panorama of green hills that surrounded them as they rode out the far end of the valley and into Whistler's Woods. "I'm simply trying to consider all aspects of my daughter's welfare."

Lily was almost disappointed when they reached the cottage. The ride had gone so quickly.

"Everything appears in order," John observed, pulling up at the end of the path. "Shall we go inside for a spell?"

"Aye, but first I want a kiss," she answered boldly, wondering where the daring words had come from.

He threw back his head and laughed. "Now there's a wench!" he shouted, and reined Greybolt to a stop with exaggerated alacrity.

By the time Lily had stopped her horse, he was at her side and holding up his arms to her. She slid into them. "Ask me again," he demanded, holding her so that she couldn't move.

She turned her face up to his. "Kiss me," she said.

He proceeded to do so, thoroughly, until both were flushed and breathing deeply.

"Ah, Lily," he said finally. "I trust you had no other urgent plans for the morning, for I'm afraid I'm going to have to make love to you in your own bed."

She grinned up at him. "I've been wondering what it would be like in a bed."

"Have ye now?" With that, he scooped her up and strode down the path toward the cottage.

"I'm too big, John," she protested, but when he seemed not the least bit ill at ease with his burden, she lay back in his arms and let him carry her through the front room of the cottage and into her bedroom.

"You don't have one of those silky things to put on, do you?" he asked, looking around the room, then added, "Never mind. The silk of your skin is all I need." He began to remove her clothing and his own, and soon they were laughing and tumbling into Lily's big bed.

"I can't believe we're doing this," Lily said. "It's the middle of the day, and we're sneaking off like a dairy maid and her swain."

John laughed. "I feel as randy as a young swain," he admitted, "but who could blame me with all this?" He lay next to her on the bed and slowly ran his hand up and down first her arm, then her side, then the curve of her hip. He turned her slightly to reach her round bottom then moved his hand up and down her back. She moaned with pleasure.

After several minutes of stroking her, he turned on his back and lifted her over him so that her legs were straddling his middle, the soft parts of their bodies pressing together. "Shall we try it this way?" he murmured. His eyes looking up at her were hooded.

Lily felt a rush in her midsection. She raised herself slightly and reached down to guide his hardened shaft inside her. When they were joined, he grasped her hips, moving her downward until he was lodged deep within. Incredible waves hit her almost immediately. She shuddered violently, held in place only by his firm hold on her. Inside her body she could feel the strong pulses of his climax.

They stayed joined as he pulled her down to the bed and into his arms. They lay side by side, letting their breathing return to normal and the sweat cool from their skin. It was long moments before he finally pulled his sated member away from her. She was vaguely aware that he hadn't made the attempt to pull away from her as he had on their previous encounter, but she was too blissful to care.

"Are you feeling better?" John asked finally.

She was almost asleep. "Better?"

"About Daphne. I know you've been worried."

"Oh, aye," she agreed with a guilty flush. She'd actually thought little about her daughter for most of the morning. Her mind had been on John.

"I did this backward, I'm afraid." He gestured to indicate the bed and the twisted covers that testified to their vigorous lovemaking. "I should have told you first that I've solved your problem."

She was having trouble following his words, but at least she'd come fully awake. "What do you mean?"

"There's no need to send her off to London. When we're married, she'll have a father and as much travel as you wish, accompanied by her parents."

She sat up. "Married?"

He pulled her back into his arms. "Aye. I imagine that Cat is going to want to plan a wedding for us, though in truth I'd thought I was too old for such folderol."

She pushed against his chest to free herself and sat

up again. "John Black, are you asking me to marry you?"

He looked up at her, a teasing light in his gray eyes. "I'm probably not doing it right, am I?" He slid out of the bed and knelt next to it, totally naked. "Mistress Lily O'Farrell, would you do me the honor of granting me your hand in marriage?" Then he jumped back into bed, pulled her down one more time, and reached for the blanket to cover them. "That will have to do, sweetheart. It's too cold for a longer speech."

Lily couldn't catch her breath. "I thought . . . you . . . aren't you going away? What about the rebels? The English?"

He tucked her head into the curve of his shoulder. When he spoke, his voice was more sober. "I can't promise you that I'll never have to leave your side, Lily. I'm probably not the best of candidates for a husband. But fighting is for young men. If it comes to a conflict again, my role will be in seeking peace, not war."

He truly wanted to marry her. The notion frightened her. Lily had spent her entire adult life rejecting the idea that this kind of happiness was ever for her. She still couldn't believe it. "Are you doing this because of Daphne? So that I don't feel I have to send her with Philip?"

John pulled away to look at her. "Lily, you have a precious daughter, and I've come to care about her deeply, but I didn't fall in love with Daphne."

"Love?" she asked weakly.

John smiled. "Damn, did I forget that part? I told you, I'm not very good at this sort of thing. I love you, Lily O'Farrell, and I'd be a happy man if I could wake up every morning of my life just like this."

He lifted the covers to reveal the two of them intertwined. Lily's disbelief was quickly being replaced by a growing bubble of elation. "Every morning?" she teased, using humor to maintain her fragile control.

"Every morning," he murmured, kissing her lips. "Every night and every morning and occasionally in between for good measure."

She lay back against the pillow and let him kiss her. She couldn't stop smiling. After a moment he stopped and asked abruptly, "Have you answered me yet?"

She grinned. "I didn't realize an answer was required. I thought you had it all decided."

He looked embarrassed. "Aye, well I did. But I suppose you should have some say in the matter."

"Then I'll say this," she said, putting her arms around his neck. "I love you, John Black."

"That'll do," he agreed, and resumed his kisses.

They were almost too lost in each other to hear the approach of the horse, but at the sound of a whinny, Lily sat up. "Someone's here. Daphne! Oh, John," she said, panicked.

John was already up, throwing on his clothes. "I'll go out and delay her, sweetheart. Take your time and get dressed. We have happy news to tell her."

Lily dressed almost as quickly as John. He was just opening the door to the visitor when she emerged into the front room. But the newcomer wasn't Daphne, it was Niall.

He took a look at their disheveled clothes and flushed faces and made a quick apology. "Forgive the interruption," he said without embarrassment. "But I thought you'd want to go with me. The stable lad's a little slow. He meant no harm, but he let her take the horse—"

"What are you talking about?" John asked.

"Daphne. She asked the stable boy if she could borrow a horse this morning to go to Lymond Castle. Said she wanted to talk with her father. The lad thought since she was a guest of the house—"

John was already out the door, with Lily close behind him.

Twenty

Veins stood out on Philip Stratton's temples as he shouted at his host. "Not only did you neglect to send word to me in London that Lily was bearing my child, Lymond, but thanks to you that child may never have been born. Your son told me part of the story, and your wife has completed it." He glanced at Maired, who stood quietly in the corner of her husband's office while the two men confronted each other. "You threw your sister out of your home and left her to have the child with no support from anyone."

Lymond was sitting behind his big desk and appeared unaffected by the Englishman's rage. "Lily had some of her own funds, inherited from our father. She was not exactly left begging on the streets."

"Perhaps she was not totally destitute, but she was left to raise her daughter in a peasant's cottage in the woods. She was forced to expose her shame to the world, excluding any chance of ever having a normal life and a marriage for herself."

Lymond stood up. "Well now, Stratton, who shall we say was the more responsible for that shame? I merely threw her out when the deed was done. You were the one who left her in that condition."

Maired took a step forward. "You're both responsible," she said in a surprisingly firm voice.

Lymond glowered at her. "Shut up, woman. I'll deal later with your loose tongue."

Stratton bristled. "Your wife only gave me information I should have been given twelve years ago, Lymond. If any harm comes to her because of it, I swear I'll see that the first estate in Killarney to be confiscated by the Crown will be yours."

"I've been a loyal ally to the queen." His tone lacked its usual arrogance.

"The queen chooses with whom she will ally, not the other way around," Stratton said coldly. "My men and I shall be leaving for London today, and the queen will receive my report on the state of affairs here. It will no doubt differ sharply from yours. The landowners I've met in Killarney appear to be peace-loving people concerned about their homes and their families. I've yet to see any of the traitorous hotheads you described."

Lymond sat back down heavily in his chair.

Philip turned and walked over to Maired, who was watching the exchange with grim satisfaction. When he reached her, he took her hand and bowed over it. "I thank you for your hospitality, Lady Lymond," he said in a much softer tone. "You are a remarkable woman, and if I can ever be of service to you in any way—" he gave a quick glance back at Lymond—"please let me know."

"I thank you, sir," she told him. "Perhaps after all Lily was not so very mistaken in you."

There was a brief warming of his eyes, then he gave a final nod and turned to leave the room. Without looking back at her husband, Maired followed him out.

"She's wandered off before, but nothing as fool-hardy as this," Lily said as the three riders neared Ly-mond Castle.

"Perhaps she was eager to explain her decision to Stratton," John suggested. "Or she may be worried that he would insist on taking her away from you. It's hard to know what gets into young people's heads."

"Why didn't she talk with me about it first?"

"You and John rode off so quickly this morning, none of us even knew where you were headed," Niall explained. "It was lucky that Cat had heard Lily say she wanted to check on her house. That's how I knew where to look for you. Though I should have guessed you two might be seeking more comfortable privacy than the floor of my library."

Under normal circumstances, John would have replied to his friend's teasing, but he was too con-cerned to engage in banter. He would not have let Daphne go riding by herself at all with the current cli-mate, but in particular he would not want her any-where near Lymond Castle, which was crawling with Stratton's English troops.

Lily apparently was as worried as he, and there was no more talk as they headed down the final stretch of road.

The old walls around Lymond Castle had no moat in the traditional sense, but they were surrounded by a series of mounds, which at some time in the past had probably served as a crude defense system. The riders had just reached the outer edge of the grassy hillocks when Lily gave a strangled cry.

Ahead of them, off to the side of the road, lay Daphne, facedown. She wasn't moving.

John spurred Greybolt ahead, then brought the stallion to a skidding halt next to the fallen girl. Jumping down, he gently turned her over, then gave a sharp intake of breath. A patch of red spread across her cloak like a bright bouquet of flowers.

"Dear God," Lily said behind him.

"She's alive," he told her. He could see Daphne's chest rise in faint, jerky breaths.

Daphne's eyelids fluttered open. She saw John and reached for his hand. Her tight grip was reassuring. "They were trying to take my boot," she said in a weak whisper.

Lily knelt beside her, looking at the blood on her cloak with horror. "What have they done to her?" she asked, anguished.

John had been wondering the same thing. He could feel the rapid beat of his heart inside his own chest, but the old teachings of his profession forced him to view Daphne with a clinical eye. It didn't take long to spot the tiny hole in her cloak. "It's a bullet," John said grimly. "She's been shot."

"Shot! What the devil!" Niall exclaimed.

"Is she going to be all right?" Lily asked, cradling Daphne's head in her arms. "Sweetcakes, can you hear me?"

"The bullet didn't hit her heart or else"—John's voice broke—"or else she'd not be talking to us. But it's lodged inside her. There's no exit wound. It needs to come out."

Lily looked up at him, her eyes swimming. "Will you do it?"

"I don't do surgery," he began helplessly. "Is there a surgeon or a barber in Banburn?" he asked Niall.

"Nay. There's no one for miles."

There wasn't really a question. He'd sworn never again to lift a knife, but he had no other choice. "We should get her inside," he said briskly. Once the decision was made, the professional seemed to take over. "We need hot water and brandy, a needle and thread, tongs, and the sharpest blade you can find."

"Does he know that he's my cousin, Mummy?" Daphne murmured. Her eyes were closed. "He tried to take my boot."

John lifted her in his arms, kissing her forehead as he did so. "Don't think about it, lass. No one is going to take your boot, and we're going to get you better soon."

He refused help from Niall as he carried her toward the castle. By now the front door had opened, and people were running out to them. John recognized Stratton and Lady Lymond, the quiet woman he'd met on his previous visit.

"What's happened?" Stratton shouted.

Niall answered. "Lily's daughter has been shot, apparently by someone here on your property."

John noticed that Lady Lymond's face went white, but then he turned his concentration back on Daphne as she groaned in pain. By the time they'd been ushered into a bedchamber inside the castle, she was unconscious.

"This is good," he told Lily, who was now holding her daughter's limp hand. "It will be easier if she's not awake when I have to cut her."

"Will she live?" It was Philip Stratton who asked the question. John gave him barely a glance. "If you clear people out of this room and let me save her. Lily can stay." He looked at Maired. "Lady Lymond, do you have a couple of strong, reliable servants who can help hold her down?"

"I'll hold her," Stratton said.

John's impulse was to refuse, but finally he nodded. "Just don't let her move when my knife is inside her."

He tried not to think about the last time he'd held a knife inside a human body. He tried not to remember the horror as he'd watched Rhea's lifeblood pouring out. The situation was different, he told himself. In Rhea's case, the baby had caused the hemorrhage as much as his knife.

Lily was still holding Daphne's hand. With her other hand she reached for his. "You won't hurt her," she said. "You'll save her."

He let the words pound in his head—*you'll save her.*

He waited, sweat starting to trickle down his temples, as the necessary supplies were gathered. Lily and Stratton sat on either side of their daughter on the bed. Daphne had not moved and showed no signs of regaining consciousness.

Finally all was in order. They'd found a thin kitchen knife with a wickedly sharp blade. It was perfect for the job. The tongs were larger than he would have liked, but they would have to do if he needed more than his fingers for the extraction of the bullet. Everything was ready. Now it was up to him.

He looked up to meet Lily's gaze. The worry showed on her face, but she smiled and gave him a nod.

He picked up the knife. His hand, at least, was rock steady, even if his heart was racing. They had removed Daphne's bloody cloak and cut away the top part of her gown so that her slender shoulder was exposed where the bullet had entered. He pressed the knife down on her soft white skin, then swiftly made the cut. Blood gushed forth, but it was surface blood, nothing dire.

Bullet wounds had not been common in Killarney when he was practicing medicine, but he'd watched many a battlefield surgeon deal with them during the years of fighting. He'd never thought to be tending one himself, but he found that once he'd begun, the skills of his profession seemed to take over. He forgot that it was Daphne lying on the bed. Nothing mattered but his objective of removing the dangerous object with the least possible further injury to the patient. He felt a surge of excitement as the tip of his knife struck metal. First try, first cut. He'd found it. With the tips of his fingers, he pulled the ball out.

It wasn't until he had sewed up the wound that he allowed himself to look across the bed at Lily, who hunched anxiously over her daughter. "We did it," he said. His throat was dry, making the words sound odd.

"*You* did it," she said. "Now what?"

His elation died. "Now we wait." Bullet wounds were notorious killers, even when the wound was clean and the bullet removed. Daphne was not out of danger. He moved over to the basin of water to wash the blood from his hands. Trying to keep the concern from his voice he turned back to Lily. "She's young and strong. Her chances are good."

For a long moment the room was silent as everyone looked down at the young girl who lay unaware that she was in a fight for her life. Finally Stratton stood up from his post at his daughter's side and asked, "How did this happen?"

Maired appeared in the bedroom door. "She was shot by my son," she said. The skin of her face looked gray. "His father bought him a pistol when we were in London. They tell me it was an accident, and I pray to God it was."

"Daphne was saying something about them trying to take away her boot," Lily said. She had not let go of her daughter's hand.

"Aye, 'twas Desmond and his friends. They saw her riding up to the castle and went out, apparently to taunt her. Desmond won't say anything, but his friends, the Crawley brothers, say they pulled her from her horse and were trying to take off her boots. She fought back, and that's when Desmond's pistol went off." She looked bleakly at her sister-in-law. "I'm so sorry, Lily."

"Don't blame yourself, Maired," Lily said.

The calm that had sustained him through the surgical procedure had disappeared, and John found himself wanting to find Desmond O'Farrell and throttle him or, at the very least, haul him in front of a magistrate who would send the malevolent boy to prison. But Desmond was the son of an earl. It was likely that he'd receive no comeuppance at all for this day's work.

As if reading his thoughts, Philip Stratton said, "I believe it's time I talked with Lymond about a commission for his son in the English army. The boy's totally undisciplined."

Lily gave him a grateful glance. Then she turned to Maired. "We'll have to impose on your hospitality until Daphne is well enough to be moved. If you could just be sure that your son stays away from us—"

"Lily, this is your family home," Maired interrupted. "You should never have been made to leave here, and you may stay as long as you wish. As for Desmond, I'll be sure that he is confined to his own quarters until you have left." She turned to leave, then paused. "I shall keep my husband away as well."

"Why does she stay with him?" John asked after Maired had disappeared out the door.

Lily shook her head. "It was the life fate gave her, I suppose, and she sees no escape from it. It's too often a woman's lot."

"You escaped. You made your own life," John pointed out.

"Aye, that I did," she said. She brought Daphne's inert hand up to her mouth and kissed it. "My daughter gave me the strength."

Heedless of Philip Stratton's presence on the other side of the bed, John went to Lily and pulled her up into an embrace. "We'll pull her through this, my love, I promise you."

Lily smiled up at him through bright tears. "I know we will." Then she resumed her post at her daughter's side.

Daphne had not regained consciousness all night, and though John had told Lily it was normal after the injury she had suffered, he was filled with the same kind of sick dread he'd had years before when he'd sat by the bedside of his first love. Rhea had been young and strong, too.

The hours had crept by while they waited. John tried to maintain a calm demeanor, hiding his worry from Lily, but several times he was forced to leave the room and walk up and down the dark corridors of Lymond Castle to compose himself. He even resorted to prayer, something he had not done since Rhea's death.

It simply was not possible that this vibrant young life would be taken, he told himself. This courageous child who faced life and her disability with such good cheer. How would any of them bear it if she died?

After a fourth trip walking the corridors, he returned to find Lily bending over her daughter in sudden alarm. John raced to the bed. "I can't see her breathing!" Lily cried.

He lifted Daphne's wrist and felt the reassuring beat of her heart. "She breathes, Lily. The breaths are shallow, but that's a good sign—she's sleeping peacefully." He put his hand on her forehead. "She's cool to the touch. If she makes it through the night without a fever, she will have come through the worst."

John moved his chair to sit at Lily's side and took her hand. They waited.

"She was so happy with her new boot," Lily said after a few minutes, tears running down her face.

"Aye, and she will be again." As he said the words, John was filled with a peculiar certainty that he was speaking the truth. Daphne would be up and walking again in her new boots. And he would be with her. After a lifetime alone, he'd come back to Killarney and found his home in Lily and her daughter. He was not about to lose it all again.

He looked out the window of the castle bedchamber. The sun was just coming up over the green hills to the east. It was going to be a bright, cloudless day like the Killarney days he remembered from his childhood.

"Mummy?" Daphne's voice was faint, but her eyes fluttered open.

"I'm here, Sweetcakes. It's morning. You've been sleeping all night."

John could hear the thickness in Lily's voice. He squeezed her hand, then let it go so that she could take hold of her daughter's instead.

"Am I hurt?" Daphne asked.

John stood up and put his hand on her forehead. The skin was blissfully cool. He grinned down at his patient. "We had to patch you up a little, but you'll be right again in no time."

"My boots—" she began.

"Your boots are fine, Princess. They'll be waiting when you get back on your feet. Remember, I've promised you a dance."

Daphne gave a dreamy smile. "I remember," she said.

Lily looked up at him, her eyes shining with gratitude. "I said you would save her," she said. "The truth is, you've saved us both."

John had heard the phrase *a full heart,* but he'd never quite known what it meant until that moment. He reached for both their hands. "And the two of you have saved me," he said.

Epilogue

John pulled the little cart to a halt at the edge of Cotter's Pond.

"Why are we stopping?" Daphne asked. "Aren't we going to our cottage to see my birds?"

"Patience, lass," John said, jumping from the seat and walking around to lift Daphne out of the back of the wagon. Lily climbed down the other side. "Would you like to go for a walk around the pond?"

Lily was as mystified as her daughter. It had taken Daphne nearly a month to regain her strength after her surgery, and each day she'd asked about her aviary. John had assured her that he was tending to her birds and other animal friends, but he hadn't allowed her to make the trip back to Whistler's Woods until today.

"Are you sure she should walk that far?" she asked John.

"I believe she can make it. Let me know if you tire, Princess, and I'll carry you," he added to Daphne.

The trio made their way around the marshy part of the lake where Lily gathered her basket reeds, then reached the wooded area on the other side. "It's not much farther," John said, turning directly into a thick patch of trees.

Lily and Daphne exchanged a puzzled look and followed him. As they walked, they could hear chirping sounds that became louder and louder. "Where are all the birds coming from?" Daphne asked.

"I suspect they're in their new home having dinner," John said with a grin.

With a flourish, he showed them through a parting in the trees that led to a circular clearing. Around the circle was an elaborate system of wooden racks that were covered with bird houses and feeders of all varieties. Some were baskets that Lily recognized from Daphne's aviary. Others were new. At the visitors' intrusion, dozens of birds flew skyward.

"It's my aviary, only bigger!" Daphne exclaimed, walking around the circle and looking at each little house. "Did you do this, Uncle John?" She'd taken to using the Riordan boys' name for him.

"I had some help from Niall and his staff."

"But I don't understand," she said. She looked over at John as if worried about hurting his feelings. "It's wonderful, but it's rather far from the cottage. I'll have to carry the seed—"

John walked over to put his arm around her shoulders. "You won't have to walk anywhere. I've placed the aviary to be right out the back of our *new* house."

"Our new house?" Lily and Daphne both said at once.

John continued his explanation to Daphne. "The problem is that your cottage is not big enough for all three of us. So now that your mother and I are to be married, I thought it would be nice if we made our house here. We're on the edge of the woods, and I'm sure all your little friends will eventually find their way here from the old place."

"You're planning to build a house?" Lily asked in amazement. She and John had been so busy attending to Daphne these past few days that they had had little time to discuss plans for a future together. Lily had more or less assumed that John would have to move into the cottage with her, since he had no property of his own that she was aware of. They couldn't continue to impose on the Riordans forever. Especially now that Philip had gone back to England, withdrawing the English troops from the neighborhood.

"Aye," John said, indicating the woods with a sweep of his hands. "It's going to take awhile to build, of course, but Niall and Cat will be happy to have us until the place is ready."

"But how—" she paused, considering how to phrase the question. "Whose land is this?" she asked finally.

"Mine. That is, it will be as soon as the papers are filed." He laughed. "Don't look so surprised, sweetheart. Did you think you were marrying a pauper?"

"I didn't care."

He stepped next to her and kissed her cheek. "I suppose you thought you'd take care of me just as you've had to take care of everything else in your life. I'm sorry to disappoint you, my independent bride, but you're marrying a wealthy man. I inherited a considerable sum from my family and have spent scarcely a farthing over the years." His face grew more serious. "I'd never found anything worth spending it on until now."

He took her hand and pulled her a few feet to an opening in the trees. "The house will be situated just here with a view of the water. Then we can put the dining hall in the back with windows that look out to the aviary." He sounded like a little boy planning a favorite game.

"We'll be able to eat right along with the birds," Daphne pointed out with a giggle.

"Aye, we can do just that. Then back there I thought we'd have the large salon." He looked at Daphne. "For the dances."

"Dances?" Her eyes were round.

"Aye. If I'm to have a beautiful young lady as my daughter, all the neighborhood beaux are going to be lining up to visit."

Lily felt dazed. It was as if everything she had once wanted for her life had suddenly been dropped into her lap as easily as a bouquet of spring wildflowers. "When did you plan all this?" she asked him.

His little-boy grin was smug. "I've been working on it in spare moments."

"Am I to have my own bedchamber?" Daphne asked eagerly.

Lily's face flamed, but John answered evenly, "That you are, lass. A proper young lady like you should have her own quarters. Perhaps we'll build you a dressing room, as well."

"My own bedchamber with a dressing room!" Daphne exclaimed. "And dances! Just think of it, Mummy!"

Lily smiled at her daughter, but mention of bedchambers had set her pulse racing. With Daphne's health their primary concern, she and John had had no opportunity to be together since the morning they had spent in her cottage. It seemed ages ago.

"I just wanted to be sure that everything met with your approval before the building starts," John said, looking well pleased with the reaction to his surprise. "Now we can go on over to the cottage, if you like."

"Not yet," Daphne pleaded. "I need some time here. Look, they've left nothing but husks in this basket. It should be cleaned out and—"

"Sweetcakes, you don't have to do that today," Lily told her.

"But I want to, Mummy. Let me stay for a while. I need to be here so that the birds can begin to learn that it's safe for them to come while I'm here."

John had been watching Lily's flushed face. "I have an idea," he said. "How about if you stay here for half an hour, Princess. That should be enough time for the birds to decide to give it a try. Your mother and I, meanwhile, will trot over to the cottage to be sure that everything is in order there. Then we'll come back here for you."

Daphne beamed and nodded approval at the plan.

Lily hesitated. "Will she be all right here by herself?"

John had already grabbed her hand and was pulling her toward the little horse cart. "She'll be fine. I'm her doctor, remember? As I tell my patients, one of the most difficult things about recovery is to convince the family that they no longer need to hover about like worried nurses."

He grabbed her around the waist and boosted her up on the cart seat. "So let her have a half hour here with her birds. She's happy."

"A half hour?" Lily asked with a touch of wistfulness.

John grinned as he climbed up beside her. Then he leaned closer and whispered in her ear. "I've been so randy all morning that the deed will be done in half that time, but I promise you a delectable, lingering encounter as soon as I can figure out how to get you alone again."

She leaned against his shoulder. It felt strong and comforting. She gave a sigh of happiness. Years ago she'd been in love with Philip Stratton, but she'd never shared her life with him. The weeks since Daphne's accident had shown her vividly what it meant to ease life's burdens with a true partner. It felt wonderful. And that was without considering all the additional benefits.

"Delectable and lingering, eh?" she repeated.

"Aye."

She looked up at him archly. "You shouldn't say such things or I'll have trouble sleeping tonight."

"Hmm. Perhaps you should ask advice from your doctor."

She leaned over on the seat and kissed his cheek. "I can't sleep, Doctor. What do you prescribe?"

"I've always felt that a good remedy for sleeplessness is to exercise the mind. You might want to consider a very fine collection of books the Riordans have in their library."

Lily giggled. She sounded like a young girl, she realized, and sitting here next to John, plotting how to find some stolen moments with him, she felt young, too. "A visit to the library? I suppose I could try that."

John pulled the cart to a sudden halt, tied up the reins, and turned to put his arms around her. "That's a good girl," he murmured. "You should always listen to your doctor."

Then he began kissing her so thoroughly that, in the end, the visit to Lily's cottage had to be left for another day.

About the Author

With family roots tracing back to both England and Ireland, **ANA SEYMOUR** has been a lover of history since childhood. She now loves writing about it in popular romances, which have been published around the world.

Ana lives in the country near one of Minnesota's fifteen thousand lakes. She appreciates hearing from readers at P.O. Box 24107, Minneapolis MN 55424, or by email at anaseymour@aol.com.